THE BOY FROM THE SEA

H. L. Macfarlane

3

For the west coast

"The sea,

The majestic sea,

Breaks everything,

Crushes everything,

Cleans everything,

Takes everything

From me"

The Sea (Corinne Bailey-Rae; 2010)

PART ONE

Lir, Age Four

There were three specific moments that defined Lir Murphy's childhood. For the first six years of his life the Irish seaside town of Bundoran had been his entire world, though Lir could remember nothing of the place prior to his fourth birthday. In another life – another reality – he would have had no cause to remember this specific birthday, either, for his early years had been decidedly happy and, above all else, unremarkable. But this *was* his life. His reality.

And this reality began on Lir's fourth birthday.

He was on the beach with his parents. Later he'd discover that it was their favourite place to go because they couldn't afford to take him to caravan parks or zoos or even to the cinema. Lir, of course, had no concept of the fact his little family was poor. He was four: what did money matter to him?

They largely had the beach to themselves, for though the tenth of May that year was particularly warm and sunny it was midweek and the local schools were not off on holiday yet. There were a few surfers out on the water – the waves were great by Bundoran – and Lir delighted in watching them ride a wave, crash, then invariably get back up to start all over again.

When lunchtime approached Lir and his parents ate buttered bread and nothing else. It was another sign of their poverty that he could not possibly have been aware of. Besides, Lir liked buttered bread. He was an easily satisfied child.

The afternoon was dedicated to making sandcastles and

playing in the shallows. His father took Lir in his arms and charged through the waves until Lir was screaming in delight, urging him to go faster and deeper. In his arms Lir felt safe from the rest of the world. He thought that feeling would last forever.

His mother watched from the beach as she searched for rocks, holding a straw hat to her head as she did so. The hat had holes in it, though when Lir asked why she didn't get a new one she merely replied that she loved this one specifically.

As the sun drew closer to the horizon and the wind picked up, Lir was bundled into a blanket and given the last of the bread and butter to eat. His parents watched the final two surfers leave with bright, attentive eyes, though by this point so late in the day Lir himself had lost all interest in them. He was growing sleepy; he wanted to go home.

The sun had almost set and the air turned chilly when his mother finally gave Lir her undivided attention, stroking his curly hair away from his face with tender fingers. "Stay here, Lir," she said. She began to fill the pockets of her jacket with the rocks she'd sourced earlier, after which his father did the same thing. "Be a good boy. I love you."

"*We* love you," his father added on, kissing Lir's forehead for just a moment. Then he nodded at his wife, taking her hand as they stood up and walked towards the sea.

At first Lir assumed they were going to play in the shallows without him and almost cried out in protest. But then they walked in deeper and deeper and deeper until the small boy on the beach could hardly make out his parents at all.

Then, between one blink and the next, a wave engulfed them and they were gone.

Lir played with one of the remaining rocks his mother had collected for an interminably long time, turning the smooth, unbroken surface over and over in his tiny hands. He bit at it, curious as only a four-year-old could be about how it tasted. He stuck out his tongue in disgust when he realised all it tasted of was gritty sand and salt.

When he heard sirens it was well and truly dark. Lir was cowering from the cold inside his blanket, slipping from wakefulness to unconsciousness just as frequently as he breathed air into his lungs. He wondered where his parents were. He wondered why the police were running towards him, shining torches into his face until he cried. He wondered why he was gently placed in the back of a car and taken to the hospital, where his Aunt Orla took him in her arms and burst into tears.

"Good lord," she wailed, stroking Lir's hair so hard that it hurt. He pulled away from her hand, tilting his chin up to stare at her tear-stained face.

"Where are mummy and daddy?" he asked. The question came out as a croak. "Where did they go?"

"They went home," she said, though Lir thought she didn't sound in the least bit happy about this. "Their real home. That's all."

Lir frowned at this concept. "In the sea?"

Another sob.

"Yes, sweetheart," Orla replied. "In the sea."

This answer was enough for Lir. He was only four, after all, and very, very tired.

His parents had returned home to the sea.

Chapter One

The first thing that came to mind whenever I thought of home was always the smell of the sea.

Not the vanilla and sandalwood of my parents' house courtesy of locally-made, beeswax candles my mother religiously bought at the market.

Not the green, heady scent of the trees and moss and freshly cut grass of Kelburn Country Park, nor the dark and loamy smell of the waterfall hidden within the forest there as it crashed into the glen.

Not even the intoxicating mixture of sugar, dairy and chocolate that permeated the air outside Nardini's Café, carrying on the breeze along the promenade and enticing tourists to overindulge on ice cream for their lunch.

No, it was the sea. The tang of it. The salt on your tongue; the brine in your nose. Every time it crashed into the shore – waves breaking on the rocks, filling the air with foam – a fresh dose of the smell hit you as if you had submerged your head in the water itself. Then the foam would dissipate, and the waves would recede, and the smell would fade until the next toss of the sea brought it back into your nose once more.

That was how the original tale of The Little Mermaid ended, with the heroine dissolving into sea foam that danced above the waves. She became a 'Child of the Air', through which she could gain an immortal soul by performing good deeds for three hundred years. But I never liked that part of the story. It seemed more fitting for the mermaid's end to be tragic, with her having failed to capture the prince's heart and yet unable to kill him in order to return to her sisters below the water's surface.

Maybe I just don't like happy endings. Or maybe I don't believe in the existence of one's soul. Either way, I always stopped reading the story the moment the mermaid turned into foam.

When I moved to Glasgow for university I left behind the slow, easy living of a beloved tourist seaside town for a bustling, high-energy city with polluted air and suffocating crowds. The River Clyde cut right through Glasgow, of course, so I wasn't completely locked in a soulless concrete jungle. It was a poor substitute for the coast but for the sake of my education I knew I had to make do.

My flat even looked out onto the river, which I knew made me incredibly lucky. Luckier still that it was a private let, and my best friend Louisa and I moved into the place before rent started hiking up and up and up. Since we were good tenants who never broke anything or had outrageous parties our landlord decided to freeze our rent so long as we remained students.

Having entered the final year of my PhD, that blissful arrangement was all too quickly coming to a tragic and inevitable end.

"What have I missed?"

I turned at the sound of the voice, smiling when I was greeted by the not-at-all flustered David Harrod. He was a third year undergrad student and always very late for the molecular methods laboratory I'd helped run since the beginning of my PhD. I used to just help the molecular biology degree group with their version of the lab – an easy three days a week for four weeks arrangement that paid better than my PhD itself – but now that the research part of my degree was finished and I'd entered the dreaded write-up months for my thesis, I'd gladly agreed to help out in the molecular methods lab for every life sciences degree group for the money.

I had no funding left, after all. Unless I wanted to pick up a thankless waitressing job or a few shifts as a cashier in the local supermarket, acting as a teaching assistant was my best and most financially secure option.

For now.

David surreptitiously necked back the dregs of his Starbucks coffee that was most likely the reason he was late, throwing the empty paper cup into the bin before the draconian technician, Jerry, could scream at him for bringing food and drink into his precious laboratory.

Though most of the students were around twenty or twenty-one years old, David had first enrolled in university almost ten years ago, dropping out and working in a Curry's hardware store for half a decade before deciding to pursue education again. That made him twenty-eight, and three years older than I was. Being closer in age to me than the rest of his peers meant we'd formed some semblance of camaraderie, though we'd only known each other for a week.

"You missed the run-down lecture for today's schedule, as usual," I answered in hushed tones so as not to interrupt said lecture as it concluded. "And, hey, no funny business this week. Georgia's off so I need to cover her lab benches."

David cocked his head and blinked, the very picture of innocent confusion. "Funny business? Me?"

"You and your entire bench," I replied, signalling towards the group of seven students in question, who were waving at David. "No *accidentally* setting Kim's ponytail on fire or writing swear words into your agar plates with *E.coli,* got it?"

"Would never dream of it. We're model students, after all. That's why we have the most experienced lab demonstrator helping out our bench, right?"

I scoffed at the comment, swatting David's arm with the manual I was holding to send him on his way. In truth I did like David's bench better than the other two I was responsible for, and most of the time I found their antics entertaining. But when I had double the number of students to take care of – on the dreaded restriction enzyme digest and agarose gel day – I had little and less patience for anything other than good, old-fashioned molecular laboratory techniques.

If only they weren't all animal biologists. Marine and freshwater biologists, to be exact.

They were still convinced that they didn't need to know any molecular biology to pursue their dream careers of working for conservation efforts or national parks. I didn't have the heart to tell them that those jobs didn't exist. Well, not enough of them to handle dozens of graduates from Glasgow every year, anyway, let alone the hundreds more that graduated from other universities alongside them.

But willing or not, the students depended on me to teach them how to perform the most essential of molecular lab techniques. And today I had double the number to look after, since the other two lab assistants present hadn't helped out with the lab before so were functionally useless outside of looking after their own benches, and the teacher, Dr Sophie Spencer, could only handle so much herself.

It was going to be one hell of a long day.

"Right, folks, who needs some clarification on what Sophie just told you?" I asked my new lot of benches, since I was aware there were at least a couple of people in my own section who always seemed to know what they were doing, and would help out the other students whilst I dealt with my new brood. I was not surprised when several hands shot up; though Georgia had helped run the molecular methods lab before she was pretty lazy and never made sure her students actually understood what they were doing.

I pointed to one of the girls who had raised their hand. "What's your name?" she asked.

The previous week everyone had been told to put on name tags but they'd been abandoned when several of the students – belying their twenty-plus years on the planet – wrote down curse words and inside jokes instead of their names.

"Grace," I replied, smiling brightly. And then, anticipating the next couple of questions, I added, "I'm currently writing up my thesis about using recombinant proteins for targeted gene therapy, so I know squat about marine biology. Luckily this is a molecular lab."

16

I could see the group relax as they realised I was easy-going and had a sense of humour. It was all a carefully-cultivated persona, though, for social interactions very often made me anxious and caused my heart to painfully constrict. But teaching was different. When I was teaching I was someone else.

"Where are you from?" a boy called out from the back of the bench. He had a look about him that suggested he didn't take the lab very seriously, as did most of his group.

All except one person.

"Um, Largs," I told him, raising an eyebrow. "Why?"

"Didn't recognise the accent," he replied, just as I realised his own accent was distinctly Dundonian.

"I wouldn't expect a sheep shagger to recognise anything over five miles away from his farm." I'd taken a calculated risk that the comment would not offend but amuse, and was pleased to see that the risk had paid off. The boy from Dundee snorted, then elbowed the tawny-haired boy to his left.

The one who seemed too serious for this particular group.

"She's much better than that other lass, Dylan," the Dundonian told his silent lab partner. "She might even answer your questions about the actual lab."

This garnered a laugh from the bench; clearly I wasn't the only one who disliked Georgia. This made the stranger called Dylan appeal to me immediately. His head was bent over the lab manual, so I couldn't see his face, but there was something about the way he held himself that suggested I'd like it.

Which was a weird thing to think about a person.

The hours passed just as slowly as I'd thought they would that day, though they blurred together just like any other day in the lab. The only moments of focus were when my eyes caught sight of Dylan; I couldn't stop watching him whenever he passed my line of sight. It wasn't that he was imposingly tall or broad or comically short, but there was a presence to him I couldn't ignore. A physicality, maybe. For he was in good shape, that much was clear simply from the way he held himself.

His tousled hair appeared dry beneath the fluorescent lights

17

of the lab and grew blonder towards its messy ends, suggesting that Dylan was a swimmer – the boys on my high school swim team all had similar hair. This was confirmed when I risked asking his lab partner about him when Dylan was putting samples into the walk-in freezer at the end of the day.

"Yeah he is, actually. One of the best members of the swim team," the boy, whose name transpired to be Max, said. He gave me a stupid grin. "Why, you interested in him?"

"Of course not!" I said, lying through my gritted teeth. "It's just that I'm friends with a lot of the swim team so I've been to a few of their socials and stuff. But I've never seen him."

Max shrugged. "Don't think he goes to most of them. I'm not even sure he drinks. Spends all his time open water swimming at the weekend and shit."

That intrigued me for sure. So Dylan was on the swim team but didn't fit into their decidedly laddish culture, and spent his free time outdoors. I wondered if he swam outdoors in winter – we'd had a bad January so far, full of snow and sleet and high-speed winds. I tried to imagine him swimming in such conditions then immediately regretted it.

Thinking about Dylan dripping wet and naked (though if he swam outdoors a lot he would probably wear a wet suit, which was somehow even worse for my brain) just as the young man in question walked towards me was a terrible decision...especially when he tilted his head to look me straight in the eye, freezing me to the spot.

My initial observation had been right: I really liked his face. There was a kind of innocence there – a softness – that appealed to my very core. It was odd because beneath the messy hair there was absolutely nothing 'soft' about the defined lines of his jaw and the sharpness of his cheekbones that gave off the distinct impression Dylan didn't eat enough.

For a moment I thought his eyes were blue, but when Dylan was but two feet away I realised they were grey. Truly, genuinely grey, like a troubled sea or a stormy sky.

I couldn't look away.

Dylan was so close to me that for one wild, insane moment I thought he was going to kiss me. Instead, he simply stood there until I noticed I was blocking the way to his seat. Recoiling as if I'd been slapped I performed a one-eighty-degree spin and headed into the office at the back of the lab, pretending that it had always been my intended destination.

As soon as I reached the office I closed the door and leaned against it, holding a hand over my racing heart as if I had to force it back inside my ribcage. I'd never felt like this before. Not when faced with any boy I'd liked at any age over my twenty-five years of existence. Not even when I was obsessed with Legolas in Lord of the Rings as a teenager and convinced myself I would somehow, some day, marry him.

If somebody told me this was love at first sight I'd have believed them. It felt stronger than lust. Stronger than desire. Stronger than any emotion I'd felt for anyone at any point in my entire life.

I'd completely fallen for a stranger, and he hadn't spoken a single word.

Chapter Two

I'd lived with Louisa ever since the second year of our undergraduate degree. We had always been of the opinion that we'd eventually get our own places once one or both of us completed our postgraduate studies - or found a long-term boyfriend. Luckily the two of us were equally as useless at keeping boys around, but neither of us cared all that much. We had each other, and late-night TV, and vodka, and that was fine.

I really hadn't relished the thought of living alone.

When Louisa finished her Masters degree and decided to embark on an impulse gap year to Australia the second she graduated I truly believed that was the beginning of the end of our happy, easy living situation. I'd be left unable to pay all the rent with no flat mate to share the financial burden - not that I wanted to live with anyone new, anyway - or I'd have to move into a smaller, more affordable one-bedroom flat - which I perhaps wanted to do even less. I loved our riverside flat. To move away from the water would be torture.

But Louisa's parents were wealthy, and she didn't want to give up her bedroom in our precious home any more than I wanted her to. It had an en suite, after all, and was ten minutes from a McDonald's. This was very important to Louisa - and me, too, if I was being honest. And so it was that her parents agreed to pay her share of the rent and bills whilst Louisa was off gallivanting, leaving me blissfully, financially secure.

For the rest of summer I discovered the perks of living by myself. Walking around naked after a shower. Having all the space in the fridge to store my food with nobody around to steal my Babybels. Playing whatever music I wanted out loud whenever I wanted to hear it.

Going days on end without talking to a single soul.

But now that the second semester of the university calendar had begun, which marked six months since Louisa left for Australia, I was forced to admit that video messaging my best friend was a poor substitute for real, physical, human interaction.

I was alone, and it sucked.

Perhaps that was why I was so drawn to Dylan from the moment I saw him. After the students had gone home that fateful day I'd immediately checked the attendance sheet to learn his full name: Dylan Lir Murphy. Lir. I'd never heard the name 'Lir' before but upon checking it out I saw that it was Irish. His whole name was pretty damn Irish, to be honest.

I tried to imagine him speaking with an Irish accent but came up blank. I'd never heard him talk, after all. I had no clue what kind of voice he'd have. Was it low and lilting? Gravelly and masculine? Or incredibly soft and unsure? I decided I liked all three of those options.

But now that Georgia had returned to inefficiently watch her section of the lab I had no good reason to wander between her benches in the hope of hearing Dylan talk. After several days of sneaky observation it was clear he hardly spoke a word, anyway.

The students all left fairly swiftly as soon as their work was done, and because Dylan was efficient with their combined lab work he and Max often left early. *Which explains why Max is lab partners with someone who doesn't seem to interact with him all that much,* I'd thought on more than one occasion. I supposed that wasn't fair; for all I knew, Dylan talked non-stop to Max outside of classes.

But when I'd looked Dylan up on social media all I'd been able to find was a perfunctory Facebook page which he hadn't updated in four years. There were no tagged photos of him, and his friend list was very, very small. Max had added me as a friend on Facebook immediately after I'd called him a sheep shagger, so that evening I'd browsed through the profiles of people he

21

was friends with whose faces I recognised from the lab until I knew most of their names by heart.

None of them were friends with Dylan, not even Max.

Using social media to learn more about him was out.

The problem with Dylan leaving early from the lab was that I never had an opportunity to 'casually' talk to him at the end of the day, and I didn't have the guts to go straight up to his bench just to talk to him during lab hours. I couldn't do that even if I'd had the nerve to, anyway – I was working.

Which left me one option: I had to find another way to see him when I wasn't teaching.

During my undergraduate degree I had a membership for the university gym that I'd used fairly frequently. Louisa and I would go for a twenty-minute run, spend some time stretching on yoga mats and then, sometimes, I would go on for a swim whilst Louisa left to have a pint in Glasgow University Union with some friends.

That all stopped after I began my PhD and Louisa her Masters. The best and most accurate excuse I could give for it was pure and simple laziness. We could argue for hours about how we were too busy to go to the gym, or too tired, or too stressed, but Louisa and I both knew that, if we'd really wanted to go, then we'd have gone. Still, we renewed our memberships every year in the vain hope that we would, indeed, return to exercise in the gym some day.

Now that day had come. For me, at least.

I felt self-conscious going to the gym for the first time in months, though it wasn't as if I was in bad shape – or, at least, I didn't look like I was. The only exercise I got was walking to and from university, and running about the teaching labs trying to help everyone at once. This kind of low level of fitness had gotten me through three years of my PhD, but I could in no way survive a five-minute run or swim more than a dozen lengths of the pool now. And that was where I was ultimately headed as I entered the gym: the swimming pool. I knew fine well why I was there, and it had nothing to do with exercise.

I hoped to catch Dylan training.

"So disappointing," I mumbled, as I finally called it quits after twenty agonisingly slow lengths of the pool. For Dylan was nowhere to be seen; I'd been naïve to think I'd 'run into him' on my first try. A cursory survey of the universe sports website told me when the swim team practised, and I was relieved to see part of the pool was still open to the public during those times. It meant I could be there at the same time as Dylan without appearing creepy.

And yet he was not there.

Neither was he at practice the second or third time I went swimming, either.

The molecular methods lab ran three times a week – all of Monday, all of Tuesday, and half of Wednesday – during which time I saw Dylan but did not speak to him. For the next three weeks I wondered if he was watching me whenever I wasn't watching him, and sometimes indulged in the delusion that he was. But I knew that, in all likelihood, he barely even knew I existed.

Sometimes I felt more confident in myself. I'd think, *This is the day. This is the afternoon you say hi to him.* But by the time it came around to acting on such thoughts my nerves pulled me back, the anxious beating of my heart making it so difficult to breathe I felt sure I was on the verge of a panic attack.

So I spent three to four days at the gym, instead, sometimes alternating swimming with running because I couldn't face going to the pool and, once more, not seeing Dylan there.

Then – after the second-from-last lab – something changed.

Dylan was at practice.

He was so beautiful I could have cried.

When I was in primary school I had swimming lessons. It was a natural thing for any parent to put their child through when they lived beside the sea, so almost every kid from school learned to swim at the same time as I did. I continued swimming throughout high school for passive exercise and fun; I never even imagined swimming competitively. Even when I took swimming seriously as a ten-year-old I hadn't been all that fast, though I did have the stamina for it, at least.

Now, having taken it back up at twenty-five years old, I was not in the least bit surprised to discover that my stamina had long since disappeared. But after three weeks of swimming constantly that stamina was finally beginning to recover. I was almost pleased with my progress...right until the moment I saw Dylan swim.

It was like watching the Olympics in real life. The rest of the swim team just could not compare. I realised, then, why Dylan was allowed to skip practice so frequently. He was miles better than the rest of them.

He cut through the water like a knife through hot butter even when he was swimming the butterfly (a stroke I'd always deemed inelegant). I'd never been the type to be attracted to someone purely for their body but watching Dylan in action changed that completely. It was a work of art, the way his tendons and muscles operated beneath his skin. He was lithe and he was efficient and he was like nothing I'd ever seen before.

Eventually I realised I couldn't continue watching him from the edge of the pool – not unless I wanted to be noticed – so I quit my own swimming early, got dressed as quickly as I could, and went up to the viewing room above the pool simply so I could watch Dylan in action. I felt like a fan girl.

I didn't care.

A crazy part of me hoped Dylan would notice me watching; a far larger and more sensible part of me absolutely wanted the opposite. Despite this, when it transpired that Dylan hadn't looked in my direction even once it made me unbelievably depressed, though I knew I'd done less than nothing to warrant his attention. Unless he'd realised I was stalking him and wanted to know why, of course, which was a conversation I didn't want to have. Ever.

When I got back from the pool that day I saw I had a message from my mum asking me to cat-sit Tom whilst they went on holiday some time in March. I hadn't been home since Christmas, and I missed my blue-eyed, dove-grey pet dearly, so I immediately told her I would.

I also had a few missed calls from Louisa. I'd missed quite a lot of her calls over the last three weeks, which I knew was because all I did with my time was go to the gym and crash out, exhausted, afterwards. This made me feel awful; my best friend clearly missed me as much as I'd been missing her, yet all I'd done lately was ignore her. And so, after chucking my swimming gear in the washing machine and going for a shower, I pulled out my phone and video called her.

She rejected the call immediately.

My heart was going a mile a minute at her knee-jerk reaction – was she angry with me? Was she *done* with me? But all my fears were assuaged when Louisa promptly called me back with no video.

"Is something wrong?" I asked as soon as I answered the call.

Louisa laughed at my concerns, just as exuberant and enthusiastic as I'd always known her to be. "God, no, Grace!" she exclaimed. There was a hell of a lot of static in the call as well as so much background noise it threatened to swallow Louisa's voice completely. "It's just – I don't have any good signal here so I can't connect to video – can you hear me?"

I nodded, then remembered I was on the phone and Louisa couldn't see me. "Yes, just barely," I replied. "Where are you right now?" I glanced at the clock hanging above the television and saw that it was four in the afternoon. Which meant it was very, very early morning for Louisa. "You out right now?"

An infectious laugh again. "At a festival, Gracie! I've tried to call you like a million times to let you know about it. It's – god, T in the Park is nothing compared to this. This is a million times better."

Louisa had gone to T in the Park several times before we met each other. I'd only been once alongside her. I loved the music, and the atmosphere was admittedly electric. But I had never been one for getting into the muck and mess of things the way she had. It's not that I wasn't an outdoor person because I considered myself very much to be one. I loved going sailing

25

with my dad, spending weekends away on the boat to fish and swim out on the open sea.

But camping in the middle of a muddy field during a torrential downpour...well, let's just say that was past my limit.

"That wouldn't have anything to do with the sunshine, would it?" I asked Louisa. "I imagine it being hot changes things a bit."

"It's not just the weather, Gracie!" she replied. "It's - look, my signal is shit but I'll send you photos and videos when I can, okay? I was really just calling to see how you are. No judgement but you're definitely avoiding my calls."

"I haven't been avoiding them *deliberately,*" I said, which was the truth. "I've just been exercising a lot lately. Trying to get into shape." That last bit was a lie, though in stalking Dylan I was in better shape than I'd been in years.

Louisa burst out laughing once more. "I thought our days of going to the gym were long since over. What gave you the kick in the arse to change things now?"

"Let's just say my impending thesis is the procrastination I needed to get me exercising."

But Louisa knew me too well. Even over the unstable connection she knew what I was saying was a load of bull shit. "I don't believe you," she said. "You're - distracted. In your messages to me. It seems like your head's somewhere else. There's a boy, isn't there? It better not be a new best friend, Grace. I'll never forgive you if you -"

"No, new best friend," I cut in, giggling at the notion. "I swear. But...yeah, I admit it. There's someone I'm interested in."

Very interested in.

There was a moment or two of silence from Louisa, aside from the static and roar of the crowd behind her. And then: "Just be careful. Don't get too obsessed."

She said it jokingly but I knew better. We were super close; she knew exactly how I could get fixated on something or someone, which was why I was careful never to get that attached to anyone other than her. I wasn't this close to anyone *but*

Louisa, because she understood me. She was my best friend and I loved her. We were all the two of us ever really needed back when we lived together.

Sure, I had plenty of friends for social occasions – all met through Louisa, who was so extroverted that it scared me on occasion. I had a great time with all of them. She'd have never introduced me to someone I wouldn't like, after all. But, now that she was gone, I realised I hadn't seen any of those friends for months. It wasn't that they'd stopped inviting me to things; I simply hadn't responded to their messages.

I'm such a terrible person, I thought, sickened by my own self-absorbed nature. I decided I should at least try to meet up with them once or twice over the next few weeks. I couldn't revolve my life around stalking a boy, even though that's currently all my life was.

"You still there, Grace?" Louisa asked, breaking me from my reverie. There was a yell from behind her – someone screaming her name. "Look, this festival will be over tomorrow and then I'll be back at the hostel. Catch-up video chat then?"

I nodded again. "Yes, absolutely. Love you."

"I love you too, Gracie. Speak soon!"

When Louisa hung up the call I threw myself onto the couch. I hadn't realised how much I'd needed to hear her voice, even if it was over a terrible connection. Now the call was over, well...I felt alone.

I considered calling my parents but the thought of doing so only made me feel worse. Was my life really so sad that the only people I could call on a Friday night were Louisa and my mum and dad? There was always Louisa's brother, Josh, whom I was fairly close to, but he was probably working a double shift in the children's ward and also had a girlfriend. It wouldn't be right for me to call him at the weekend just to talk.

A heavy sigh escaped my lips, and I glanced at my laptop sitting innocuously on the coffee table. I'd looked for Dylan on social media before. He was a ghost; it was pointless to search again. Yet there was a twitch in my hand urging me to do so anyway. *Stop this,* I thought. *Do something else. Write your thesis. Watch Netflix. Do literally anything else.*

I grabbed my laptop.

Chapter Three

The final day of the molecular methods lab ended the way most teaching labs did: students impatient to leave for a pint on Ashton Lane or in one of the unions. For this lab that held particularly true, as most of the students couldn't wait to see the back of their weeks of molecular genetics training.

I'd spent the morning talking to my section about how a large chunk of jobs within biology these days involved using molecular lab techniques, having finally given into my desire to be frank with them. I told them if they tried to get summer projects that increased their experience with said techniques they'd be far more likely to find employment after graduation or get onto the more interesting PhD placements.

Despite this, come 2pm when the lab ended, it seemed as if most of the students couldn't wait to get rid of the knowledge that had been pushed into their brains for the past month. 'What use is PCR or protein purification to marine biologists?' they told each other. I had to stop myself laughing every time I heard the students say such things. They'd find out soon enough that what I'd said was the truth.

As usual, my eyes found the group that sat on the same bench as Dylan as they tore off their lab coats and headed for their lockers. I supposed they were actually friends with him; they laughed and joked together as if they were, at least. Or, rather, Dylan smiled and nodded along to their loud conversations.

There was something about the careful way Dylan held

himself – the smallest of distances he kept between him and the rest of the people on the bench, even Max – that told me he didn't consider them friends in the same way they considered *him* a friend. I wondered how they couldn't see it for themselves. To me it was obvious, like there was a gulf between them.

Dylan was unreachable.

In some ways that made me feel better, though in many more ways it made me feel worse. For if his supposed friends didn't appear to mean that much to him then how could I, a random girl Dylan had never spoken to, hope to get closer to him?

I had to give up on my obsession. Three weeks was more than enough. I had never found the courage to bridge the silence between us and that was on me.

It was time I moved on.

There was no motivation left within me after the lab to even try and make some progress with my thesis, so I decided to head to the gym once I was finished teaching instead of going to the library. At least then I could say I'd done *something* productive with my afternoon rather than heading home and crashing out.

As I exited the lab, however, I noticed that David was leaning against his locker waiting for me. His friends were standing a little ways further down the corridor, watching us. David waved, indicating for me to join him.

"I thought you'd all had enough of me and my love of protein purifications," I joked, for lack of anything better to say.

David chuckled, pushing his glasses back up the bridge of his nose when they slipped a little. At the beginning of the lab he'd worn contacts but after a close call with some acid he'd opted to switch to glasses for the rest of the lab. I *had* told him that's what safety goggles were for – I wore contacts, after all, and had never even come close to getting anything terrible in my eyes – but the near miss was enough of a fright for him to abandon lenses in favour of glasses nonetheless.

"We've had enough of the protein chat, sure," he said, "but

somehow not of you. Shocking, I know."

"Lovely."

"Join us for lunch?"

That was when I noticed David was nervous. His legs were crossed one in front of the other, and he shifted his weight from his left foot to his right every two seconds. There was a hopeful cast to his face that I didn't want to crush. Truly, I didn't. But after spending the morning surrounded by people the last thing I wanted to do was spend even *more* time with them. And besides, I wasn't hungry.

"I'm sorry, David," I said, making sure my expression was suitably apologetic. "I'm actually just on my way to the gym. Another time, maybe?"

A moment of disappointment, then David configured his features into a completely manufactured, unbothered smile. "Didn't have you pegged as a gym bunny, Miss Ferguson."

Because I'm not. I put on just as manufactured a smile as David's. "People can surprise you. Anyway, I best be off -"

"Grace."

David grabbed my elbow as I began to move past him, though he dropped his hand immediately and grimaced when he realised what he'd done. I knew he hadn't meant any harm but the shock of his hand gripping my arm sent my brain into a wild state of panic. I forced myself to swallow down my uncalled-for fear.

"Sorry, I didn't mean to grab you," he said, very quietly. He leaned forward, clearly not wishing for his friends to hear what he was about to say. "I just...I don't know how to ask this without seeming weird. Can we keep in touch? As friends?"

I begged my heart to stop thumping so hard. I needed friends, and I liked David. That he was literally *asking permission* to keep in contact with me rather than pushing his own agenda regardless of how I felt deeply endeared him to me.

If only I wasn't so damn anxious all the time.

"Of course," I replied, crafting my previous smile into a far

31

more genuine one. "I'd love that. But I really *do* want to get to the gym whilst there's a post-lunch lull. First dibs on equipment and all that."

David laughed nervously. "Of course. I'll – see you around, I guess. Or I'll message you!"

"I look forward to it." And then, because I didn't think I could handle any more, I gave the rest of David's friends a perfunctory nod before scurrying past them. I could hear them making fun of David behind my back, which suggested he'd wanted to ask me to lunch for a while. It made me feel terrible for reacting the way I had when all he'd done was simply try to stop me from running off long enough to ask me a damn question.

I was the worst.

By the time I reached the gym I no longer had even the slightest iota of energy to exercise. My skin was itchy and *wrong*, which was how I always felt after bad social interactions. I needed to relax – preferably alone for hours and hours and hours – and exercise was anything but relaxing to me. Yet I was already here, and I knew fine well that leaving without doing anything would make me feel even crappier than I already felt.

So I slid into my swimming costume and braided back my hair, relieved to see that the pool had just three people currently using it. One was an older man I thought might have taught me chemistry back in my undergrad; the other two were girls younger than I was taking selfies by the edge of the pool. I clucked my tongue in disgust. I wasn't in the mood for people like that.

Glancing at the steam room I realised I *could* relax instead of exercise, so long as it wasn't full of people. So I padded across the wet floor around the pool, a blast of balmy air hitting my face when I opened the opaque glass door to the steam room an inch. I was beyond relieved to see that nobody was inside the small, dark space.

Thank god, I thought, gladly entering the safety of the steam and closing the door behind me. *Some peace and quiet.*

I winced at the scorching ceramic of the tiled seat I lowered myself onto, though it wasn't long before I got used to the heat emanating from it. With a sigh I reclined against the wall. The steam was full of eucalyptus, which calmed my nerves and cleared my sinuses.

Since most of my previous visits to the gym coincided with the swim team being present, the steam room had always been full of laughing, pushy lads winding down after practice whenever I thought I might like to use it. I could never face going in there with a group of strangers...even less so had Dylan been one of them.

Ugh, I had to stop my thoughts from always leading back to him.

I forced myself to think of something else and inevitably ended up on the not-so-pleasant topic of my uncertain career prospects. But as I breathed in another heady quantity of steam and allowed the heat all around me to relax my muscles, I discovered that I could broach such a subject without going into a panic.

The marine biology students were the last group I was teaching this semester. Now there was nothing between me and my ever-looming thesis deadline and the ordeal of applying for jobs. I was such a hypocrite; I'd only just been criticising the undergrads and their unwillingness to get the right experience for a good job when in truth I had no bloody idea what I wanted to do with my 'sensible' PhD.

Did I want to pursue a post-doc? Move into industry? Medical technology? Or did I want to settle for some kind of technical writing or corporate job that had little if anything to do with the years and years I'd spent studying a field I was so enthusiastic about?

It was hard to remember being enthusiastic about my subject area now. The drudgery of finishing a PhD and trying to remember research I'd completed three years ago in order to write it up had taken its toll on my love of molecular biology. I wondered if all I needed was some time off – a proper break spent doing anything but applying for jobs – for my adoration of the subject to renew itself.

"I could move back to Largs," I whispered, the words billowing the steam in front of my face. I knew my dad would eagerly let me do so. My mum, on the other hand...she was enjoying her semi-retirement too much to have to deal with an adult child. A flash of irritation caused my temples to twitch at the thought. I was their *only* child. Surely they had to help me find my feet, even if only for a while.

But then I let out another sigh, and all my anger faded into the darkness around me. It wasn't fair to push myself on my parents. My dad climbed up the ranks of a phone company with no higher education to fall back onto. He'd worked tirelessly, and endlessly, to save up the money to leave the firm at the age of fifty-three. My mum was a private accountant and could definitely have afforded to retire completely if she hadn't enjoyed her job too much to give it up entirely.

I was proud of them. Of course I was. But the notion that they didn't need me in their lives haunted me. I wondered if, when Louisa returned from Australia – if she ever did – she would no longer need me, either. Was I destined for a life of anxiety whenever I was faced with the prospect of making friends for myself, even when they literally did all the hard work for me, like David? I didn't want that. I wanted to change.

It was so easy to think that. It was another thing entirely to *do* it.

When the door to the steam room opened and a shadowy figure sat down opposite me I immediately closed my eyes and tilted my head back against the wall. It was the only way I could continue to sit in comfortable silence with a stranger in such a situation; so long as I kept my eyes tightly shut I could enjoy the steam as it detoxed my mind and body as if I were still alone.

After several minutes of deep breathing I finally allowed myself to fall into a kind of semi-slumber. My muscles truly relaxed, and I wondered for how long I could remain in such humid conditions before collapsing from the heat. But, then, though there was no reason to believe such a thing, the atmosphere around me changed.

I became all too aware of the person sitting opposite me. It

34

was not as if they were breathing heavily – in truth I could hardly hear them breathing at all – nor were they shifting on the spot or fidgeting with their hands or feet. No, there was nothing that had transpired to make me more aware of them in the past two minutes. But something had changed nonetheless.

I opened my eyes.

Through the steam I saw Dylan.

He was unabashedly staring at me as if challenging me to explain my presence there, sharing the steam room with him. Fearfully I imagined what he was going to say now that I knew he was there. 'Why are you following me? Why were you asking Max about me? What are you doing stalking one of your students?'

That last question I'd rationalised to myself time and again on the pretence that I couldn't be more than four or five years older than Dylan, but I knew that wasn't the point. If I discovered one of my teachers was watching me the way I'd been watching him I'd have been scared and upset.

Yet Dylan said nothing. He remained completely and utterly silent, staring at me through fronds of steam with grey eyes that appeared to suck up what little light there was in the room. I opened my mouth to speak to him, instead, only to discover that my throat and tongue were so parched I seriously doubted I could've talked at all even if I'd known what to say.

There was plenty I could have said. Plenty I *should* have said, especially if I was a completely normal lab assistant who was not in the least bit thinking inappropriate thoughts about the oblivious tormentor of her heart currently sitting mere feet away from her.

I could have said, 'Hi, you're from the lab, right? Did you enjoy it?' It was a valid question. In fact, the more I thought about it, the more I realised how weird it was that I *hadn't* said something like that already. It was the kind of thing teachers said when they found themselves in bizarre situations with a student they saw every day.

I knew this from personal experience; a few months ago I'd run into the head of molecular biology in the bakery aisle of my local supermarket. Another time, three years ago, Louisa and I met one of our lecturers singing his heart out at a karaoke bar we'd gone to for her birthday.

'What did you think of the experiments?' was another thing I could have said. 'Is there anything that could be improved? Do you think you might be inclined to get into the genomics side of marine biology?'

Just like Dylan, I remained silent.

Overwrought with painful chest constrictions and a heart that threatened to burst, it took me an excruciatingly long time to fully absorb the situation I had found myself in. But as the silence stretched out further and further between us, I found that I was – unbelievably – beginning to calm back down. I realised that I was sitting bolt upright, hands protectively clutched to my chest and my legs pressed together as tightly as I could physically manage. I wasn't even aware I'd assumed such a position.

Dylan, on the other hand...Dylan was the picture of ease, reclining on his seat with his legs outstretched. They were so long my feet would have been touching his had I not blindly recoiled the moment I'd opened my eyes.

Steam clung to his hair, plastering it to his forehead in dark, heavy curls. Dylan's expression gave away nothing of his intentions, and when I found my eyes wandering from his face to take in the rest of his disgustingly fit body he did not turn away.

What is going on? I wondered, finding myself slowly but surely relaxing back against my seat. My hands fell to my lap, then to my sides, and I opened my legs just an inch. It felt as if my attraction to Dylan must have been obvious – I was mirroring his body language, for god's sake – but still, he said and did nothing.

Except stare. I stared right back, challenging *him* to give away his intentions. Had he been the one following me this time? Or had he come to the steam room right after me by chance? I was torn between the logical part of my brain saying that coincidences happened and the desperately lonely part of myself that wished nothing more than for Dylan to have directly sought me out.

36

And it was so hot. Steam swirled around me, turning my vision hazy and indistinct. Sometimes I could hardly see the lines of Dylan's body at all, but I could always see his eyes. A burning filled my core that had precisely nothing to do with the steam. I wanted him; I knew I did.

I wanted him to know I wanted him.

Then, just as I consigned myself to finally say something, Dylan turned his gaze away. He got to his feet, stretched his arms above his head like a lazy cat waking from a sun-drenched nap, and left.

That was it. With a blast of cold, chlorine-scented air as he opened the door he was gone.

I bashed my head against the wall and my foot against the floor, chewing the inside of my mouth to hold in a frustrated scream. "You fucking idiot," I said, close to tears. I had been given a perfect opportunity to talk to Dylan – my first and perhaps my last – and I'd absolutely squandered it.

I could never forgive myself for this.

Chapter Four

I never used to go to the university library. I always studied well enough at home. But *studying* and *writing your thesis* were two entirely different things, and I found it impossible to sit in my flat, alone, with nobody working beside me for company.

So I began going to the library...only to discover that it was so busy during the day that I couldn't find a single seat next to a plug socket for my laptop charger. Thankfully I found it easy to adjust my sleep schedule to become a bit of a night owl, and in this way confirmed that the library was much emptier later in the evening.

I had, of course, shamefully scoured each of the thirteen floors of the building whenever I visited just on the off-chance that Dylan was there. He was a good student, after all. It was reasonable to think he might be there. But I'd not once run into him – not even in the week after our strange encounter in the steam room – much to my dismay.

On this occasion my visit to the library occurred at midnight. I hadn't been able to sleep, tossing and turning in bed and restless beyond belief. The air outside my flat had been too still. Too quiet. It had unnerved me past all reason. So I got dressed, wrapped myself up in my favourite black, fluffy jacket, grabbed my laptop bag and walked the thirty minutes to the library through dimly-lit, abandoned streets.

Nearly every floor of the library was almost empty at this time of night – it closed at two in the morning – but I took the lift up to the tenth floor, anyway. There was a table I liked in the annexe there, surrounded by shelves of barely-if-ever-read books that was also, conveniently, close to a plug point. Some anonymous saint had actually plugged in an extension cord the previous week. If I ever found out who it was I swore I'd buy them a coffee or a Red Bull or something.

I crashed down onto a chair without looking to see if anyone else was sitting at the table first. It was large enough for eight people, after all, and I liked my regular spot here too much to give it up because someone else may or may not have been present. It was in this way that I got out my laptop, brain serenely filled with the sound of early 2000s Pop Idol music, and began reading over the progress I'd made the night before on my thesis.

For around half an hour I managed to focus. But when the playlist I'd been listening to ended and I had to choose some new music to listen to, I became aware of the sound of a pen scrawling across paper. It wasn't the regular strokes associated with writing, though; it sounded more like the person in question was drawing.

I looked up and gasped.

How had I not noticed that *Dylan* was sitting two seats to my left on the opposite side of the table? In all honestly I didn't even know if he'd been sat there before I arrived. Either way, I promptly lost all desire to work as my brain went into overdrive about how I currently looked: no make-up, hair pulled back into a half-hearted ponytail, terrible posture as I slouched inside the fluffy jacket I hadn't bothered removing. I sat a little straighter and fiddled with my hair in response, willing it to not look like I'd tried and failed to sleep on it.

Dylan, by contrast, looked great in an unassuming way, dressed in a grey jumper with the sleeves rolled up to his elbows. His messy hair tumbled over his forehead and threatened to touch his eyelashes as he frowned in concentration at his drawing.

Should I move? I wondered. I wasn't sure if Dylan had noticed me. He was so engrossed in his blue biro dancing across a lined piece of notebook paper that I reckoned he wasn't aware of *any* of his surroundings.

I focused on the paper to work out what he was drawing. A dark, stormy sea, crashing against a shelf of rock whilst a gull flew overhead. In the foreground I could make out a collection of shells and broken mussels, and when I narrowed my eyes I thought I could see a crab.

Every line Dylan drew seemed full of intent. The waves were powerful and disastrous; the delicate, pretty shells at the mercy of that power.

It felt as if I watched him draw for hours. I *could* have watched for hours.

"That's beautiful," I said, covering my mouth when I realised I'd been so entranced that I'd stupidly spoken out loud. Dylan's eyes darted from the paper to my face in an instant. *This is it,* I thought, certain. *If he didn't know before that I'm a stalker then he definitely knows –*

"Thank you."

I blinked, too shocked that Dylan had responded to take in what he'd said. His lips curled into the smallest of genuine smiles, and when he didn't immediately return to drawing I took it as a sign that it was okay for me to speak again – intentionally this time.

"Do you...do you like the sea?"

Dylan's expression changed slightly, though I had no idea what the look on his face meant. "I think that might be an understatement."

"Is that why you're studying marine biology, then, Dylan? Because –"

"Lir," he interrupted, in hushed tones that felt like he was telling me a secret. "My name is Lir."

There was a moment of silence as I processed this. Lir was his middle name; I hadn't heard anybody use anything other than Dylan to refer to him up to this point. I dared to believe that I was the first to learn this about him.

I tried the name out. "Lir." It felt good on my lips, as if it belonged there. "Lir. I like it."

The way Dylan's – Lir's – face lit up was like seeing the sun in the middle of the night. I could hardly stand to look at his luminous smile; his wide-eyed delight. I recalled that my first impression of his face was that there was an innocence about it. Now I could see why.

"So is that why you're studying marine biology?" I asked again, not knowing what else to ask – though there were countless other questions rushing a mile a minute through my brain.

"Yes," he said, as if that was all there was to it. I supposed that *was* enough. But then Lir elaborated. "I feel...more myself... when I'm in or near water. I don't feel right trapped inside a city."

It was my turn to smile. "I'm exactly the same. I grew up in –"

"Largs. I remember."

The fact Lir had remembered such a small, inconsequential nugget of information about me from a group conversation in the lab weeks ago did strange things to my stomach. Well, lower than that. It told me he deemed me worth his notice. Worth his brain retaining facts about me.

Fuck, I had it bad.

"Yeah, Largs," I said. "I spent most of my summer out sailing and fishing with my dad. What about you? Your name is pretty Irish but you don't *sound* that Irish." It was only in saying this that I consciously processed what Lir's voice was like. There was definitely an Irish twang in it, to be sure, though not enough to know from where it originated. But it didn't matter; his voice was beautifully low and lilting. *Like a storyteller,* I thought, *weaving impossible tales by firelight.*

Lir ran a hand through his hair and replaced the lid on his pen before replying. "I lived in Ireland until I was six in a tiny place called Bundoran that nobody's ever heard of. Then I moved to Campbeltown."

"*Campbeltown?* Of all places, why there?"

41

He narrowed his eyes. "You seem to find that funny. Why?"

"Oh, no, it's not – okay, it's funny," I admitted, "but that's just because I grew up surrounded by folk making fun of the place. Campbeltown is really lovely though, even if it *does* take forever to reach, what with it being in the middle of nowhere and all."

"Which is exactly why I like it," Lir said, returning to his heart-melting smile. "The surfing's good there."

"You surf?"

"As often as I can."

"Ah, so it's not always open water –"

I stopped myself from finishing my question, horrified that I'd almost revealed I'd asked Max for information about him. "Do you like swimming outdoors, too?" I asked, instead, to cover my tracks.

"Far more than in the pool, though I imagine you probably surmised that already."

The way Lir eyed me up told me he already knew I'd been asking people about him.

I was mortified.

"I've seen you in the pool sometimes," he added on when I didn't reply. "You're not bad, though your back stroke could use some work."

Okay, if I was mortified before I was even more so now. I hung my head in shame, mumbling an, "I hate back stroke," in response.

To my complete surprise Lir burst out laughing, eliciting a *shh* from someone several tables away. He simmered his laugh down to a gentle chuckle. "Hey, Grace," he murmured. "Look at me."

I'd never heard him say my name before. I had no choice but to look at him.

Lir's grey eyes were soft and commanding in equal measure.

"It's all fine," he told me. "You haven't done anything wrong."

I absolutely had. Hearing Lir say otherwise only made me more ashamed of myself. "Uh - thanks, I guess," I said after a while, no longer able to hold his gaze. His face was too honest; I couldn't stand to look at it right now.

A long, uncomfortable silence stretched out between us. Perhaps Lir was waiting for me to say something. Perhaps he'd said what he needed to say and was content with our one and only conversation ending where it ended. Either way, I didn't break the silence, though I desperately wanted to.

Then, after five minutes, Lir packed up his belongings and stood up. "I hope I'll see you around," he said, before walking away so silently I had to turn my head and watch him leave just to make sure he wasn't standing right behind me.

"See you around," I mouthed.

I had no idea when that would be.

It seemed, however improbable it may have been, that Lir very much did.

Chapter Five

One morning in late February, which at first appeared to be just like any other dreary winter morning, I received an email that changed everything for me.

It was from my PhD supervisor, handing me a blessed opportunity for paid work that he knew I so desperately needed. I had nothing but a rapidly-depleting savings account acting as a buffer between me and homelessness as I forced out my thesis, so any kind of paid work was a god send. This particular work, however, seemed like a literal miracle.

The email read:

Hi Grace,

Figured you could do with the work. Professor Reynolds, who runs the marine and freshwater biology degree, needs an extra pair of hands for the group's upcoming Millport trip in March. The students spend a week gathering research samples and doing wet lab work in prep for their final year projects, so you won't be doing anything complicated. She said it's basically glorified babysitting, and since Sophie told her the marine students got on well with you in the molecular methods lab she thought you'd be a good fit. Would you be interested in helping out over there?

Let me know what you think,

Mark

I had to read the email over three times before what was written before my very eyes sunk in. A week with the marine and freshwater biology third year students.

With Lir.

I hadn't seen him since our conversation in the library, which felt entirely like a dream rather than a real thing that happened a mere week ago. It had been so late, and the tenth floor had been dark and silent all around us. Since then I'd become a ball of nervous, manic energy, especially because Lir told me he'd see me around. But, seven days later, I hadn't laid eyes on him even once.

I emailed my supervisor back saying yes.

The Millport trip was in two weeks. Fourteen days to prepare my heart and my nerves, as well as write as much of my thesis as I physically could. Something told me that if I didn't do much of it now I would struggle to get back into the swing of things when I returned.

I certainly wasn't going to do any of it in my parents' house, that much I knew for a fact. No, I'd spend my time eating all the food in the kitchen, soaking in the bath (which had jets), and watching anything and everything on their surround sound, fifty inch television whilst taking up all the space on their expensive corner sofa.

After all, what else was a poor student supposed to do when faced with the simple luxuries in life that came from spending the week in a nice house right on the promenade of a tourist town? Not work on her thesis, that much was for sure.

So I pulled my head out of my ass and locked myself down in the library day after day, only pausing from writing my thesis in order to exercise in the gym – which, for once, I wasn't doing simply to catch Lir. Well, I suppose I was doing it to catch Lir's *attention* once we were in Millport; I was now in the best shape of my entire adult life.

By the end of the two weeks I only had a final results chapter and a closing discussion left to write. When I sent all the work I'd done to my supervisor he responded with surprise at my burst of productivity, which I'd expected. I was pleased with myself. When left to my own devices I tended not to be all that dedicated to deadlines until the literal night before said deadline.

Perhaps I was finally growing up. Maybe this was the beginning of me becoming a responsible, forward-thinking adult, who could talk to people that she liked and socialise with large groups on a regular basis.

"One thing at a time," I said as I carefully packed my bag for a week in Largs. I'd originally intended to pack almost entirely pyjamas and lounge wear, but now everything had changed. I needed to bring pretty clothes, hair curlers and make-up.

One thing at a time, then another and another. I had to finish writing my thesis and pass my *viva* before anything else could happen with my life. And, before that, I had to work out if Lir was interested in me the way I was interested in him. It certainly seemed that way in the library and – I gulped at the memory – when we'd been in the steam room at the gym.

I had goals. Small, manageable goals. That was good. I didn't feel so anxious when I broke down what I needed to do like that.

After I packed I checked my Facebook account for messages. I'd uninstalled all social media apps from my phone to stop them distracting me whilst I wrote my thesis, so I cringed in anticipation of a deluge of missed conversations.

To my relief there weren't many. I had several messages from David, which included a gif of a cat and a video of a fainting goat. I responded to the video, apologising for being terrible at messaging for the last fortnight. He replied almost immediately saying he was looking forward to seeing me again during the Millport trip. To this I merely said *me, too,* and left it at that.

Aside from David I had seven missed video calls from Louisa. And several messages on WhatsApp, Instagram and Snapchat.

God, I felt terrible. I hadn't been avoiding Louisa deliberately, since I'd been genuinely working or in the gym, but still. I could have found the time to call her at least once over the past two weeks yet I hadn't. So I fired over a quick apology, stating that I'd call her when I reached my parents' house the following day. Hopefully that would be enough to make it up to

Louisa and assuage my guilt in the process.

Things were changing in my life, that much was certain. Good things – great things – felt just within my grasp. But my relationship with Louisa was the one thing I never wanted to change. I had to be a better person and make more of an effort.

And besides, how could I expect her to like Lir if all she ever knew about him was that I ignored her in favour of him? I was determined that they should meet when Louisa came back from Australia. They *had* to. I wanted them both in my life, after all.

I just had to make Lir part of said life, first.

Chapter Six

When I was fourteen – perhaps to apologise for never giving me a sibling, though in truth I never wanted one – my parents bought me a kitten. He was an adorable thing, all grey fluff with white-tipped ears, white underbelly and three white socks on his feet. I'd called him Tom, for the cartoon, because I wasn't all that imaginative as a teen. He followed me everywhere, and when I left for university I cried for days over leaving him. I loved him down to my very core.

After keeping me up half the night, he was seriously testing that love to within an inch of my life and my sleep-deprived, frayed nerves.

"Tom, get down here!" I yelled. "Your damn breakfast is ready."

The fact that Tom didn't immediately come skittering into the kitchen the moment I opened a tin of food was telling. He was asleep on my bed, I knew, having exhausted himself exhausting *me.*

Tom cried and screamed in the garden whenever anyone came close. His mad behaviour actually saved the house getting broken into on a dark November evening two years ago, when my parents were out and our neighbour, Terry, was keeping an eye on things.

It was an instinct I should have been grateful for. But, now that Tom was almost twelve years old it seemed very much as if he was starting to go senile. No matter how many times I opened the door to scope out the garden and the street in front of the house there was nobody there, yet Tom just wouldn't stop yowling even when I locked him up inside.

It meant I had been blessed with about three hours of sleep collectively, which was at least five hours less than I needed. I'd wanted to be fresh for the lab and reach the ferry that was taking the students over to Millport with time to spare; instead, I was scrambling about knowing that I was cutting it fine to get to the pier before the damn boat left.

I thumped up the stairs, arms crossed over my chest as I spied Tom sprawled on his back on my bed. "Fine," I told him, not trying to keep my voice down in the slightest, "sleep the day away and keep me up at night. Talk about love, you useless cat." Then I grabbed my jacket and left the house, making sure to double-check that both the front and back doors were locked.

Just in case.

It was a lovely morning, blustery and sunny. The mid-March air held the promise of spring, though there was still a biting edge to it when I passed beneath the shade of a tree. If I'd not been so tired and running so late I'd have been tempted to get an ice cream from Nardini's Café for breakfast.

"For dinner, then," I promised, stomach rumbling and mouth watering at the mere thought of coconut and vanilla ice cream melting down the cone and onto my fingers. God, it had been too long since I'd been home.

The ferry was just over ten minutes from my house – I could see the pier from my bedroom window – so though I'd been worried about missing the boat I still reached it with a minute or two to spare. When I boarded and caught sight of the students I couldn't help but smile. There was an obvious split between the ones who were excited to be on the boat and those who had already grown uneasy. Though it was a sunny day the water was, as it often was, choppy, with frequent waves causing the deck to shift beneath its passengers' feet.

At least the students had an easy morning getting settled into the Research Station and listening to a few introductory lectures. I had a hectic morning of sample preparation and aliquoting reagents ahead of me.

As the ferry left the pier the original enthusiasm for being on a boat was washed away from many of the students, who were now faced with inevitable seasickness. "David!" I called when I saw the man in question. His eyes were closed, and he had removed his glasses to pinch the bridge of his nose. "The ferry ride is barely fifteen minutes long. You'll be fine."

True to my promise after the molecular methods lab I had kept up my friendship with David, though at times I felt unsure about his attentions. I knew I only saw him as a friend, but it was becoming apparent that wasn't all he saw me as. I didn't want to risk our friendship by calling him out on it: I'd met a lot of men who, when faced with rejection, no longer had any interest in being my friend. I didn't imagine David was that kind of person. However, I had so few friends currently that I had no intention of risking the loss of this one just on a hunch.

In any case David did not respond to my comment verbally. He shook his head, and that was it.

When it became clear David was in no condition for conversation I headed to the passenger cabin to check my phone, as I knew my schedule for the day was too busy to check it later. Louisa had sent me a few photos on Instagram, showing me that she was busy fanning herself on the beach whilst nursing a mojito, then playing volleyball on the sand with several handsome strangers. *Classic Louisa,* I thought, *making friends at every turn. I wonder if she'll even remember their names tomorrow.*

As I mindlessly scrolled through my feed another familiar redhead appeared – Louisa's brother, Josh. He'd uploaded a photo of himself drinking a coffee; below it was the caption 'Am I doing the fake candid thing right?'

I was curious. Josh never posted photos like that. But a quick search of his profile suggested that he'd recently broken it off with his girlfriend, for up until a week ago every photo was of the two of them. Now it seemed as if she had been all but eliminated from his life.

There was a part of me that was satisfied about the apparent break-up. The night Louisa left for Australia Josh and I got drunk together and he admitted he'd always liked me as more than a friend, but because he was five years my senior and my best friend's brother he hadn't wanted to push his feelings on me.

He was already seeing his girlfriend at the time. When I'd brought her up, though, Josh said that their relationship was casual. Convenient. They both needed something to satisfy their physical urges whilst working full-time in a demanding job. I could never imagine being in such an emotionless relationship when in every other respect you were closer to them than anyone else.

But, like I said, I was drunk and I was lonely, and so was Josh. We slept together several times that night and, when we were too exhausted to continue, I cried against his shoulder about Louisa leaving. He'd stroked my hair and told me everything was going to be okay; all I had to do was go to sleep.

In the morning, through the pounding of a hangover-induced migraine, I watched Josh get out of bed and collect his clothes. "I'll call you during the week," he'd said, but then he never did.

A week later he set his status on Facebook to 'in a relationship', and that was that. It had taken some time for us to get on somewhat easy ground again, knowing that things would never be the same between us. Our common link was gone and, with it, most of our reasons to see each other. I never mentioned what happened between us, and neither did Josh. We were friends, nothing more.

I didn't know back then if I'd wanted things to change between us. Even now I still didn't. But friends checked in with each other so, though part of me still felt weird about doing it, I sent Josh a message asking if he was okay. I didn't mention his girlfriend. I didn't mention the fact he told me he'd liked me for years, or what had happened between us after that, or that it hurt when he didn't call.

No, it was a nice, simple message making sure he was in good health, with no indication whatsoever that I wanted things between us to be complicated, because I didn't.

51

Very quickly the passenger cabin became full of students who had grown tired of recreating the scene from Titanic where Jack and Rose stand at the bow of the ship. With so many people inside the small compartment the air grew suffocatingly hot. I found it difficult to breathe, resulting in me putting my phone away and deciding to head back outside.

"You're insane if this rocking doesn't bother you," David muttered just as I reached the door. He was sitting at a tiny table, nursing his head in his hands. There was a distinctly green tinge to his pale skin. I could only laugh at the comment, though I knew doing so was kind of cruel. David was a born-and-bred city boy with limited experience of boats and ferries. But I wasn't.

I grew up on them.

When I reached the bow of the ferry my heart began to soar. It was a giddy feeling, to have the floor beneath you shiver and shake as the waves tried their level best to unbalance you. I lived for this. No concrete. No sky-high blocks of flats shielding me from the weather. The wind eagerly whipped my hair across my face, and the sun reflecting off the waves back onto my skin threatened to burn me even in March.

Above me seagulls followed the path of the ferry in wide, lazy circles, cawing and screaming obnoxiously loud. I smiled up at them then breathed in deeply, savouring the tang of seawater overwhelming my senses until I could almost taste it. There were lots of people I knew who hated the smell. They couldn't stand the brine, the fish, the salt. I couldn't get enough of it.

Then, just as the ferry slowed as it neared the pier on Millport, a large wave sent the vessel veering to the left. Water came crashing over the side, soaking me down to the skin in an instant. I hadn't been at all prepared; it filled my lungs and blocked my ears and stung my eyes into blindness. I could feel my body shivering against the freezing water, though my brain hadn't yet caught up with my nerves telling me I was cold.

As my vision went from non-existent to blurry to normal, and my ears popped themselves free of water, I noticed somebody was laughing at me. I recognised the voice immediately, and in turning to look to my right I realised they weren't laughing *at* me.

Lir was laughing with me, even though my mouth was still a silent *o* of shock.

He, too, had been hit by the wave, his arms outstretched as if welcoming the water to crash into him again. His eyes were closed, chin tilted up towards the sun. Even though his hair and clothes were plastered to his skin he didn't seem to care in the slightest.

He looked completely and utterly mad.

Maybe I am, too, I thought, dizzy with the overwhelming urge to laugh just as Lir was. So I did, savouring the sound of my voice joining his against the roar of the wind and the waves and the ferry's engine. Lir opened his eyes and locked his gaze on mine, a dazzling smile on his face that was for the two of us and nobody else.

We didn't talk. No, neither of us said a word.

We didn't have to.

Chapter Seven

It was Thursday, and the previous three days of working in Millport and cat-sitting had passed by in a blur. I fell into a routine that seemed to have been specifically created to destroy my brain: struggle to sleep whilst Tom yelled all night; drown my fatigue in coffee; try to look put together and not-at-all-tired; get the ferry to the Research Station; work until I'm dead on my feet and then, finally, get the ferry back and collapse on the couch in my parents' living room and pretend to watch television.

I hadn't spoken to Lir once. Georgia had insisted on each of the demonstrators 'looking after' the same students they'd been in charge of from the molecular methods lab, which Professor Reynolds thought was a good idea. I didn't mind – I liked my lab section a lot, after all – but I'd been disappointed nonetheless.

Of course, I could have hung back when work was over to talk with the students and other teachers, but since I had to get the ferry back and Tom was keeping me up all night I was far too tired to even try and socialise. So I made do with watching Lir from afar, though I knew things were different between us compared to when I'd done the same thing back in the molecular lab.

For I knew he was, sometimes, watching me back.

The weather had gotten worse since Monday. It wasn't raining, but the air had cooled to wintry January levels, and the sun was obscured behind what felt like miles of thick, dark clouds. The stretch of coastline the students were gathering rock pool samples from was drained of almost all colour, which seemed appropriate to my current mood.

I huddled into my fluffy jacket deciding that, tomorrow, I'd throw on one of my dad's trusty anoraks over the top of it for extra warmth and protection from the cutting wind. I tried and failed to stifle a yawn, holding a hand over my mouth when it became clear I could hold it in no longer. God, I needed coffee. And my bed.

The students themselves were largely, woefully unprepared for collecting samples outdoors. They'd been warned to bring appropriate outdoor clothing, of course – they were due to go out on boats tomorrow to collect even more samples – but most of them hadn't listened. The ones who by and large hailed from the countryside and the coast were fine, which wasn't surprising. They owned proper waterproof jackets and thick-soled boots that were all function over form, as opposed to the 'fashionable', paper-thin anoraks and ankle-high wellington boots many of the city kids were wearing.

They'd probably bought them for a festival or something, immediately throwing them into the back of a cupboard afterwards never to be seen again. Until their next festival, of course. That was the only reason Louisa had ever owned wellies.

"Oh my god, Dylan, are you insane?! Get out of there!" one of the girls from Lir's bench called out, catching my attention. Lir was having a terribly great time, in stark contrast to many of the students currently shivering through the freezing cold afternoon. He had waded into one of the deeper rock pools, peering into the murky water for whatever he was searching for. Lir did not even seem to feel the bite of the water as it seeped up his jeans to his thighs; perhaps he simply didn't care. I suspected the latter.

"Come on, get out of there," Max said, waving a hand at his lab partner to urge him out of the rock pool. But Lir ignored him, and turned his gaze to me for half a second with the flash of a grin on his face. I almost thought I'd imagined it, though I had learned enough about him to know that I hadn't.

He could say more with one wild, wide-eyed look than he

ever could with words.

When it became clear that he was going to continue collecting samples as if he were oblivious to the people around him, everyone slowly got back to their own work and left Lir to his madness. I wished I could be as unselfconscious as he was.

It must be so freeing, not caring about what anyone thinks, I mused on my way to the laboratory an hour later, arms stacked high with box upon box of the samples the students had collected. Georgia was supposed to have helped me but, in classic Georgia fashion, she begged me to do it so she could reply to a missed call from her mum. She didn't see me notice her sneak off to have a cigarette, but I couldn't be bothered calling her out on it. I had too much on my mind.

I wonder if Lir cares what I think of him?

After storing the samples in the large walk-in refrigerator I checked the time. It was only four; today's work had ended blessedly early. I was exhausted from my lack of sleep, and a late afternoon nap sounded heavenly, but it felt like I was looking a gift horse in the mouth if I didn't use this time to try and find Lir and...I didn't know. 'Talk' to him didn't sound like enough anymore, though in truth we had only spoken once. But I wanted more.

Needed more.

When my phone buzzed I jumped so badly that I slipped on the floor and almost fell over. Cursing aloud, I pulled out the offending device and saw that I had a text from David inviting me to join his group for coffee in the social area. I knew I should accept, not just in the hope that Lir would be around but also because it would be good for me to socialise.

I declined.

"Fucking useless," I berated myself, choosing the coward's option of going home early for my longed-for nap. With any luck I'd fall into such a heavy sleep I wouldn't wake until morning, even with Tom's yowling.

When David responded telling me to live a little and get drunk with him and his friends I no longer had the energy to feel bad about my decision, so I left his message on 'read' and didn't reply.

When I finally got back to Largs I realised, with a cry of frustration, that I needed more cat food. There was literally none left which meant I couldn't leave it until tomorrow morning. So I made a beeline for the supermarket, grabbing a couple of spicy chicken pizzas, a carton of orange juice and a bottle of prosecco for definite future use. When I passed the toiletries aisle I remembered I basically had zero mascara left so I quickly chose one Louisa liked that I'd occasionally borrowed.

Then I saw the hair dye. More specifically, turquoise hair dye.

I grazed the side of my neck with my fingertips, pulling a lock of hair over my shoulder to inspect it. Though most of my hair was its natural dark brown colour, the underside was bleached. Months and months ago it was pink – at Louisa's behest, of course – and there was still more than enough of it left white blonde that the turquoise dye would take to my hair quite well.

Would Lir like it?

I bought the hair dye before I could stop myself, hating how obsessed I'd become but at the same time not caring one bit. So what if I wanted mermaid-coloured hair for the boy who adored the sea? My eyes were green; it would suit me.

"You've gone mad, Grace Ferguson," I said in my mother's tone of voice, paying for my shopping before gritting my teeth against the wintry air as I left the shop. It seemed to take forever to get back to my house, though in truth it was barely a quarter of an hour since the shop was right by the pier. But by the time I reached the kitchen I was dead on my feet, barely able to keep my eyes open as I put away my shopping and opened a tin of food for Tom.

"Where are you, silly cat?" I called out, banging a fork against his bowl for a few seconds until it became clear Tom wasn't going to respond. "Don't you dare hide from me right now."

After searching the house I discovered that Tom hadn't

returned from his walkabout yet. But I wasn't worried, not really. Tom spent half his time outdoors; there was more than one occasion from when I still lived with my parents where he had disappeared for an entire day.

"Come back soon, Tom," I whispered as I wrenched off my freezing clothes and pulled on a giant t-shirt I'd left hanging on the radiator. It was gloriously hot, since I'd had enough sense to put the central heating on a timer to turn on an hour before I returned from Millport.

I barely got out a yawn before I crawled beneath the feather duvet on my bed and closed my eyes, feeling lonely without Tom's presence but also inordinately happy that he wasn't around to scream me awake.

I fell asleep thinking of Lir in the rock pool, and the way he'd smiled at me for but the smallest of moments.

In my dreams, that smile stretched on for ever.

Chapter Eight

"...third mugging in a week, Joe."

"I heard nothing was taken from the victims, so are they really muggings?"

"That's not confirmed. I think we can both agree, though, that if the attacker wasn't *after* anything then these assaults are even more a cause for concern."

I shivered out a yawn, forcing another gulp of scalding coffee down my throat. Between the torrent of rain outside, the whip-like wind battering the kitchen window and the dreary news on the radio, I felt tempted to call in sick and curl back into bed for the entire day. But I wasn't the type to lie just because I didn't feel like doing something, so I searched through the coat cupboard for one of my dad's trusty anoraks to protect me from the worst of the weather once I stepped foot outside.

Millport wasn't exactly a cesspool of crime; hearing about not one but three attacks in a week was unusual. But there was more to it than that. The so-called muggings had begun the moment the students from Glasgow had settled into the Marine Research Station, which I'm sure hadn't escaped any of the teachers' notice.

"It better not be anyone I know who's responsible," I muttered, searching through the pantry for cat food only to remember that Tom was yet to return from his outdoor adventure, so hadn't eaten the last lot I'd put in his bowl. I wasn't used to him being gone this long. Then again, I'd spent most of my adult life in Glasgow. Tom could spend his days roaming the streets and I'd never know unless my mum and dad told me. I resolved to call them about it when they returned from holiday.

"And now for the weather report," Joe-from-the-radio said, interrupting my thoughts. "The occluded front moving over the west coast is expected to bring with it further unsettled weather in the afternoon that will linger until tomorrow morning. The last ferry back to the mainland is expected to leave at two."

"God damn it!" I slammed my hand down on the kitchen counter-top, causing concentric circles to ripple across the surface of my coffee. Tomorrow morning was the final lab for the students before they spent the afternoon (and evening) drinking, returning to Glasgow no doubt hungover the following day. Which meant *today* was their proper final day, during which time they'd be working with their samples in the lab until close to six this evening. Georgia had already left for Glasgow, which left only me to help out as a student assistant.

Meaning I had no choice: I had to stay in Millport at the Research Station tonight.

"It might be fun," I reasoned, inhaling the rest of my coffee before running upstairs to hurriedly pack an overnight bag. I got on well with the students, and this way I could sleep a little longer in the morning and have more time to get ready before having drinks with them in the afternoon. My heart fluttered at the thought.

Drinks with Lir.

Okay, not drinks *with* Lir, but he would be there. And he would be there tonight, too. Staying over meant I doubled my chances of being able to talk to him and get to know him better.

If he let me.

If I had the nerve to.

God, I was so pathetic. If Louisa could see me now she'd probably punch me in the face and tell me to man the fuck up. But Louisa wasn't here, and I had nobody else to push me into making a move. I had to rely on me and me alone.

After throwing more clothes than I could possibly wear in a twenty-four hour period into a bag I added in a pair of curlers, my make-up, toiletries and, perhaps against my better judgement, the box of hair dye I'd bought the other night. My dad would go mental if I used it in the bathroom and dyed the sink, anyway. Better for me to use it elsewhere or not at all.

Shrugging into his forest-green anorak on top of my own fluffy and not-at-all waterproof black jacket, I pulled the hood over my head and braced myself for the storm outside. The wind blew me down the front path the moment I left the safety of the porch, threatening to push me straight into the steel-grey, stormy sea if I wasn't careful. I had to fight hard against it to reach my neighbour's house and knock upon his door.

Terry Jones was a decade or two older than my parents, with a bad back and arthritis in his joints. He used to cat-sit for them before the arthritis started getting worse, but I figured one night couldn't hurt him. And besides, if Tom didn't show up he wouldn't have to do anything at all.

I rang the buzzer several times but Terry did not respond. Wondering if it was broken, I banged my fist against the door for a minute or so until, finally, I heard the slide of a lock and the door inched open.

"Hi, Terry," I said, trying to keep my voice bright as I smiled at him. Because of the weather it came out more like a frozen grimace.

He returned my smile with a very genuine one of his own. "Little Gracie. Your parents mentioned you were watching the house. What can I do you for?"

I pointed in the direction of the ferry. "I've been working over in Millport all week and there's no way I can get out of it today," I began explaining, "but the ferry's only running until two, so -"

"Do you need me to feed Tom?" he asked, predicting my request.

My shoulders relaxed. "Yes, please. He's actually been on a wander for a few days so he might not even show up. But if you could keep an eye out for him it would be much appreciated!"

Terry's smile widened. "Of course, Gracie. Now you get

61

yourself on the ferry before the waves capsize it!"

With a nod and another round of thanks I all but sprinted towards the pier, gritting my teeth against the freezing rain as it pelted my face. It stung so much I thought it might have been hail. More than once a wave came crashing over the promenade, soaking through my leggings and boots immediately.

By the time I reached the Research Station I was drenched from head to toe, though my dad's anorak took the worst of the damage. I wasn't looking forward to an entire day of working in the lab looking and feeling half like a drowned rat, even after changing into dry clothes, but I got through it all by holding on to the thought that tonight I might finally, *finally,* talk to Lir again.

Yet after the working day was over and I'd had dinner with Professor Reynolds and the other teachers, all thoughts of talking to Lir vanished. I was desperate for a hot shower and literally nothing else.

"The en suite rooms were allocated already," Professor Reynolds apologised when she opened the door to the twin room she'd had the Research Station staff prepare for me. "But the communal showers are just down the hall. They're all cubicles, though, so they're still private."

I held up a lock of painfully tangled hair. "At this point I wouldn't care if it was one huge shower used by ten people at a time. I just need hot water."

With a chuckle Professor Reynolds left me to my own devices, so I quickly dumped my bag on one of the beds and hung my dad's jacket on the back of a chair. I'd been to the Research Station before – back in the third year of my undergraduate for an overnight trip with my degree group – and the room I was in now was exactly as I remembered the one I'd been in then with Louisa.

It didn't matter that the mattress on the bed was thin and probably uncomfortable, or that the only furnishings were the two beds, the chair, a wall-mounted mirror, a wobbly desk and an equally unstable-looking wardrobe. I was only here for the night, after all, and if one night of bad sleep was the price I had to pay to talk to Lir then I would gladly pay it.

If I had the capacity to talk to another human being after a shower instead of falling dead asleep, of course.

I knew from my time here before that the communal showers didn't have space anywhere to change, so I stripped out of my clothes, wrapped myself in a towel and grabbed my toiletry bag and the box of hair dye. To be honest I couldn't be bothered with something as cumbersome as dyeing my hair right now, but if I *didn't* do it now I knew I never would. I was colouring it like the sea to catch Lir's attention, after all. It was pointless if I didn't dye it now.

The corridor was blessedly empty on my way to the showers, since almost everyone was either hanging out in their own rooms or socialising downstairs. Nobody was even having a shower – another stroke of luck on my part. The third stroke of luck came in the form of a beautifully high-pressured, burn-your-skin-off-hot shower, which was exactly what I needed.

I spent far too long simply standing beneath the torrent of hot water, thinking that I could quite easily fall asleep where I stood. But then I shook away the fatigue, forced myself to shampoo my hair and then lathered the bleached underside of it with turquoise dye. It was fiddly business, trying to keep it out of my natural hair colour, but this wasn't my first dye-at-home rodeo.

The most boring part was having to stay out of the water for twenty minutes whilst the dye worked its magic, so I kept the shower running to languish in the steam and leaned against the cubicle door to keep my hair well away from the water.

"I'm as well shaving my legs," I murmured, taking out my razor and softly singing along to some song playing in my head as I did so. It might have been from Hamilton; I'd found a bootleg recording of the Broadway production online the week before.

By the time it came to wash out the dye somebody else had turned on the shower in the cubicle directly on my left, so I stopped singing and finished up as quickly as possible. I tied my hair up into a dripping wet, messy-as-hell bun, figuring I'd just dry it as soon as I got back to my room, then wrapped my towel around me and left the cubicle to check I hadn't accidentally dyed my neck in the fogged-up mirror. Pleased that I hadn't, I gave my toiletry bag a once-over to make sure I'd actually brought everything I needed with me, since I hadn't checked it before I left that morning.

I'd forgotten my contact lens solution.

"You idiot!" I cried at my steamy reflection. I'd brought the damn case for my lenses but no solution; if none of the students had any then I'd have to make up some salt water for them and I hated doing that. I *always* got the salt concentration wrong, and when I put my lenses back in they stung my eyes until they were streaming.

Without thinking, I left the shower room and made a beeline straight downstairs to the social area, intending to make a blanket request for saline solution from any students down there. It was only after I opened the door and was met by no fewer than four wolf whistles that I remembered I was wearing a damn towel and nothing else.

"Well this has just made my day!" David called out, laughing as my face grew as red-hot as the fire he was relaxed in front of. I couldn't believe what I'd so foolishly done. These were my *students.* Sure, most of them were only four years younger than me – and some, like David, were the same age or older than me – but having them see me half-naked was mortifying. It was more embarrassing than getting wasted in front of them, I imagined.

"I – uh – forgot my contact lens solution," I said, forcing out a self-conscious chuckle to show that I, too, found the situation funny. "Does anyone have some?"

"Oh, I do," David replied, just as two other students raised their hand in response to the question. "Want me to grab it for you now?"

"If you could, thanks."

David got up from his seat – which was swiftly stolen by Lir's lab partner, Max – winking at me as he passed me by and left the social area. I only grew more flustered and uncomfortable standing there waiting for him, so I turned to wait in the corridor instead and –

Walked straight into Lir.

Similarly dressed in a towel and nothing else.

"I thought it was you singing in the shower," he said, though I wasn't paying attention to what his gentle, lilting voice was actually saying. This was only the second time he'd ever spoken to me after that one late, late evening in the library weeks ago. "*Say No to This* from Hamilton, right?"

I nodded, though I wasn't sure what I was agreeing with. Lir's towel was slung around his hips, so un-self-consciously bare-chested that I had no choice but to stare at the lines of his body, from his collarbone all the way down to his obliques. Memories of the time we'd both been in the steam room at the gym – Lir's grey eyes watching me watching him through the haze – filled my brain. I knew I had to look away. I knew I was being inappropriate.

There was not a single part of me that wanted to look away.

"What were the two of you getting up to in the shower, eh?" Max called from behind me, bringing me starkly back to life.

I let out a nervous laugh and bowed my head, not daring to look directly at Lir's face after I'd so unashamedly ogled him. "Being overheard singing, clearly," I replied, making to bypass Lir and attempt a swift escape.

But then David reappeared in the doorway and I was boxed in by Lir's left-hand side. I could feel droplets of water sliding down his arm against my skin; every hair on my body and his was stood on end. I knew, instinctively, that he was looking at me.

Don't look at him don't look at him don't look at him.

"The sacred solution," David said, handing me over a contact lens case filled with the stuff. It had googly eyes stuck on the lid, which looked at me as if they were aware of the filthy thoughts that were currently circling inside my head. "Aliquoted by yours truly. You can keep the case; it's my spare."

"Uh, thanks," I mumbled, grabbing the case from David and all but pushing him aside to flee the social area. I could hear everyone laughing at me, no doubt highly amused by my extreme embarrassment. They were good students, though, so I knew they wouldn't be cruel about it when they doubtlessly made fun of me for it at the pub tomorrow.

But still.

When I reached my room I collapsed on top of the lumpy, uncomfortable bed that I'd get no sleep in for the night, burying my head in the pillow and willing the sea to swallow me up.

So much for turquoise hair and having the confidence to actually talk to Lir.

I couldn't even look him in the eye.

Chapter Nine

The morning lab passed by in blessed, uneventful quiet. I was beyond shattered thanks to the - as predicted - horrifically uncomfortable bed I'd tried and failed to get any sleep in, though once the lab finished and I fell onto its lumpy surface once more it felt as luxurious as the memory foam mattress I had at my parents' house. Everybody was currently eating lunch and getting ready for the pub; I figured an hour-long nap couldn't hurt.

"Just for a little while," I said, readjusting the pins in my hair so it wouldn't get messed up when I lay on it. I'd curled my hair very early that morning when it became apparent I wasn't going to get any sleep, then carefully spun it into a bun to keep the curls from falling out before the afternoon...and so none of the turquoise was visible.

I wasn't ashamed that I'd dyed it - I was well past that - but I simply couldn't be bothered dealing with people commenting on my hair whilst I was working on very little sleep.

I'd be happy and social after a nap. I knew it. I just had to close my eyes for forty minutes. An hour, tops.

It ended up being just over three.

"You fuckwit," I cursed, rubbing my forehead as I groggily emerged from unconsciousness. I threw my phone to the floor after I checked the time (David had messaged me: *don't you dare be asleep*). It was already five in the evening; most of the students and teachers would have been in the pub for two hours already. "You stupid, stupid girl."

So much for feeling better after a nap. Though, admittedly, I did feel decidedly more alert now that I was fully awake, I had no time to waste. For all I knew Lir was a lightweight and had already passed out drunk. I surprised myself when a giggle escaped my lips at the thought, for it seemed so unlikely as to be impossible.

"Stop thinking of Lir and get ready," I scolded my reflection, wrenching off the jumper and leggings I'd been napping in as I spoke. Given that I had negative time to get ready I chose the first matching outfit I pulled out of my bag: turquoise camisole, high-waisted black miniskirt with silver buttons, black tights and black boots with silver heels.

My underwear – not that I thought in a million years it would ever matter what it looked like – was all barely-there blue lace. A gift from Louisa before she left for Australia, with the threat that I had better use it whilst she was gone. It was by far and away the sexiest underwear I owned and, up to this point, had seen no action whatsoever. If ever there was a time to wear it, today was it.

"Guess I really am playing up the whole 'sea' thing," I muttered, drawing black eyeliner along my lash line before blending silver eyeshadow into blue and green across the lid. The colour palette matched my eyes as well as my hair, top and lingerie, though I'd always considered my eyes to be more of a forest green colour. Now, though, with all the eyeshadow, they could almost pass for seafoam.

It had been a while since I'd cared so much about my outfit and make-up. Since before Louisa left, probably. It felt good to concern myself with something so...normal. Even if it was all for a boy. Well, I guess wanting to look good for the person you like is pretty normal, too, though liking Lir felt anything *but* normal.

Finally, I pulled out the pins from my hair and ran my fingers through it until it was loose and bouncy down my back, adding a pair of silver hoop earrings for good measure. I whistled at my reflection in the mirror, turning on the spot to check myself out with a pout firmly on my lips. I looked good; I wasn't afraid to admit it. But it didn't matter what I thought about how I looked. What mattered was what *Lir* thought.

Glancing through the window I saw that though it wasn't raining there were still dark, gloomy clouds obscuring the sky. The storm had dissipated as promised by Joe on the radio, but I didn't trust that it wasn't windy along the promenade towards the pub. This was the west coast, after all. It was *always* windy.

So I slid into my big, fluffy jacket, tucking my hair beneath the collar and buttoning the thing all the way up to my neck. It covered my entire outfit and made me look like a black sheep on spindly legs but I didn't care. It was imperative that my hair was still pretty and my outfit remained dry by the time I reached the pub. Then I further covered my outfit with my dad's anorak and bundled my bag into my arms, since I had to take all my stuff with me so I could catch the last ferry later that evening.

I was not surprised to find the rest of the Research Station abandoned as I made my way outside: even the teachers had been looking forward to some well-earned downtime after a week of educating nursery school children disguised as twenty-year-olds. It made me wish I'd brought some vodka or wine or something to drink on the way to the pub to keep me company, though the journey wasn't all that long.

When I opened the door and let the cold evening air hit my face my heart started racing. Something was going to happen tonight. I could feel it in my bones. The only problem was, I didn't know *what.*

I could only hope that it would be a good thing.

By the time I reached the pub I thought I was going to have a heart attack. I didn't think I'd ever been so nervous before in all my life, which only made me feel stupider than ever. *Get a grip,* I thought, over and over again. *You're just drinking with your students and colleagues. So what if you can't stop thinking about one of those students? Nobody else knows that.*

There wasn't a single person standing outside the pub smoking or fighting or talking on the phone, so I spent a while lingering on the pavement with my eyes closed against the chilly sea air. I blew a low whistle through my teeth to centre myself, knowing I was wasting precious time. One second passed. Two. Three.

69

When I finally found the courage to open the door I was blasted by a wave of hot, sticky air. It was full of the scent of spilled beer, sweat and the ever-lingering stale bitterness of cigarettes from years long past. It didn't matter that over a decade had been and gone since smoking was banned indoors in Scotland: small-town pubs would *never* be rid of the smell. There was something heart-warming about that, though. Something permanent and ever-lasting, though in truth my nose wrinkled at the acrid stench.

"There you are, Grace!"

I spotted David standing by the bar immediately. I smiled at him, then waved to Professor Reynolds and two of the other teachers who were sitting in the corner. Going by their ruddy cheeks and the eight empty pint glasses on the table in front of them I could only conclude that they were well past tipsy.

Sheepishly I approached David and dropped my bag to my feet just as he handed me one of the two drinks he was nursing. "Sorry I fell asleep for so long," I said. I indicated towards the glass he'd given me. "What's in this?"

"Vodka lemonade. Figured it was a safe bet. I'm more of a vodka orange person, myself."

"To be honest anything but beer is a safe bet," I replied, swallowing the contents of the glass in a matter of seconds. A satisfied sigh escaped my lips when the vodka began to burn my throat. "Right, next one's on me. What's your poison?"

David stared at me in disbelief. "I didn't have you down as a big drinker, if I'm honest."

"Then you don't know me very well," I laughed. "So what'll it be?"

He picked up his glass, which was still half-full. "I'm sorted for now. Were you really asleep for three hours? The beds in the hostel are hell on my back."

"Oh god, yes," I said. "I needed it. Did I mention before that my cat was yowling non-stop and keeping me up all night?" David nodded. "Well, three days ago he decided to disappear so now his silence is keeping me up, instead. Which meant I could have slept on concrete this afternoon, I was so tired."

A frown of genuine concern shadowed David's eyes. "I hope he shows up soon. Does he disappear like this often?"

"Maybe for a day at a time back when I still lived in Largs," I replied, ordering a gin and tonic when the barmaid asked me what I wanted. "I have no idea what his habits are now, though. When my parents get back from holiday I'll ask them. But enough about my cat...where is everyone?" It was only in asking the question that I realised almost every student I'd come to know from the marine and freshwater biology degree group was missing.

"Oh, they're in the karaoke bar in the next room over," David said, indicating towards a door at the back of the bar with a thumb. "I figured I'd wait for you in here so the teachers didn't steal you away to complain about how terrible we've all been this week."

A cheeky smile played across his lips. David was what Louisa would have called 'second glance handsome' – none of his features stood out but the more you looked at him, the more you realised he was good-looking. Especially without his glasses on, which he'd chosen to forgo this evening.

For a moment I imagined him holding my hand, embracing me, kissing me...then immediately stopped. Trying to picture being like that with him caused a jolt of nausea to pass through me. I could never be more than his friend. Could never let him touch me the way his eyes currently told me he wanted to.

"I don't reckon the teachers will be all that capable of good chat for much longer," I joked, side-eyeing Professor Reynolds as she let out a hiccough. "Or maybe their best chat comes when they're steaming? Perhaps I should go over and – "

"Let's go to the karaoke room," David cut in, laughing softly, picking up our drinks so I could hold my bag in my arms and follow him through the door.

The room we entered was dark save for a multi-coloured projector bouncing lights off every surface. Max and a girl called Julie were rapping Love the Way You Lie as loudly and as angrily as possible down a single microphone. I was somewhat impressed by the fact neither of them seemed to breathe during their entire performance.

Circular booths and tables lined the walls so that the main floor was kept clear for dancing and karaoke, though the room was so full a lot of folk were simply standing around talking to one another. Since all the booths were taken David and I headed to the stools at the bar, which was smaller than the bar in the main pub.

David pointed to a corner of the room where a pile of jackets lay abandoned just as I put my bag on the floor. "I think everyone shoved their stuff over there," he explained. "Why don't you do the same? You must be roasting."

In truth I was. However, now that I was surrounded by people who knew me I grew self-conscious about the fact I'd put so much effort into my appearance. It wasn't as if nobody else had dressed up – plenty of the girls had and some of the boys, too – but I always felt this way when I was with people who didn't often see me in full make-up and nice clothes.

And dyed hair.

But then I saw Lir through the hazy air and changing lights, waving Max over to the booth he was sitting in with their lab bench once Max's song finished. When he caught my eye I looked away, knowing I was blushing.

"You're right," I told David, necking back my gin and tonic just as quickly as I had done the vodka, "it's a bloody sauna in here." I shirked out of my two jackets and took them and my bag over to the corner, rearranging my hair around my shoulders on my way back to the bar.

David stared at me, open-mouthed. "That's...wow," he said, waving towards me somewhat uselessly. "Grace, you look stunning tonight."

I gave him a nervous smile. "Um, thanks. Felt like I should put in some effort given that I was unconscious for most of the afternoon."

"When did you dye your – *oh!*"

Someone bumped into David, knocking his drink all over

his white shirt in the process. When the offending person raised their head of tousled hair to look at me I was torn between laughing and staring at them in horrified silence.

"Christ, David, I'm sorry," Lir said, sounding so authentically apologetic I almost believed him. He grabbed a napkin from the bar and handed it to David, who took it with numb fingers. "I wasn't looking where I was going. You should probably wash that out before it stains."

David grimaced at the large yellow spill down his clothes. *If only he'd had a vodka lemonade,* I thought, still trying hard not to laugh. He fired an almost accusatory look at Lir before heading for the toilets.

"What're you drinking?" Lir asked, who was suddenly very, very close to me. When I flinched he chuckled, then moved a respectable two feet away. He raised an eyebrow, holding up his own glass of what looked like whisky. "Well?"

"Gin," I said, remembering how to speak, "and tonic."

Lir ordered me a double. I didn't correct him.

Now that we were standing beside each other I could see him far more clearly. He was dressed well and simply, in a navy, long-sleeved t-shirt and tight-fitting, charcoal grey jeans. Lir's hair was just as messy as usual; I was beginning to suspect he cared very little about it. Regardless, I liked the way it looked.

"– have you been?"

I blinked, taking a sip of the drink the barman handed me without once taking in what Lir had asked. "Sorry, what did you say?"

"I asked you where you've been," Lir repeated. He leaned easily against the bar, inviting me to take a step closer to him so I could hear him better over the cacophony of the newest karaoke singer. "David seemed beside himself with worry."

I narrowed my eyes at him. "Do you dislike him?"

"Nope," Lir replied immediately. "He's a nice enough guy, I suppose. But he's head over heels for you. Surely even *you* have noticed that by now?"

73

Such a blatant comment on my usual obliviousness would ordinarily have rankled me to no end. From Lir, however... hearing that he understood my personality made me inordinately happy.

"I guess I had a notion," I admitted, finally taking the step towards Lir he was waiting for me to take. It really *was* too loud to talk two feet away from each other without shouting. "But David hasn't actually said anything to me about it."

"He was going to ask you out tonight. Good thing I got in his way."

I didn't reply. It felt cruel to say I was happy Lir had deliberately spilled a drink on David and interfered with him asking me out, but I was. I was over the moon Lir would do something like that of his own accord.

When we finished our drinks I bought another round, and the two of us talked about the last week at the Research Station. It was a general, boring conversation – not the kind of conversation I'd wanted to have with Lir at all – but as the evening progressed I found that I didn't care. *Any* kind of conversation with him was good.

When David reappeared from the toilets and saw that Lir was still talking to me I caught him skulking back to his friends out of the corner of my eye. I felt bad though, in truth, I hadn't done anything wrong. Then I heard a few people tipsily shout things like 'poor David' and 'I didn't even know Dylan and Grace were friends' at him.

Lir and I both tilted our heads to listen in just as Max replied, "Are you joking? It's about bloody time they got together!"

I turned my back on the students, hunching my shoulders to my ears in a desperate attempt to disappear to another plane of existence where I wasn't being spoken about. But Lir moved a few inches closer to me, just barely grazing my arm with his.

"Does it bother you when people talk about you?" he asked.

I let out a short bark of humourless laughter. "I think most people are bothered by that, not just me."

"Maybe so," he mused, "but you *really* don't like it. Why is that?"

I turned my head ever-so-slightly towards him. Lir's face was impassive, though his grey eyes were alert and attentive. He was genuinely curious about my answer.

"I just..." I began, thinking hard through the beating of my heart for an answer. "Being around lots of people makes me anxious. So when they all start talking about me, well...it makes me feel worse. Even if what they're saying is nice or whatever. I'd rather nobody spoke about me at all."

"Would you ever want to be invisible?"

"I – what? Invisible?"

Lir nodded seriously. "Would you? Nobody would ever know you were there. You could do anything you wanted with no repercussions."

"That would be incredibly lonely, don't you think?"

"I suppose so," Lir admitted, taking a long draught of his whisky. "Maybe if someone else was invisible with you it wouldn't be so bad."

I regarded Lir's face carefully. It didn't look like he was discussing invisibility as a joke. "What would you want to be invisible for, then?" I asked.

The smile that curled his lips was decidedly mischievous. "It's a secret."

"That's not fair!"

"You'll just have to get to know me better and then you can work it out."

It sounded like a challenge – one which I'd gladly step up to meet.

After a few minutes the comments about me and Lir died down, and we returned to companionable silence for a while. I *wanted* to say something. Of course I did. But here, in the bar, felt like the wrong place. I didn't want to be surrounded by other people with him.

I wanted us to be alone.

Eventually I realised Lir's eyes were on my hair. "Did you dye it last night, in the hostel showers?" he asked, reaching out to touch a lock of turquoise before pausing an inch from it. But I leaned into the touch, and when his fingers met my hair he ran them through it all the way to my neck.

"I – yes," I replied, heart thumping in my throat as Lir began stroking my skin very, very slowly. "I didn't want to get any dye in my parents' bathroom. My dad would have killed me if I did." I knew I was rambling. What did Lir care about my parents' bathroom?

But Lir smiled softly and bent a little closer towards me. He ran his hand around the back of my neck as if he was going to pull me in, closing the last few inches between us. "You're like a siren," he murmured, so quietly I almost didn't hear him. My eyes were on his lips, watching them form words even as I wished he'd do something else with them entirely.

God, I wanted him to kiss me so badly I could cry.

I shivered when his lips brushed my ear. "So does your underwear match your hair, too, or is just your eyes?"

Fuck, fuck, fuck.

It took me far too long to realise my phone was buzzing in my bra, where I had stored it for safekeeping when I moved my stuff over to the corner. Achingly aware of what Lir had only just said, I pulled my phone out – his eyebrows were lost beneath his hair as he watched me, they rose so high – and saw, in horror, that the last ferry to the mainland was due to leave in fifteen minutes.

"I have to go!" I exclaimed, jerking away from Lir and his devilish touch as if he had burned me. His eyes narrowed in confusion, and he straightened his back to face me properly. "I – ferry. The last ferry. I need to get it. I – bye."

Without waiting for a response from Lir – or anyone else for that matter – I grabbed my stuff and fled the pub for the blessed outdoors. The bitter night-time air was a welcome relief against my skin. I was so hot.

Too hot.

Lir had made his intentions abundantly obvious, and I'd responded by running away without even getting his number or arranging to see him again.

I was so stupid.

Chapter Ten

It was closing in on ten in the evening and the bottle of prosecco I'd bought a few days ago was now half-empty. I hadn't bothered changing into pyjamas yet, though curling up on the couch still dressed in a miniskirt and heeled boots wasn't exactly comfortable. Perhaps it was self-inflicted punishment for running from Lir in a panic.

I was still hitting myself over it. All I'd had to do was say, 'Hey, I actually have to go home now but do you want to meet up tomorrow before you go back to Glasgow? My parents won't be back until Monday so we'd have their place to ourselves.'

There. That was it. Succinct, to the point and very obviously an invitation for him to see if my underwear *did* match my hair. Oh, well. There was nothing I could do about it now except continue to drown my sorrows in bubbly alcohol.

When I returned I'd stopped by Terry's to ask him if Tom had returned. My mood fell even more when he said no. I was beginning to seriously worry – what if my cat had been run over somewhere and I had no idea?

With a grunt I shifted off the couch and wandered over to the large bay window, pulling the curtain back in order to peer into the darkness. There was no sign of Tom in the garden.

"Damn cat," I grumbled, turning from the window to slide into my dad's anorak (which by this point I was seriously considering 'borrowing' to take back to Glasgow) and grab a torch from the utility room. I had to bang it against the counter-top several times before it flickered to life.

It was actually warmer outside than it had been when I'd returned from Millport; clearly the wind had changed direction in the past few hours. The air was unnervingly still.

"Ten minutes," I told myself. "I'll look for ten minutes." To be honest I didn't expect to find much of anything in ten minutes but I had to at least *try* to find Tom. I let out a low whistle as I searched the back garden. "Tommy, come out," I begged. "Come on, Tom. This isn't funny. I'll never shout at you again for keeping me up at night, I swear." It was a lie, of course, but at this point I'd promise anything for my cat to return before my parents came back from holiday.

When it became clear that Tom was nowhere in the garden or the shed I moved onto the street. He wasn't skulking along the promenade – the ornate, wrought-iron street lamps meant even at night visibility of the entire seafront was good. So I decided to check the side streets, instead, turning up the road our house shared with Terry Jones.

No sooner had I turned the corner than a scream rent the air. I froze to the spot, terrified, listening as the scream was followed by another and another. Then something inside me kicked into life and I ran towards the screaming, calling the police in the process.

The road was dark when I found the source of the screaming, for the street lamp had been broken. A shadowy figure loomed over another, brazenly hacking away at their victim right in front of me. The silver of their blade was all I could hone in on, flashing and glinting and then disappearing as it entered the victim's body.

I tried to find my voice to warn them off but nothing would come out. My entire body was shaking.

My torch had burned out.

I knew I couldn't stand there, silently watching as some poor soul was stabbed and stabbed and stabbed again. So, using some kind of courage I never knew I possessed, I threw the dead torch with all my might at the attacker, hitting them across the back with a dull thump.

"The p-police are coming," I stuttered, my voice painfully

insubstantial but just loud enough to carry across the street.

Without a word or even a glance in my direction, the perpetrator fled.

I wasted no time in running towards their victim, though part of me worried the attacker had pretended to run off with the intention of stabbing me, too. But no such thing happened and, as I skidded to my knees beside the person currently bleeding out on the ground, I realised in horror than I recognised them.

"*Terry!*" I cried, desperately searching for the worst of his wounds to try and staunch the bleeding. He was wearing a thick jacket and cable-knit jumper that seemed to have taken the worst of the damage from the blade's attacks on his chest and stomach, but there was a serrated opening on his neck that was bleeding out far too quickly.

I wrenched off my dad's jacket and pulled off my camisole to hold against the wound, not caring about the way the night-time air cut through my skin. "Hold on, Terry," I said, blindly trying to check his pulse but realising I was in too much of a panic to count it out.

Terry's eyes were wide and glassy. He tried to grip my arm but there was no strength behind it. "W-watching your house," he said, voice thick with blood. He coughed up thick globules of red.

"Shh," I soothed, wiping my hand across his forehead, "don't try to talk. Help is on its way. Just hold on, Terry. Hold on."

"*No,*" he tried again, desperate. "Watching your –"

His voice was cut off by the sound of sirens, and all around me I became aware of the porch lights of nearby houses blazing bright as concerned neighbours came outside to see what was going on. Before I knew it I was pulled to my feet and Terry was bundled into an ambulance.

As the police questioned me I felt more and more useless. "My torch broke," I told them. "I didn't see the attacker's face. No, I couldn't see any defining features. No, I don't know if it was a man or a woman." All I knew was that they'd used a serrated blade, like the one my dad had in his fishing kit.

I should have changed the batteries in the damn torch.

By the time I returned to my parents' house I was numb and cold and shaking. My tights were ripped; I wrenched off my boots then tore the ruined material from my legs. When I unbuttoned my skirt and threw it in the washing machine my fingers came away wet and red.

My hands were covered in blood well past my wrists. I turned on the kitchen tap to clean them, thrusting my hands beneath the faucet without acknowledging what I was doing. It was only when the water became scalding hot that I pulled my hands away.

I didn't know what to do. What to think. My neighbour had been attacked – viciously, mercilessly stabbed – right before me. This was Largs, not Glasgow. Things like this didn't happen here.

Dully I thought of the muggings in Millport that hadn't really been muggings at all. Were they related? I didn't know enough about the cases to form a good hypothesis.

"I...need a drink," I mumbled, collapsing onto the couch in my underwear and pulling a thick, woollen blanket over my skin. I'd been so excited about the prospect of Lir seeing my lacy blue lingerie. But it had been Terry, old and bleeding and possibly dying, who'd seen it instead.

I wanted to stop such a ridiculous train of thought but I couldn't. My mind was a mess of impulses and emotions and sheer, overwhelming terror. If I hadn't gone out looking for Tom – if I'd stayed in Millport for another night to spend more time with Lir – Terry would in all likelihood have died.

He might still, my brain chimed in unhelpfully.

"Shut up shut up shut *up*," I cried, banging my temple with my fist in a useless attempt to sort myself out. I barely managed to pour a glass of prosecco with a violently shaking hand, bringing it to my lips and forcing it down with desperate gulps.

I wanted to call my parents. I wanted to call Louisa. But they were all in time zones several hours ahead of me and long since asleep; I would not get a hold of them no matter how much I longed to hear their voices.

But I didn't want to be alone. The silence was deafening, like the still air outside. If I was by myself I would cry until I got a migraine and threw up and then I'd cry some more. I didn't want that. I wanted to stay in control of myself.

The doorbell rang.

"What the fuck?" I murmured, tightening the blanket around myself and wondering if I could simply ignore it. But then I figured it was probably the police needing a second statement, so with some effort I got to my feet and dragged myself to the door.

But when I opened it I discovered it wasn't the police. Nor was it a neighbour checking that I was okay, or a misplaced pizza delivery, or any other person I could imagine calling on someone at eleven in the evening.

It was Lir.

Lir, dripping wet, barefoot, teeth chattering as he forced a smile on his face.

"Can I come in?"

Chapter Eleven

I stared at Lir, mouth agape and silent, for far too long. My mind was blank. I couldn't comprehend that he was standing right in front of me even though all evidence pointed to the fact he very much was. Eventually I asked what seemed to be the most pressing question, given the fact that he was dripping wet.

"How did you get here?"

"Well, it's o-only 1.2 miles across," Lir replied, sounding nonchalant even though his voice was shaking. "It was pretty easy for me to -"

"You *swam* here?"

"How else w-would you explain why I'm dripping wet?"

He had me there. Yet my brain wasn't working; it was torn between the attack on Terry and Lir's bizarre, impossible appearance in front of me. Truly, I didn't know what to say or how to feel.

When it became clear I wasn't going to respond he elaborated on his presence at my front door. "I didn't like the way our conversation ended so abruptly," he said, gazing at his feet. Then he lifted his head, bright, keen eyes locked on mine. "Something told me you felt the same. So can I come in?"

It took me another moment of processing Lir's soaking clothes and shaking shoulders before I sputtered, "Y-yes! Yes, come in. You must be bloody freezing. I'll turn the shower -"

"Grace." Lir reached out for my elbow beneath the blanket I was hiding in, brow furrowed in concern. I cringed at the touch of his frozen fingertips. "Are you alright?"

There was no point in lying to him. My entire evening had been too unreal – too terrifying – for me to ignore. "No," I admitted, "I'm not. But...I'm glad you're here."

I really was.

I was just about to ask Lir to take off his shoes when I remembered he didn't have any on. I didn't have it in me to ask where they were. "Up here," I said, indicating for Lir to follow me up the stairs to the bathroom. "There are some fresh towels on the radiator already; leave your clothes by the door and I'll stick them in the wash."

With my blood-covered skirt.

He gave me a careful smile. "You don't have to do that." And then: "What happened to you, Grace? You're so pale. Did –"

"Shower first," I cut in, pointing towards the bathroom without looking at him. "I think I can find an old pair of my dad's pyjamas for you to wear."

A pause. Then: "Thank you."

It was with the same numbness that had carried me through the evening since Terry's attack that I searched my parents' bedroom for some clothes for Lir. I didn't even put the light on, though it would have helped my search immensely.

Eventually I found a pair of Ferguson tartan pyjamas. They had a drawstring on the trousers so they'd at least fit Lir okay... even if the top half ran the risk of swamping him. My dad was in good shape but he was a giant of a man, after all. From observation I knew Lir was just under six foot tall.

When I returned to the hallway I saw that Lir had found the wicker basket my mum used all my life to take the washing downstairs. It was waiting by the closed bathroom door, wet clothes neatly folded inside. For some reason this made me laugh a giddy, uncalled-for laugh that felt entirely inappropriate for my current mood.

I picked up the basket and replaced it with the pyjamas, resting an ear against the door to listen for...I didn't know what. I could hear the sound of rushing water and literally nothing else. *What was I expecting?* I wondered, heading downstairs towards the utility room. *For Lir to be singing? Reciting his intentions for showing up at my door out loud? How did he even know where my parents' house was, anyway?*

That last question finally seemed to spark my brain back to life, and I became far more aware of what I was actually doing. I picked out Lir's top from the basket – it smelled of salt and dark water and cold air. I knew that was because of the sea but, for some reason, I figured his clothes would have smelled like that even without the night-time swim.

After I turned on the washing machine I curled up on the couch, then paced the living room, then went into the kitchen to grab another champagne flute in case Lir wanted some prosecco. It occurred to me that he probably wanted something stronger – he'd been drinking whisky in the pub – but when I scoped out my dad's study I saw he only had his 'special occasion' whisky on a glass shelf, which I absolutely didn't dare touch.

When I returned to the living room I found Lir relaxing on the couch, curly hair gently steaming from the shower. He was wearing the trousers part of my dad's tartan pyjamas but not the top half. He'd rolled the cuffs up a couple times; clearly they were much too long on him.

"What happened to the rest of the clothes I gave you?" I asked, perching myself down a respectable distance away and rearranging the blanket I was still huddled into. I should have changed whilst Lir was in the shower – now I was stuck in lingerie with nothing but the blanket to protect my modesty. God, I was an idiot.

He huffed out a laugh. "It absolutely drowned me. Besides, it's roasting in here. How can you even stand being under a *wool* blanket?"

I didn't reply, though my reddening cheeks answered Lir's question without a need for words. His eyes lowered across my frame then back to my face, and he laughed harder than before.

"You're so weird, do you know that?" he said, leaning back against the couch without taking his eyes off mine. They were

85

creased up in genuine amusement. "I don't understand you at all."

"There's not much to understand," I replied, somewhat discomfited by his amusement. I pointed at the prosecco. "Do you want some?"

Lir shook his head. "I had plenty to drink in the pub. Drowning my sorrows after you ran away and all. Max said David and I were the most pathetic pair he'd ever seen."

"I find that hard to imagine."

"You're very honest tonight."

I stilled at the drastic change in conversation, then chose to pour myself a glass of prosecco in lieu of giving Lir my full attention. "What do you mean by that?"

"I mean," he said, sidling over on the couch a few inches in my direction, "that you're not thinking of your responses before saying them. You normally over-think everything to death, don't you?"

Earlier, when we'd been drinking in the karaoke room, I'd been pleased that Lir understood my personality. But now I realised he knew far more about who I was as a person than almost everyone in my own damn family – and he'd done it all with barely a word spoken between us.

"That's...true," I admitted. My hands were shaking, which meant my glass was shaking. "I guess I'm just not myself tonight."

"Grace." Lir spoke my name the way he'd done earlier: a plea for me to answer his questions.

"My neighbour was stabbed tonight. Repeatedly. I saw it all. I don't even know if he'll make it to morning."

There. I'd said it. Now the horror I'd witnessed earlier had spilled from my own mouth, which meant it had to be real and I had to face it. My hands shook so much I could no longer keep hold of my glass; gently Lir extricated it from my grip and placed it on the table.

I couldn't bear to look at him. I was so afraid I'd burst into tears.

"We don't have to talk about it if you don't want to," he said, which was somehow precisely the right thing to say. I *didn't* want to talk about it. I just didn't want to have to face the rest of the night alone, either, knowing my life had been forever altered by what I'd seen.

"Thank you," I murmured, hanging my head for a long moment before throwing myself back against the couch. I let out a long sigh, then turned my head to give Lir the smallest of smiles. "Really, thank you. I was literally just thinking that I didn't want to spend the night alone when you rang the doorbell. What was swimming in the dark like?"

"Kind of scary, actually," Lir said, slowly moving back into a relaxed posture when it became clear we were moving back into normal conversation. Well, as normal as swimming 1.2 miles across the sea at night just to talk to someone could be. "I've swam in the dark plenty of times before but always in lochs or secluded bays and stuff. This was a little different."

"You don't have hypothermia, do you? The water must have been so cold."

"Nah, it might have been a foolish thing to do but I'm used to swimming outdoors, even in winter. I know what I'm doing."

I raised an eyebrow. "Something tells me you don't usually go swimming in jeans."

"You would be right," he laughed. "Well, regardless, it was worth it. I'm glad I could be here for you after what happened. And..." Lir shifted over until he was but a foot away from me. There was no doubting the seriousness of his gaze on mine. "I really, really wanted to see you. You left so quickly I couldn't ask you something I've wanted to ask you for a while now."

For some reason this took me aback. I fumbled with my words trying to respond. "You – what did you want to ask?"

Lir cocked his head to the side. "You *do* like me, don't you? It isn't just wishful thinking on my part?"

There was a moment, then, when I honestly felt as if my heart had stopped and all the air had been stolen from my lungs.

This was the moment for me to panic and run away, terrified by the notion of being honest with my feelings and being rejected in the process. But there was no point in denying my feelings or being coy and charming about them.

Not now.

"I've felt so foolish these past few weeks," I admitted, running a hand through my hair when it fell over my face. "There wasn't much about you on social media, and then, you know, I went total psycho and tried to 'run' into you in the library or the unions or at swimming practice. I'd like to say I'm not that much of an idiot around people when I like them as much as I like you, but it would be a lie. Well, half a lie. I think the last time I liked a guy as much as you was...possibly never. Ugh, I'm not good at this," I complained, balling my hands into fists over my eyes so I didn't have to look at Lir. 'Mortified' couldn't even cover how I currently felt.

I expected Lir to laugh in my face at such an overt confession of inexperience. Instead, he stretched out a long-limbed leg towards me and curled his foot around my ankle, turning me to face him directly. His hands wrapped around my wrists and pulled them away from my face.

"Was my 'I want to fuck you' face back in the steam room not obvious enough for you, Grace?" Lir asked, all stormy eyes and low, troubled voice that rumbled like the waves outside the window. "Because I'll be honest: it kind of hurt when you just sat there, not responding to me in the slightest."

"I – I didn't know what to do," I panicked. "I thought you were going to tell me to stop following you. I thought –"

"You thought, but you never asked. Then I sat beside you in the library and even tried to get you on your own in the shower room at the hostel and you just...ran off."

Oh. Oh. *Oh.*

"So you...you like me, too?" I asked, barely daring to vocalise the question.

Lir shook his head and clucked his tongue, clearly impatient with my slow, plodding brain. "Yes, you fool! I don't know how I could have made it more obvious. I mean, I literally asked you about your underwear in the bar and you totally ignored it. Kind of hurt my ego, if I'm honest."

"I...had to get back home on the last ferry," I said, which was true but somehow still felt like an excuse. "Not all of us can swim over a mile in the dark."

The ghost of a smile crossed Lir's lips at my comment. When he didn't say anything I decided to do something utterly outrageous by my standards. Pulling my wrists from his grip I shrugged off the woollen blanket that had thus far protected my modesty, blushing furiously and averting my gaze from Lir's all the while. "And...yes," I mumbled. "I *did* match my lingerie to my hair."

I glanced up through my lashes when Lir did not respond after a disconcertingly long time. His eyes roved across my body, setting goosebumps on my skin even though I was burning.

"Back in the bar," he said, slowly bringing his gaze back to mine as he pulled on the drawstring of the ridiculous tartan trousers I'd given him, "when I said you were a siren. I wasn't being specific enough." He slid a hand around the back of my neck just as he had done hours earlier. Only this time Lir properly closed the distance between us until our lips were almost touching and his breath was hot on my skin.

"You're *my* siren, Grace," he murmured, "put in my life to lead me to my doom."

I kissed him first, that much I was sure of.

The moment Lir said I was his drove all reason and inhibition from my mind, and I pressed my mouth against his with an earnestness that felt pathetic. But I didn't care. I *wanted* Lir, and from the way he pulled me into his arms and moulded his body to mine I had no doubt he felt the same about me.

There was power in his hungry frame, barely suppressed beneath the surface of his skin. I felt sure, somehow, that he could shatter my wrists and bruise my skin if he'd felt inclined to do so. Yet every one of Lir's touches as he pushed me onto my back and planted kisses along my jawline were gentle, as if he was afraid he might break me.

89

I *wanted* to be broken.

In an unexpectedly smooth, cocksure moment I rolled on top of him, pinning Lir beneath my hands and thighs. His eyes widened in delicious surprise.

"If I'm a siren luring you to your doom," I said, voice low and heavy with longing, "then be desperate with me. Hurt me. Don't be careful with me."

It was all the consent Lir needed. With a snarling grin that was so at odds with his innocent grey eyes he broke free from my hold, grabbing my waist and toppling me once more beneath him with a strength I knew I couldn't escape from.

Lir was mine, and I was his. So long as his hands roved over every inch of me I could forget all about the horrors that lay just behind my front door.

PART TWO

Lir, Age Five

The second moment that defined Lir's childhood occurred one month after his fifth birthday. The boy had become fixated on water after learning his parents returned to the sea, so Orla bought him a tropical fish tank full of a wondrous assortment of brightly coloured fish.

A dozen blue tetras. Ten threadfin rainbow fish. Eight blood orange mollies. Four red swordtails, who often tried to jump out of the tank whenever Lir removed the lid to feed them. Three stripy loaches, who rooted around the plants and gravel like dogs picking up a scent. Two dwarf gouramis, that were inseparable from one another.

He very quickly learned how to look after his aquatic pets, cleaning the tank, feeding the fish and checking the thermometer and water filter unaided after a mere two weeks of helping his aunt do it. Lir adored the fish, naming each and every one of his new friends after the Greek gods and heroes Orla liked to tell him about before bed.

His relationship with his only human friend suffered as a result of the fish. Cian Byrne lived next door to Lir's aunt; Lir met him at pre-school and was due to start primary school with him after summer ended. Lir didn't think he was looking forward to school – all he wanted to do was watch his fish and listen to Aunt Orla's stories.

This upset Cian. He hated being ignored in favour of a tank of fish, especially since Lir carefully guarded them so that Cian never got to press his nose to the glass and watch the animals swim the way Lir did. And he wanted to. He thought the fish were cool.

But Lir didn't want him anywhere near the tank.

One afternoon, Cian knocked upon the door and invited Lir to play gods and monsters in the back garden. It was just about the only game that interested Lir these days – so long as he got to be the god. They fought and laughed and shouted almighty curses at one another until, after about an hour, Cian ran inside to use the toilet. Lir didn't think anything of it; they used the bathrooms in each others' houses all the time when they played outside.

Another two hours of playing passed by before Cian was called back next door for his dinner. Lir was hungry, too, so he perched himself on one of the stools in the kitchen and happily watched his aunt cook him fish and chips. Then he fell asleep in the living room watching Animal Planet, clutching his favourite plastic tiger shark to his chest like it was a soft and fluffy teddy bear.

It was in this way that Lir did not check on his fish for six hours. When he finally roused from his nap – Orla was sprawled out beside him, softly snoring – he gambolled up the stairs, eager to feed his friends and watch them compete for the largest flakes of food.

The fish were all dead.

Orla awoke to the sound of Lir screaming. She was immediately concerned; her nephew was a very quiet boy. The moment she found him hugging a tank full of dead, floating fish Orla knew something had gone horribly awry, so she checked the thermometer and saw that the water temperature had increased far beyond safe limits. The filtration system had also been turned off.

"Oh, Lir, what happened?" she asked, gently pulling the boy away from the tank to sit on his bed, where she curled him protectively against her chest. Orla could feel every one of Lir's sobs wracking through his body and into her own, making her want to cry with him.

"He did it," Lir eventually got out. "He *killed* them." His words were a snarl, even through his tears. Orla had never heard such vehement fury from a child before.

Orla knew Lir could only be referring to Cian. Lir hadn't been playing with his friend much lately, and it was clear that had upset the other boy. But doing something so awful to get back at him Orla simply couldn't fathom. He was just a child, after all. Killing Lir's fish was too cruel. Too vindictive.

"There must have been a technical issue," she told Lir. "This was a horrible accident. But it's okay!" She forced a smile on her face. "Tomorrow we'll go to the pet shop and buy you some new fish to replace the ones who returned to the sea. How about that?"

When Lir looked up at his aunt she was struck by how empty his grey eyes were. "Like you replaced mum?" he asked, voice as chillingly devoid of emotion as his eyes.

Orla was horrified by his words, but she knew she couldn't show that on her face. "Hush, Lir," she soothed, stroking his hair and leaning both of them against the stack of pillows on his bed as she did so. "I could never replace her. But I love you so, so much. You know that, right? So let me tell you a story. There once was a fisherman who fell in love with a selkie -"

"A what?"

"A seal that could turn into a human by taking off her skin."

Lir wrinkled his adorable little nose in disgust. "She took off her *skin*?"

"Her seal skin, of course," Orla laughed. Lir had begun to calm down, much to her relief. She had no idea how to deal with conflict or death or anything else complicated regarding real life; Orla had always been that way. The one thing she *could* do was tell a story.

Luckily, it was the one thing that seemed to matter most to her beloved nephew.

"So he fell in love with a seal?" Lir asked, amused by the notion.

"She wasn't a seal, though," Orla explained. "She was a selkie. A mythical being. They liked to come to shore and strip off their seal skins and bask in the sunshine as humans. Well, anyway, the fisherman caught sight of a beautiful woman near his house one afternoon and immediately knew what she was. It was love at first sight for him and...well, people do strange things when they're in love. He found the selkie's seal skin and stole it, hiding it in his house so she could no longer return to her friends in the sea."

Lir gasped in outrage. "But that isn't fair!"

"I know, child," Orla said, wiping the remaining tears from Lir's face. "The woman, scared and alone after discovering her skin was missing, came upon the fisherman's house to ask for shelter that night. He gladly took her in, and the woman came to love the man."

"For years they were together," she continued, "and though she bore him several children she never stopped longing for home. She would stand on the shore and look out across the sea, mourning her brothers and sisters for hours on end. Now, her youngest son, who was her favourite –"

"How old was he?" Lir interrupted.

Orla ruffled his messy hair. It needed cut; she made a note to call her hairdresser the following morning. "Why, about your age, I imagine," she told him. "So her favourite child saw how sad his mum was, and he didn't know what to do. Then, one day, he found a strange, silky coat like a seal's hidden deep in the cellar. He took it out and showed it to his mum, who immediately knew what it was."

Lir's eyes lit up. "Her skin!"

"Indeed it was. Now, the fisherman was still out catching fish when this happened, so he had no idea what was going on. The woman took her youngest down to the beach and told him to look after his father and his brother and sisters, kissed his forehead and said she loved him. Then she put on the skin and turned back into a seal, sliding into the water never to be seen again."

When it became clear that was the end of Orla's story, Lir extricated himself from her arms to confront her. His face was contorted in anger, his hands balled into fists. "Why did she do that?" he demanded. "Why did she leave her favourite son? She said she loved him! She –"

"The world can be cruel, Lir," Orla replied sadly. "So cruel that, in order to be granted what we truly long for, we often must pay a terrible price. For her freedom and her home, the selkie's price was her children...and the fisherman, whom she loved despite what he had done to her."

Lir considered this for a moment. He scrunched his brow, concentrating hard on processing the story. "And that's...is that what happened to mum and dad? They had to pay a price to go home?"

"Yes," Orla replied. "And it was a terrible price. But they paid it, anyway, so we can only hope it was worth it."

They sat in silence together for a long time after that, Orla feeling just as lost in their situation as the boy in front of her was. In truth she could never forgive her sister for what she'd done to Lir. To her. But Lir did not deserve to suffer more than he already had by learning that his existence was not enough to keep his parents alive.

No, she would take the secret to her grave, and in the morning she would buy Lir a new tank full of fish.

Chapter Twelve

I woke with a start, sitting bolt upright when I discovered that I was in my bed with no memory of having gotten there. It was still dark outside.

What was I doing? I wondered, trying to force my brain to work out why I was naked and in bed when my last conscious memory was on my parents' couch with –

"Go back to sleep..." a voice murmured from my left, low and soft and heavy.

Lir.

In my bed. With me.

I looked down at his tousled hair, sprawled around his face like a messy halo. He hardly seemed conscious. "Did you –"

"Carry you up?" he murmured, rolling onto his side to run his fingers across my waist. He didn't once open his eyes. "Yes. Now *go to sleep.*"

So I did.

*

The next time I woke up there was a dull grey light filtering through my window. Peering at the clock on the opposite wall I saw that it was just before six in the morning.

I was alone in bed.

"Was I dreaming...?" I wondered aloud, rubbing at my throat when my voice came out croaky and sore from thirst. No,

I was sure I hadn't imagined my previous evening. Arriving to the pub late, Lir spilling a drink on David, fleeing for the ferry, witnessing my neighbour getting violently stabbed, Lir showing up at my door soaking wet, Lir telling me he liked me, Lir taking off my clothes and –

No. It definitely wasn't a dream. Through the awful moments and the blissful ones, everything was real. So where was Lir?

"Oh, you're awake."

I turned my head from the window to the door so quickly that I cracked my neck. Groaning, I massaged the top of my spine as I slowly blinked focus into my eyes. Which was weird, because I couldn't usually see immediately upon waking.

"I – did I sleep in my contacts?" I asked, feeling groggy and useless. The image of Lir swam before me, holding two bottles of water in his hands as he stood a respectful distance from the bed.

"Yes," he replied. "Do your eyes hurt? Do you want me to get some saline solution from –"

"No, it's fine," I cut in, waving for one of the bottles of water in his hands as I rubbed my eyes. My contacts could wait until later. "You do realise the tap water is fine to drink in Largs, right? You didn't have to raid the bottled water."

Lir looked bashful and embarrassed as he sat down on the bed. He was wearing my dad's tartan trousers, though I was sure they'd been abandoned in the living room the night before. "I didn't know where the glasses were, and I didn't want to raid your cupboards. When I saw the bottles of water in the fridge I panicked and took them."

His answer pushed another question into my head. After taking a large, much-needed gulp of water I frowned at him. "How did you even know where my parents' house was, Lir?" I asked. "I hadn't told anybody – not even David."

At this he looked incredibly guilty. "You can't judge me because you were stalking me first, okay?"

I didn't say anything.

"I may have looked into your student records," he explained, holding my gaze beneath his thick lashes. "Are you mad at me?"

Anyone else would have been. But, as Lir had so astutely pointed out, I was guilty of stalking him for weeks and weeks. So what if he used the university's records to find out where my parents lived?

I could only laugh. "Not mad," I said. "Just...surprised you went that far, I guess. What else did you find out?"

When it became evident I truly wasn't angry at him, Lir fluffed the pillows beside me and relaxed against them, a contented smile plastered across his face. "Oh, just that you're twenty-five, and your birthday is the seventeenth of September, and your parents earn *way* too much for you to qualify for student assistance, and you failed second year inorganic chemistry, and –"

"Okay, okay, okay!" I cried, horrified. I held my hands over my face. "That's mortifying."

"Why did you fail?"

"I didn't like it."

"So you just...didn't study?"

I glanced at Lir between two of my fingers. "I guess so. Is that terrible of me?"

"It's a waste of tuition to be sure," Lir said, though he was laughing. He ran a hand through his hair, though it was so messy the gesture did nothing to tidy it up. "I guess I should give you some free passes to ask me questions, since I found out so much about you."

"Are you – are you sure?"

He nodded. "You were terrible at stalking me. I mean, did you even find anything out?"

"Rude."

"Says the stalker."

"You were clearly stalking me, too!"

Lir chuckled. "Touché. So, what do you want to know?"

I thought about this for a moment. What *did* I want to know? When the wind battered against the uncurtained window I shivered, then burrowed further into the duvet until only the top half of my head was visible above the covers. "How old are you?"

"Are you worried you're a cradle snatcher?" Lir asked, an amused smile twisting his lips.

"Should I be?"

"I'm twenty-three. Twenty-four on the tenth of May."

"Then you're hardly younger than me at all!" I exclaimed, surprised and delighted in equal measure. "Why did you start uni so late?"

Lir shrugged. "I travelled for a while. Next question."

"Umm..." I thought hard about it. What did I want to ask him? I'd been so obsessed with Lir for weeks now; why was it so difficult to come up with reasonable questions? "Where are your shoes and jacket?" I ended up asking.

Lir stared at me, incredulous. "*That's* what you want to know?"

"I guess so."

"Back by the pier in Millport," he said. "Hiding in a plastic bag. I'll get them when I return to the hostel in a few hours."

Oh.

"I suppose you kind of have to return," I muttered, feeling my mood drop considerably. Fanciful dreams of spending the day with Lir cooking in my parents' kitchen and watching stupid cartoons and whiling away most of our time in bed were dashed in one fell swoop.

When Lir turned onto his stomach and bent his head down to touch his lips to my forehead, I was sincerely glad for the duvet pulled up to my nose hiding my blushing cheeks. "Unfortunately so. But..."

"But?"

100

"I hope this wasn't a one-time thing," Lir said, with enough doubt in his voice that I knew he was genuinely fearful that it *was.*

Of course it wasn't.

Slowly, then with more conviction, I raised a hand to touch his cheek. Lir closed his eyes, leaning into the touch as if he had been starved of physical human interaction for years and years. "I don't want this to end," I admitted, not caring if I sounded desperate.

He kissed my palm. "Neither do I."

"Then let's never let it end."

When Lir opened his eyes once more they were earnest and happy. I always wanted him to look at me with such an expression on his face – like I was the first and only person that could give his life meaning.

With a newly rekindled desire I lowered the duvet, pulling Lir down to kiss him and instigate a far more sober repeat of the night before. But then a buzzing to my right and, then, to my left, caught my attention, and I paused with my lips a hair's breadth away from Lir's.

Both of our mobile phones were overloaded with notifications.

"Just ignore them," Lir purred, rubbing his nose against mine. "I don't want to let in the rest of the world right now."

I couldn't do such a thing. Not when I was waiting for news about Terry. About whether he'd survived the night...or hadn't. So I rolled onto my side and grabbed my phone, Lir sighing as I did so. I was beyond relieved – and a little annoyed – to see that I had precisely zero notifications about my neighbour. All of my messages were from Max, of all people, as well as the Facebook group for the marine and freshwater biology degree group.

But any relief I might have felt at knowing Terry hadn't died yet crumbled in the face of what I then read.

"Oh my god – David was attacked last night," I gasped, more to myself than to Lir. "He was airlifted to hospital to get treated. Fuck, it must be bad."

101

Lir was out of bed in a second. "Where are my clothes?"

"Um, probably still in the machine," I said. "I put a drying cycle on after the wash. Are you going?"

"I was one of the last people to see him before he left the pub," Lir explained. "I should get over there in case I have any useful information for the police."

"I – I'll come with you!"

"No. Stay here."

Lir's tone brooked no argument, though his face softened when he saw the hurt in my eyes. "There's no point, Grace. Just message David and see if he's okay. I'm sure he's fine. In fact, I'm sure he'll be ecstatic to get your attention."

I knew he meant it jokingly. Right now, in this moment, I didn't find it funny at all.

"You don't think it was the same person who attacked my neighbour?" I asked, following Lir down the stairs and uselessly watching as he wrenched his clothes from the washing machine and pulled them on. "Do you need shoes?" I added on, looking at his bare feet in concern.

He laughed softly. "I'll be fine. The ferry's less than fifteen minutes from here and it's dry out. And no, I don't think it's the same person. Unless they swam across the sea to commit one attack after the other."

"Oh, very funny," I said, though my lips curled into a smile at the ridiculous notion that anyone else was as mad as he was to swim over a mile in the dark, in March. When Lir moved to the front door and made to open it I reached out towards him, realising there was a question I very much needed an answer to. "Lir, wait!"

He looked back at me over his shoulder, hand hovering above the door handle. "Yes?"

"Can I have your number?"

He waited far too long to answer, though by this point I was beginning to understand Lir did such things for dramatic effect. Eventually his face broke into a grin.

"It's about time you asked."

Chapter Thirteen

Three weeks passed in a blur. Lir and I fell into an easy routine: I'd try and fail to write the rest of my thesis or go to the gym whilst Lir went to class or trained, then I'd eagerly open the door around seven to let him into my flat for the night. After week two I gave him a key.

Once, I asked Lir why he always came to mine instead of the other way around. In response he pointed to my large, plant-covered terrace which overlooked the river, and I laughed. I'd gotten so used to my flat that sometimes I forgot how much nicer it was than most of the places students could afford in Glasgow. Thank god for a good landlord and Louisa's parents still paying her rent.

When the teaching semester was over it would have been so easy for Lir to come round much earlier, but we both agreed he shouldn't. Perhaps we were pretending that we were capable of some restraint. That we didn't need to spend all our time together.

What I wouldn't have given to throw that pretence away and spend every waking second with him.

But the fact remained my thesis *did* need written, and Lir needed to study for exams, so I did my best to do the work I needed to do. Unsurprisingly, my progress was incredibly slow, and by the time the weekend rolled around I was eager to spend a shameless amount of time with Lir under the excuse that we'd worked hard all week and needed a break.

The weekend, however, was when Lir disappeared, leaving

Glasgow to surf and swim along the coast no matter the weather. Both Max and Lir himself had told me about this, of course, but still it came as a surprise that he *always* left. I understood that this was clearly Lir's alone time so I never asked to come along with him even though I wanted to. Eventually, I hoped, he'd be the one to invite me on his adventures out of the city.

Until then I could impatiently wait.

It was on one such lonely Sunday afternoon when Lir was away that Louisa video called me. It was a gorgeous spring day, so I was sitting out on my terrace basking in the sunshine whilst drinking a gin and tonic, listening to music and half-reading a paranormal romance novel that Louisa herself had left behind in her room many months ago. Checking the time I realised it was pretty damn late for my best friend to be calling. Curious, I put her book on the little table beside me and propped my phone against it, fixing my hair using my reflection on the screen before accepting the call.

"Hey, Lou," I said, chirpy and carefree. The sun had made it impossible for me to be in a bad mood, even though I missed Lir. "How's it hanging?"

Louisa rolled her eyes at me. "You finally tore yourself from your boyfriend long enough to talk to your former best friend?"

"You know fine well I have no other best friends," I replied, "nor really many other friends to speak of." I spared a thought for David, who had been discharged from the hospital the week before and had yet to message me with any of his pre-attack enthusiasm. I guessed I couldn't blame him; if he'd really been planning to ask me out that night in Millport only to discover Lir got there first he was probably not very happy with me. I did want to remain friends with him, though, so I hoped that whatever feelings he'd developed for me would quickly dissipate. Until then, I continued to send him memes and funny videos to let him know that I very much still valued talking to him.

"And it's not as if I've ever really had a boyfriend before," I added on as a valid afterthought. "Surely I'm allowed to lose myself in the honeymoon period for at least a little while?"

My best friend sighed magnanimously. "Of course you can.

I don't want you to be lonely, especially when I'm over here having the time of my life. But Grace....just be careful not to fall too hard, too fast, okay?"

Something about Louisa's comment irked me. Who was she to tell me how to go about dating a guy? True, in the past, whenever I began to date someone the person in question pretty much always ended up being a narcissistic arsehole. They liked that I didn't say much so they could talk at length about their own life and, when it transpired that I wasn't nearly as quiet as I was in public, they stopped calling. I'd never been all that good a judge of character when it came to who I was attracted to, and each and every time Louisa had warned me against putting my heart on the line.

But Lir was different.

Lir was good.

"I know you're just looking out for me," I said, choosing my next words carefully. "Really, I do. But I *am* an adult, whether either of us wants to admit it or not." I laughed a little, and was pleased when Louisa joined in. "I really, really like him, Louisa. Lir isn't like anyone I've ever met before."

A smile spread across Louisa's tanned face, and she relaxed into the sun lounger she was sitting on even though it was night-time over there. She almost looked like a stranger to me now – her skin used to be ghostly pale, stark against her red hair. Now she was darker than the group of girls in Lir's class who were overly generous with their fake tan all year round. Her arms and legs were toned, too, which meant even though she'd made fun of me going to the gym she had clearly been working out herself.

"Well, if you're happy then I'm happy," Louisa said. "But in other news – the literal news – what is going on over in Scotland right now?"

I grimaced at the change in subject. But it was all over social media, TV and radio right now. More and more senseless attacks were spreading up and down the west coast of Scotland, with some of them even encroaching into the Central Belt. People were wary about leaving their homes at night, even in Glasgow. Glasgow, which was once the murder capital of

Europe. That people were being more careful than normal here was really saying something.

"It's pretty scary," I told her, which was an understatement.

"Any news about Terry?"

Louisa had met my neighbour on several occasions when she'd come to stay with me in Largs during our long undergrad summers. Of course I'd told her about him being attacked... only, I'd left out the small fact that I'd witnessed said attack. I had no desire whatsoever to relive that particular moment of my life, and I didn't want Louisa unnecessarily worrying about me, either.

"He's still in a coma," I said, drooping my head. "He's doing well, though, the doctors say, but they have no idea when he's going to come out of it. They don't want to try anything to wake him up because they're worried he won't react well to the shock."

Louisa said nothing. I could tell from her face that she hoped as much as I did that he would wake up.

"Maybe he'll be able to identify his attacker," I thought aloud. After all, I knew I'd seen nothing of the person in question that would have helped anyone identify them. I didn't even know if they were a man or a woman. "And if it's the same person responsible for the attacks happening everywhere else, then –"

"Yeah, that would help a lot," Louisa finished for me. "In any case, Gracie, be careful. Have that boyfriend of yours accompany you everywhere. Especially after dark," she added, which was ironic coming from her. Louisa had never been one to be careful around Glasgow after nights out, staggering home barefoot, spilling chips and cheese on the pavement and singing loudly down the street as she proclaimed she definitely didn't need a taxi.

"I've always been the careful one," I reassured her. "And, besides, I have my thesis to finish, remember? You're the one outside enjoying mountains of free time."

Louisa gave me the finger. "You act as if I'm not working as a barmaid forty hours a week, bitch. It's exhausting!"

"Clearly," I said, pointing towards the mojito she was nursing even though it was after midnight.

Louisa laughed. Then, unexpectedly, I heard the front door unlock, and I jumped so badly I almost knocked both my drink and my phone to the floor. "Is that you, Lir?" I called out, nervous for some reason.

"Who else would walk into your flat uninvited? Don't tell me you've given other men a key?" he called back, chuckling at his own joke as he tossed his battered, once-red-but-now-almost-black rucksack onto the couch. When he saw I was sitting out on the terrace he came bounding over like a golden retriever, standing behind my chair to wrap his arms around my neck and nuzzle my cheek.

I was more than pleased by the attention.

"Missed you," he whispered into my ear. Then he propped his chin on my shoulder and took notice of my phone, waving to the camera with a stupid, lop-sided grin on his face. "Hey, Louisa," he drawled, as if this wasn't the first and only time he had ever met my best friend before. Then he turned his attention back to me. "I didn't expect to get back from Rothesay so early. Did you get more lemon tea?"

I nodded, so with another kiss on my cheek he left the terrace to put the kettle on. When I locked eyes with Louisa it was clear she wasn't happy. "What?" I demanded, crossing my arms over my chest protectively. I sensed a lecture coming on.

Louisa glanced over my shoulder. "You gave him a key? Isn't that a bit..."

"A bit what?"

"Well, *early?*" she pressed. "You've barely known the guy two months – you've literally only been going out three weeks – and he has free access to the flat?"

"He's my *boyfriend,* Louisa, not some crazy stalker." Because the stalker was me. "And you gave Josh a key."

Louisa rolled her eyes. "He's my brother."

"Yeah, but he's not *my* brother, is he?" I countered. "And all things considered I'd really rather he –"

"What do you mean, *all things considered?*"

"...never mind," I muttered, remembering just in the nick of time that I never told Louisa about what happened between me and Josh. I'd been too ashamed of it, especially when it became clear he was never going to call me. And she'd have yelled at him to make things right with me, and that would have made things even worse.

"Look," I sighed, "it's late for you and Lir is back, so I better go."

My best friend looked very much like this particular topic of conversation was not over, simply delayed for another time. "Remember what I said, Gracie," she warned. Another glance over my shoulder. "About everything."

I ignored her not-so-hidden meaning. "Love you, loser," I said. "Talk soon."

"We better. It's impossible to get hold of you these days!"

Before I could respond an arm reached over my shoulder and turned off the call. Lir perched on the armrest of my chair and clucked his tongue in distaste. "She's so clingy for someone who just left you to live on the other side of the world."

I swatted his hand. "What were you doing, eavesdropping?"

He shrugged. "Had to do something while the kettle's boiling. Why is she so over-protective?"

"We're best friends," I said, as if that settled things. "How else would you expect us to be?"

"More independent from each other?" Lir suggested. "You're your own person after all. Are you so integral to Louisa's daily life that she can't go through a single twenty-four-hour period without constantly calling you?"

Lir was exaggerating – it wasn't as if Louisa called me *every day* – but he still had a point. I always thought I was a hindrance to Louisa, who was trying to fit in calls to her friend around her hectic Australian lifestyle, which only made me feel awful when I missed said calls. She was all I'd had here in Glasgow, even though she was half a world away surrounded by new and shiny friends.

But she wasn't all I had now. Perhaps she never should have been. It hadn't occurred to me before that our relationship could be considered unhealthy, but through another person's lens I could clearly see how it very much was.

"Well I guess her leaving was the best thing for us, then," I said, taking Lir's hands when he pulled me up to my feet, enveloping me in his arms as if trying to protect me from the wind. When he loosened his grip I grinned up at him. "I don't reckon she'd have ever let me get away with stalking you for so long."

Lir chuckled, his grey eyes soft and warm on mine. He gently trailed a finger down my cheek. "God forbid she was around to stop you from doing that," he murmured. "We'd probably have never gotten together."

I didn't want to think about my life without knowing Lir. It felt like he was always *supposed* to be in it – that, for twenty-five long years, all I'd been doing was waiting for him.

A life without him now was unfathomable.

Chapter Fourteen

It was Wednesday, and mid-April, and a gloriously warm afternoon. Since Lir was away to Islay at the weekend and we didn't want to waste the weather, we'd forgone studying and thesis writing for a walk around Glasgow. Walking through the city was our usual routine when we weren't in my flat – even when the weather wasn't as nice as it was today. Lir wasn't much of a pub and club-goer, and he didn't like shopping, and he only liked going to the cinema if it was for a film he really, really wanted to see.

I didn't mind. I liked walking. And I liked talking to Lir for hours on end even more. It was therefore to my surprise when he told me he wanted to visit an old book shop on Great Western Road, which had the kind of worn-away sign and window display that I would have looked at and immediately forgotten had I been out on my own.

"What is it you're looking for?" I asked, naturally curious as Lir led me through the door. A little bell went off as we did so, which I thought was pretty old-fashioned and charming.

"Just a couple of things," he replied, already too distracted by the tomes surrounding us to really hear what I was saying. Though the last four weeks had shown me that Lir was actually more than happy to talk at length, he often had spells where he would disappear into his own head without speaking more than a word or two for ages – even when I was with him. Since I was a massive over-thinker I'd originally thought this was because he was already tired of me, but Lir was quick to reassure me that, sometimes, all he needed was silence.

Such as right now, browsing the book shop.

Dust motes floated in and out of streams of sunlight filtering through the window; I sneezed a couple of times as I got used to them. All around us were what seemed to be thousands and thousands of books, impossibly packed into the tiny shop. They were bursting from old, wooden bookcases, organised into boxes or literally stacked on the floor in precarious piles that threatened to tumble over when I brushed past them.

The shop was sort of organised into sections and genres, but not in a strict way, and when we crept down the rickety staircase to the basement floor we found even more books, all largely non-fiction. Sheet music, atlases, historical accounts and the like. Lir ran his index finger along the spines of the atlases for a minute or two, a small frown of concentration furrowing his brow that I adored watching. But then he turned from them to wander back up the stairs, pausing to scan the spines of the expensive, decorative volumes of fairy tales that adorned a shelf as he ascended to the ground floor.

Eventually I left Lir to his own devices, winding through the narrow shop in search of whatever it was he was looking for. I contented myself by looking at a shelf full of pulp fiction-style paperbacks from the nineties, whose hand-painted covers were simultaneously terrible and beautiful. They were the kind of books Louisa liked, alongside her trashy paranormal romances, which meant I recognised several of them. I'd even read a couple of them.

I picked up a Point Horror book with a particularly ridiculous cover, thinking that I might send it over to my best friend to make her laugh. But then I considered the postage costs and pulled out my phone to take a picture of the book, instead, sending it to Louisa along with the message, 'Have you read this one?'

Since it was very early afternoon here, Louisa was still awake on the other side of the world. She replied immediately with an excess of heart-eyed emojis, saying the book was one of her favourites but Josh had accidentally thrown it out when she was seventeen during a parent-mandated household clear out. I was

112

aware my face contorted at the mention of Josh, so I closed my eyes, took a deep breath and forced him out of my head.

I'd buy the book for Louisa, I decided, but keep it back as a homecoming present if – when – she ever returned.

When I reached the counter to pay (the counter in question was just as covered in books as the rest of the shop) I was surprised to find Lir already there, carefully placing two paper-wrapped books into a bag. He grinned at me.

"I was wondering where you went," he said. "I think we both lost track of time."

When I looked at my phone and saw that it was past two I realised Lir was right. We'd spent close to an hour in the bookshop and I hadn't even noticed.

He indicated towards the book in my hand. "What are you buying?"

"Oh, it's for Louisa," I replied, lifting the book up so he could see the cover.

A flash of displeasure crossed his face. "You're spending your money on her instead of yourself? Why don't you buy a book *you* actually want?"

"I'll read this, anyway," I said. "I'm not giving it to her until she comes back."

"That's not the point and you know it."

I did know it. But I didn't buy things for myself all that often, since I usually didn't have the money to and, to be honest, I wasn't even sure what I'd buy if I *did* have the money.

Then Lir sighed, a smile playing across his lips that screamed *What am I going to do with you?* "What do you like to read?" he asked. "I couldn't really work it out from the books in your flat. They basically cover every genre."

I shrugged. "I'll literally read anything. Most of those books are Louisa's, anyway, or books my parents gave me. The sailing ones I stole from my dad. I guess I don't have a preference. I don't think I even know any of the authors of the books I've read."

"That's not in the least bit helpful."

"Hey, if I'd known you wanted to go book shopping together I'd have warned you of my unfaithful nature towards the art of reading," I joked, paying the doddering man behind the counter who looked to be as old as the shop itself in the process. When my stomach grumbled loudly my face flushed. "Look, we can come back another day with the specific purpose of buying me books, but for now I'm starving. Lunch?"

Lir looked at me like I was a lost cause. But then he chuckled softly. "Fine. Next time. Sushi?"

I made a face. "Again?"

"It's good for you."

"It's practically *all* you eat. We've never gone anywhere but sushi restaurants together. Can't we change things up?"

But Lir stood firm with his choice. "I have to watch what I eat to stay in good shape. Is that so wrong?"

"Can we at least go to a general Japanese place rather than strictly sushi?" I asked, hoping for a compromise. "A katsu curry or teriyaki would be amazing right now."

At this Lir brightened immediately, which made my heart sing. When Lir was happy it was the greatest thing in the world – his eyes lit up, transforming his serious face into something angelic. It felt as if I somehow cured cancer or solved world hunger whenever I made him look like that.

Though, right now, I'd settle for solving my *own* hunger.

Because it was midweek the restaurant we went to was blessedly quiet. I ordered my katsu curry, and Lir ordered an assortment of sushi, as usual, and we relaxed into the easy atmosphere of the quiet, inoffensive music filtering through the air.

"Why is it always fish you eat?" I ended up asking, when our food arrived and I realised most of the things Lir ordered contained it. Salmon, tuna, yellowtail, mackerel. There was an absolute minimal amount of rice, and hardly any vegetables or greenery that didn't derive from the sea.

114

There was an odd pause before Lir answered, as if he was working out what to say. "I've always been fussy," he eventually explained. "There's not really much more to it than that."

I wasn't one to question someone on their oddities but something told me that there was probably a hell of a lot more to it than what he told me. Lir had remained very quiet on his childhood, though, aside from during our very first conversation when he told me he'd lived in Ireland before moving over to Scotland. I didn't want to pry – his childhood was his business and his alone. If he ever felt comfortable enough to talk about it then I would eagerly listen. Until then, I didn't plan to push him to tell me anything.

"So what did *you* buy in the book shop?" I asked between mouthfuls of curry. I pointed to the bag by his feet. "They looked pretty big. Were they expensive?"

Lir put down his chopsticks and dabbed at his mouth delicately with a napkin, then pushed his many small plates away to bring out the books. He unwrapped them as if they were treasures which, when I looked at them, I supposed they were. One was fresh and new, with a gorgeously ornate, illustrated gold cover and sprayed blue edges on the paper. The other was old and beaten; I could hardly make out the title at all.

"They're the same book," Lir explained, handing me over the much newer copy to peruse. "I'd been waiting for a copy of the original edition to become available for years. When the bookseller told me it was in pretty frail condition I figured it was worth buying the new version so I could read the text without further damaging the original."

"Greek myths of the sea," I read, opening the book to a random page. It was illustrated just as gorgeously as the front of the book, depicting a bearded, tightly-muscled man in the process of turning into a seal in front of several wild, crashing waves. "Does the original have all the same drawings?"

Lir nodded enthusiastically then very, very gently searched through the old tome to find the equivalent drawing to the one I was looking at. The illustration had lost some of its lustre – the colour had faded in places – but that somehow, inexplicably, added to the piece. It made it ancient and unknowable. A mystery. A myth.

"This particular story is about Proteus," he told me as I scanned the picture, marvelling at the detail in the piece.

"Proteus?" I wasn't familiar with Greek mythology at all.

"Proteus was a prophetic sea-god who could change his shape at will," Lir said, pointing to the man – the god – changing into a seal. "Because he could foretell the future, people often sought him out to know their fates, but he would only do so if they could capture him. Given that he could change form, this was almost impossible."

I realised, as I listened to Lir talk with his soft, lilting, born-for-stories voice, that there was something about the very way he held himself that had changed. He relaxed in his chair, head tilting to the side as his eyes grew hazy. It was almost as if Lir was recalling a memory rather than narrating a piece of fiction.

It was strange and enthralling.

"But then Menelaus," Lir continued, completely oblivious to the way I leaned across the table towards him in rapt attention, "who was struggling to reach home after the Trojan War, successfully captured Proteus. The god changed into many things to avoid him – a lion, a serpent and even water itself. Yet Menelaus prevailed, and he demanded to know which gods he had so offended that they would prevent him from journeying home, and how to appease them. Proteus had no choice but to give him this information. If you could find out that you had displeased the gods and how you could fix things, would you, Grace?"

The question was spoken in Lir's normal tone of voice and so utterly took me by surprise that I stared at him, mouth agape, for far too long.

"I – I'm not sure," I eventually, rather uselessly, managed to say. I searched for a better answer. "I guess, if my life had gone horrendously wrong, I'd want to know if there was some outside force responsible for it. But what if the price to set my life back on course was something I couldn't, or wouldn't pay? Aren't Greek myths full of sacrifices and stuff?"

"I suppose it depends on how badly you want something," Lir mused, more to himself than to me. "Some prices must be paid, even if they're unspeakably evil in some eyes."

The conversation had grown too serious in a way I didn't entirely understand. "Only eating fish, spending all your time swimming and surfing, reading legends about the sea...are you a mermaid?" I joked, trying to lighten the mood. "Or merman, I suppose."

Lir was silent for a long, contemplative moment. The hint of a smile coloured his face. "...something like that."

I didn't know how to respond, so I didn't.

Chapter Fifteen

When Louisa messaged me on Monday evening to say that Josh was coming to pick up some of her stuff I wasn't much in the mood to see anyone. Other than Lir, that was. *Especially* him. They'd just announced on the news that they'd found a body on Machir Bay on Islay, and they were treating it as a murder.

The victim was a young man in his twenties.

Lir had spent the weekend on Islay. He was late in returning, and hadn't replied to any of my calls or texts for two days. The prospect that he was the victim didn't seem real. He *couldn't* be gone. He just couldn't.

When I heard the door unlock my heart leapt. *Lir!* I thought, skittering down the hallway to throw myself at him. But it wasn't Lir.

It was Josh. A wave of disappointment mingled with rekindled fear for my boyfriend's fate washed over me. "Hi, Josh," I said, voice flat. I couldn't even look at him. "Come in, I guess."

"Well, hello to you too, Gracie," he said, smiling brightly as he waltzed past me so I could close the door. He hadn't been back since the night we slept together straight after Louisa left. It was weird having him standing here with me.

I followed Josh through to Louisa's room in silence, not knowing what to say and not really wanting to say anything, anyway. He dropped his head when he walked through the doorway, which he always did when passing through them. Though they shared the same auburn hair, fair skin and green eyes, Josh was tall where his sister was notoriously short. He was taller than my dad, even. But his head never would have actually touched the wooden beam above him if he'd stood up straight. I used to think it was endearing, the way he made himself smaller to 'fit' through the space.

Now I thought it was stupid.

"So how have you been?" Josh asked me as he opened Louisa's wardrobe and knelt on the floor to sift through the wreckage of her belongings that I'd stuffed in there.

"What are you looking for?" I asked, ignoring his question entirely. When Louisa had still lived here her room was a travesty at all times. Clothes were strewn across the floor from an overloaded washing basket, rumpled bedsheets hid whichever novels she was reading late into the night, and her university notes poked out from beneath a pile of plates on her chair. She hoarded mugs and glasses like a fiend, only returning them to the kitchen when I complained about the distinct lack of any drinking receptacles.

Even when she decided to de-clutter it only ended up worse than before, as she'd get distracted from pulling a pair of shoes or a dress out of the wardrobe that she hadn't seen in forever and laugh at her previous, 'uncultured' fashion sense. This would go on for hours until, finally, she'd get too hungry to continue and would invariably give up.

During that time I'd have scrubbed the rest of the flat clean, and Louisa always acted surprised when she saw how much work I'd done. 'You didn't have to do all that on your own!' she'd exclaim, though we both knew I did. But then she'd buy us a takeaway and a few bottles of wine to celebrate a 'job well done', so I didn't mind. I liked cleaning, anyway. It kept my mind busy.

The only time Louisa had ever cleaned her room properly was the day before she left for Australia, and even that was mostly her throwing everything into boxes that she could get away with leaving under the bed. The rest was shoved into the wardrobe and the chest of drawers, though I knew by the time she returned she'd have no use whatsoever for her old clothes and folders full of study materials and research papers from university.

With Louisa gone I hardly had to clean at all to keep things in an orderly fashion in the flat. It had felt lonely, not having anyone's mess to tidy up. But that was before Lir – who was just as clean as I was – and I realised it was the presence of another person that I'd missed, not the clutter.

God, I hoped he wasn't dead.

Josh glanced over his shoulder from where he was kneeling, a pair of biker boots in his hands. He sighed. "Nothing in particular. Louisa wanted me to see how you are, in truth. She's worried about you, Grace. Which means *I'm* worried about you."

When I rolled my eyes it was possibly the biggest eye-roll of my entire life. "What could either of you possibly be worried about?" I asked, moving over to the window to focus my attention on the river. The weather wasn't great; the surface of the water was rough and unpredictable. If it was worse along the coast than it was in Glasgow then maybe Lir was delayed because of it. Maybe it was making it impossible for him to get any phone signal. That *had* to be it. But still...

Young man in his twenties found dead on Islay beach.

I didn't notice Josh joining me by the window until he was literally right beside me. I clenched my jaw and refused to look at him, so he took a careful step away. "She told me you're spending all your time with some guy you only just met."

"I met Lir in January; it's mid-April now. I'd hardly say I just met him." Every word out of my mouth was clipped and careful.

"She said it doesn't seem like you've been seeing any of your friends for months."

"You mean *Louisa's* friends?" I corrected, finally looking at Josh just to glare at him. "You know fine well she's the outgoing one. I found it really hard to socialise with all those people on my own." *I never even had the guts to see them.*

"Did you actually give any of them a –"

"Did you honestly come here to lecture me, Josh?" I fired back, temper rapidly rising. "Because I seem to remember you completely, selfishly avoiding me when you were my only real friend."

Josh stared at me like I'd just shot a puppy. I didn't care. "Grace, I –"

I waved off his protest. "You do realise what it looked like to me, right? You told me you'd always liked me, then slept with me, *then* went back to your 'totally not serious' girlfriend who you were going to break up with as if nothing had happened. You said you'd call but you never did. I don't think you get to judge me on who I decide to spend my time with."

There was a long, drawn-out silence as Josh absorbed what I said. He kept his eyes on the window, resolutely not looking me just as I had done to him two minutes before. "You're right," he said, very quietly. "I've been awful. A total dick. I'm sorry, I really am."

The most annoying thing was that I could see Josh meant it, even though I wanted nothing more than to be angry at him for ever and always. But he was clearly genuinely worried about me, even though there was nothing to be worried about – well, not in the way he thought. That my boyfriend may or may not have been murdered was decidedly not something I wanted to speak about out loud, and certainly not with Josh.

"Things were always going to be weird between us after Louisa left," I eventually said, which caused Josh to turn his gaze from the window to look at me. His eyes were such a lovely shade of green – closer to blue than mine were – but they weren't the eyes I wanted to be looking at. Those eyes were as grey as the unsettled river outside, and weren't capable of sleeping with me only to return to the arms of another.

"Even *without* us sleeping together," I continued, wincing at the notion, "it was really naïve to think that we would be fine after she left."

"Yeah, but it's still my fault," Josh insisted. Well, at least he was owning up to it. "Can we please try to be proper friends

121

again? No awkwardness, no avoiding each other. Just...friends?"

Slowly, very slowly, I nodded. Friends I could do. Friends was all I'd ever wanted to be in the first place, before my loneliness made me susceptible to Josh's drunk confession and insistent fingertips on my skin.

Then he ran a hand through his hair, which was a sign he was about to push his luck and most probably say something stupid. "You know," he began, "I'm as well just coming out and admitting this. I was gutted to see you started dating someone just as I manned up and broke it off with Lauren. I -"

"Don't," I warned, before Josh ruined everything by speaking another word. "Don't even go there. You want us to be friends? Then keep your feelings in the past."

Josh fidgeted with the zip on his leather jacket. "You're right. Again." He reached out a hand and grazed my elbow. "But something is clearly bothering you. I'm not blind. We used to be able to talk to each other about anything. So just tell me whenever something is bugging you. I really mean it this time." He let out a self-deprecating chuckle, which was sincere but still sounded manufactured to my ears. It would take time for us to get back to normal, if such a thing were at all possible.

But I was willing to try if he was.

Then I thought of the attacks, and if Josh had any knowledge about them since some of them had occurred in Glasgow. I wondered if he'd had to deal with any of the victims directly. But that would mean some of the victims were children, which sent a shudder rippling through me.

I truly hoped that wasn't the case.

I forced a smile on my face. "There's nothing you need to worry a-"

The sound of the front door unlocking stole the rest of the words from my mouth, replacing them with a new one. "Lir!" I exclaimed, bolting out of Louisa's room so quickly I skidded on the floor and almost fell over.

And there he was, standing in the doorway, shaking from head to toe and so frail-looking it was a wonder the wind outside hadn't blown him out of existence. Lir's upper lip trembled as he looked at me, mere seconds away from crying, so I threw my arms around his neck just as Lir wound his around my waist. He squeezed the very air out of my lungs in his desperation to get as close to me as possible.

"I was so worried," I whispered into his ear, stepping up on tip-toes to do so. "Have you – did you see the news?"

"Who is he?" Lir asked instead of answering my question, voice flat and emotionless. His expression had entirely changed from one of fragility to dark, stormy suspicion; I twisted in his arms to see that he'd locked his eyes on Josh, who was awkwardly standing behind us.

"This is Louisa's brother, Josh," I explained, pulling away from Lir to introduce the two of them properly. "He was just collecting some things from her room to send over to her. Josh, this is my boyfriend, Lir."

"It's great to meet you," Josh said, holding out his hand for Lir to shake. For a long, drawn-out moment I thought Lir wouldn't take it, but then he grabbed Josh's hand and shook it as quickly as he possibly could.

"I wish I could say it was good to meet you, too," Lir said, "but being held back on Islay because of the weather and then getting caught in it hasn't left me in the best of moods. So if you don't mind..."

Josh smiled at Lir, though it was tight and superficial as he replied, "Of course!"

Lir bowled past him and locked himself in the bathroom without another word, which was closely followed by the sound of the shower turning on.

"Does he have much of a temper?" Josh asked me, frowning at the bathroom door in obvious concern.

I didn't like his question at all, not least because Lir was perhaps the gentlest person I'd ever met. "No. Not even a little bit. How would you feel if you'd been trapped in a storm?"

His face softened. "I guess after Louisa saying she was worried about you guys I kind of set myself up to immediately dislike him," he admitted. "Not fair, I know."

I didn't reply.

After a minute of silence Josh's shoulders fell, and he moved past me towards the open front door. "I'll get going, then. But I'll call you soon, Grace. That's a promise."

I let just the hint of a smile cross my lips. "I guess only time will tell if that's true."

Then Josh left, leaving me alone in the hallway and wondering if everyone who was close to me was going to immediately dislike Lir. It was just as Josh said: it wasn't fair. But when I tried to picture my parents meeting him my mind drew a complete blank. It was an impossible thing to predict.

After standing there for far too long I kicked myself back to life and turned on the central heating, then grabbed every blanket I had stored in my wardrobe and threw them on the couch before putting the kettle on. When Lir got out of the shower I handed him a mug of lemon tea, then the two of us cuddled up and watched a film. I couldn't for the life of me take in what it was actually about, even when the credits began rolling two hours later.

I resisted the urge to ask Lir what had shaken him up so badly; his expression made it clear that he didn't want to talk about it. But he clung to me like he was drowning and I was his only means of survival, so I smoothed his hair away from his face and kissed him until the dead look in his eyes slowly dissolved and he finally relaxed against my side.

I didn't need to know what happened to him. I was just glad Lir was safe and sound and, most importantly, back here with me.

Chapter Sixteen

When I was a child my parents had a boxy, unattractive Volvo Estate for a car. I knew by around age eight or nine that they could definitely afford a much nicer car, but they unconditionally loved the battered vehicle no matter what anyone said.

Back then most of our holidays together were spent within the UK, since my dad wasn't keen on flying. We drove everywhere in that Volvo - the Highlands, Aberdeen, the Lake District and, once, all the way down to Cornwall. We'd stayed overnight in a roadside hotel to split the journey down there in two, but on the way back my dad insisted on driving the entire way home in one go. It took him four cans of Red Bull to get through the journey and, when we returned to Largs, he slept for almost two full days.

He never insisted on driving for so long across a single day again.

I loved our Volvo trips. My parents would bundle a duvet into the back of the car for me to cuddle into and I'd serenely pass the time playing my Gameboy or reading a book. Eventually I'd feel so motion sick they had to stop the car so I could get some fresh air - or risk me throwing up everywhere. We'd stop every two hours for food and toilet breaks, and sometimes they let me scramble across the little play parks the service stations had just so I could stretch my limbs.

It never occurred to me that these holidays may have been improved by having a sibling. I was content all on my own, with just my parents for company.

Once we went to Center Parcs with some of my parents' friends; the couple had two children of their own. It became clear quite quickly that they didn't like me very much, though the feeling was mutual. They left me out of their games at the swimming pool and tried to kick me when we were cycling. In retaliation, I started cycling far faster than the two of them and disappeared in the pool to ride the flumes on my own, showing them that I was actually much better than they were and completely above their immature antics. After that trip, my parents and I never went to Center Parcs again.

When I was twelve – around the time my parents knew they were never going to have another child – they finally retired the Volvo Estate to the garage, where my dad kept his fishing gear and my mum stored spare light bulbs and other household items. They replaced it with a Ford Fiesta, which was far smaller than the Volvo and gave me hardly any space to cuddle up into a duvet in the back seat. But that was also the year we started going abroad on holiday once my dad had been convinced to give flying a second chance.

I loved visiting new countries, though part of me keened for our old road trips whenever the summer holidays rolled up.

When I was seventeen my parents gave me the Fiesta and bought themselves a hybrid Toyota Yaris, finally buying a car that identified them for what they were: well-off, middle class and responsibility-free. I thought I'd drive everywhere once I started university, though it became apparent very quickly that there was little point in having a car when public transport was often more efficient than using the congested city roads.

And so the Volvo Estate was left in the garage to gather dust, since both my parents didn't have the heart to sell it. When I was back home for the summer before my PhD started I went into the garage to grab a spare bulb for my dad and was filled with a bizarre desire to get into the car. I slid into the front seat (the doors were all unlocked) and sat in front of the steering wheel, dreaming about having my own child wrapped in a duvet in the back seat and a husband complaining about directions beside me.

126

It was an odd thing to dream about. I didn't want children; I wasn't even sure I wanted to get married. But I dreamed it nonetheless, and it made me ache with a sadness I couldn't quite understand. But then I got out of the car, left the garage and never thought about the Volvo again...until my mother called me, one afternoon when I was having a cup of tea whilst watching the rain outside batter my plants on the terrace.

"What do you mean the car is missing?" I asked, not taking in what my mum was saying. "How does a car go missing?"

"That's why I'm asking *you*, Grace," she said. "The police called saying they've spotted the Volvo in several places along the west coast. Apparently they noticed it in some of the towns where folk have been attacked over the past few weeks, so they ran the plates and obviously traced it back to us. We didn't even know it wasn't in the garage, Gracie. It must have been stolen when you were watching the house."

This rubbed me the wrong way. "If you didn't even know it was gone then it could well have been stolen while *you* were there, not me," I countered. "Why does it have to be my fault?"

"Your father has been stuck in the house every day since we got back from holiday with that bad leg of his," she explained slowly, as if she was trying to teach a particularly stupid child something achingly simple. "You know that. But you were gone for large parts of the day when you were here, weren't you? You were teaching."

I gulped. My mum was speaking the truth. The car could well have been stolen on my watch – I never went into the garage even once when I was staying in Largs.

"But the alarm never went off," I insisted, still trying to work out how this could not be my fault. "And if it had gone off when I was in Millport then Terry would have called me."

"So how do you explain this?" my mum demanded, temper very clearly lost. "Tell it to me in a way that makes sense."

I didn't have an explanation. The car being stolen was bad enough; that it had been spotted close to several of the attack sites was scary and unnerving. That meant the person responsible had been in my house...possibly when I was there.

127

The night Terry was stabbed flashed through my head, sending a wave of nausea roiling through me. I clutched a hand to my chest and closed my eyes, concentrating hard on my breathing.

My mum noticed the change in me immediately, even over the phone. "Gracie," she soothed, all anger gone in a moment. "I'm not angry with you. I'm just - well, I'm bloody terrified, that's what. After what happened to Terry so close to the house..."

I let her ramble on without really listening. My parents knew I'd witnessed the attack, unlike Louisa. It wasn't as if I could hide it from them when the police came round to the house looking for a new statement from me the day my parents returned from holiday. They hadn't wanted me to travel back to Glasgow alone; I reasoned that it was safer than staying on the literal street where Terry had nearly been murdered.

"Have you seen Tom yet?" I asked, abruptly changing the subject, though not really. For Tom had been yowling non-stop until he went missing. I had dismissed it as him going senile. But if he'd actually spotted the attacker scoping out the house...

My mum sighed, which I knew meant she hadn't seen Tom at all. "I think we have to accept that Tom is either dead or just not coming back," she said, not unkindly. And then, "Look, I have to go, but if you can think of anything that might help us work out what happened to the Volvo then please, *please* let me know. Okay?"

"Yeah, okay," I promised. "Of course I'll let you know. I love you."

"Love you too, Gracie."

I stood staring at the sheets of rain outside for a long, long time, forgetting about the cup of tea that was going cold in my hands. The evidence was stacking up that the attacks - as well as the murder on Islay - were not only performed by the same person, but were also premeditated. If the perpetrator had stolen my parents' car to travel around anonymously...

"Tom knew," I murmured, certain.

It did not occur to me until much later, when I was hugging

the person in question that night, that the only other soul who had been in my house that week had been Lir. But I'd been with him the entire time he was round. It couldn't have been him.

Of course it wasn't him.

Chapter Seventeen

I hadn't thought it possible. Really, it felt as if the end was never within my grasp. But, as we moved into the third week of April, haunted by Terry's stabbing, the attacks on the news and the theft of my parents' car, I finally finished my thesis.

I wanted to celebrate but I didn't know how. It's not as if I had a group of friends to get riotously drunk with at one of the university unions or a bar in the city centre. I didn't exactly have the money to do that, anyway, even if such a group of friends had existed. If Louisa were here she'd have borrowed money from her mum – who doted on her baby girl – to fund our festivities. But she wasn't here, and I had to be capable of celebrating without her.

I sent Josh a text to tell him I'd finished my thesis, though he was working and therefore unlikely to reply. Since his impromptu visit to my flat last week we'd messaged each other almost every day, slowly but surely getting back onto 'banter and insulting Louisa' ground. It was nice to have that again, though I was constantly a little on edge that Josh would say something that would take things too far.

When my phone buzzed a few seconds later I was surprised to see that he'd responded to my message. There was no stopping the snort of laughter I emitted upon seeing that he'd sent me a photo of himself in full scrubs and a face mask giving me a thumbs up. He followed this up with a message that we had to celebrate in person when he next had a weekend off.

Then I sent a similar message to David and to Louisa,

hoping that the former would reply and that the latter's response wouldn't involve telling me to celebrate with people who were not my boyfriend. But when David replied simply saying 'Congrats' and Louisa replied exactly the way I'd hoped she wouldn't I sagged onto my couch, thoroughly deflated.

"Should I go home?" I wondered aloud, thinking that my parents, at the very least, would be happy to celebrate with me. But the notion felt pathetic, especially because I knew I was but a few days away from giving into the urge to ask them if I could stay in Largs with them for a few months whilst I applied for jobs. It's not even like I *wanted* to specifically move back home; I didn't want to live so far away from Lir, for one. But I was fairly certain I couldn't stand to stay in Glasgow anymore...at least for a while.

Not wishing to feel sorry for myself – and full of too much restless energy to continue sitting on the couch – I wandered over to the terrace door and slid it open. When the wind blasted me back an inch or two I grinned. It was blowing from the west, and smelled faintly of salt. The combination of the smell and thoughts of my parents made me homesick.

I longed to be anywhere but the city.

That was how Lir found me, leaning against the railing of the terrace, staring at the river but dreaming of the sea.

"I heard someone finished their thesis!" he announced from the kitchen. I turned to see him pulling white paper packages out of a plastic bag from which the mouth-watering scent of fried foods began filling the air, competing with the wind. Lir gave me a small smile. "Sorry I didn't pick up your call earlier. I was already in the chippy so couldn't reply."

My ears perked up at the word. "You? In a chip shop? That sounds preposterous."

Lir could only laugh. "I figured you'd want something loaded with salt and caked in fat to celebrate," he mused. "I got some wine, too. Unless you want to go out somewhere?"

But I shook my head. Lir's presence – along with chips and wine – had improved my mood exponentially. "Staying in and pigging out sounds great to me," I said, heading back into my flat to fix my windswept hair in the bathroom mirror before helping Lir plate out the food and pour the wine.

We spent the next two hours cuddling on the couch, eating, drinking and not quite watching whatever was on the television. It might have been Antiques Roadshow. Lir seemed distant, which had been an increasing occurrence since his trip to Islay. I mean, he was here beside me, contributing to conversation and listening to what I was saying, but I could tell his mind was elsewhere. He kept glancing at his phone before, eventually, pausing from our conversation entirely to read something on it.

Now that the remains of the chippy had been thrown out and the terrace door was closed I realised that the distinct smell of salt and seawater had not dissipated from around us. It was odd to be sitting inside but able to smell fresh, blustery air and a hint of brine. It wasn't quite the same smell as the wind outdoors, by the river, carrying a diluted version of the scent.

No, it was the very authentic smell of the coast.

I shifted my gaze to Lir, too absorbed in his phone to realise I was staring at him. I tried to pinpoint a change in his appearance - an indicator that he'd been anywhere but campus today - but came up blank. His tawny hair was just as messy as usual, and he had on his favourite grey jumper and dark jeans combo.

Stretching my arms before feigning a yawn, I casually toppled into Lir's side and nuzzled my face against his neck. It *was* him who smelled like the sea. I didn't understand. If he was going to leave Glasgow for the day why didn't he mention it to me? He'd told me he was going to spend the morning studying and then the afternoon training in the swimming pool. But there wasn't a whiff of chlorine about him, only salt.

"What are you reading?" I asked, kissing Lir's jawline until he turned from his phone long enough that I could kiss his lips, instead. His eyes were glassy and faraway as he just barely reciprocated the gesture. I wanted to ask him where he'd been today - not what he was reading - but something was stopping me from asking. I didn't think it was fear, but...

It was something.

Maybe I was just being paranoid. I'd certainly have *sounded* paranoid if I demanded to know his whereabouts at all times like a jealous, untrustworthy girlfriend. I didn't want to be that kind of person. I wanted things to remain easy and wonderful between us.

"Ah, just an essay reinterpreting Celtic myths for the modern age," he replied smoothly, kissing me a final time before returning his attention to his phone. It was a valid response. A very *Lir* response: it was the kind of thing he always read in his spare time.

I knew he was lying, anyway.

"If you read any more of that stuff I'll be inclined to think you actually believe in it," I murmured into his ear.

When Lir jerked away from me, threw his phone on the couch and stormed off to the bathroom I was beyond surprised. My comment had obviously been in jest. I'd just wanted to break through the wall of silence between us and return things to the way they'd been before. But Lir had clearly taken offence from my joke.

I sat motionless for a few seconds, my eyes locked on his phone the whole time. Even though I knew I'd hate myself if I got caught snooping I grabbed the device, anyway, turning it around to see that the screen was still on. But Lir hadn't been reading about the modernisation of Celtic mythology.

He was reading about the attacks.

Why would he lie to me? I fretted, placing Lir's phone in the exact place he left it just as he returned to the living room. He seemed to have returned to being in a good mood, though, wrapping his arms around me and happily wasting time joking about all the jobs our degrees qualified us for that we'd never want to do in a million years.

He didn't pick up his phone even once for the rest of the evening, and I didn't dare ask him why he'd lied to me. Something told me some things were better left unasked.

Much, much later, over an hour after we'd retired to bed, I became aware of the fact that Lir was definitely not asleep. He wasn't even pretending to be. I spent the best part of that hour with my back turned to him, trying to ignore the fact that I could practically feel Lir's eyes boring holes into the ceiling. Eventually I could take the oppressive silence no longer.

I rolled over.

"What's bothering you?" I whispered, sliding a hand across Lir's cheek until he turned on his side to look at me, too. His eyes were just as glassy and faraway as they had been when he was reading about the attacks. "Look, I didn't mean to upset you earlier," I tried to apologise. "It was a joke. I –"

Lir swallowed my apology with his mouth on mine, pulling me in close and burying me beneath his lean frame. I reciprocated for a while, running my hand through his hair and urging him closer as I got lost in the sensation of his skin on mine. But I knew he was trying to distract me. Perhaps it was his silence, or the darkness all around us, but I finally found the courage I'd lacked earlier to call him out on his odd behaviour.

"Lir," I mumbled against his lips, though he only kissed me more insistently. My tongue grazed his teeth as I tried to speak. "Lir, I – *ow!*"

I pulled away immediately, bringing my fingers to my stinging tongue. They came away wet and smelling of metal.

Blood.

Not quite knowing what had happened, my eyes scanned Lir's face and stopped on his teeth. His canines were gleaming in the darkness. Perhaps it was *because* it was dark, but it almost looked as if he'd...sharpened them.

I'm imagining it, I thought, desperate to assuage my paranoia and uncertainty. *I must be. Why would he sharpen his teeth? I just caught my tongue. It's fine.*

"I'm sorry I hurt you," Lir mumbled, genuinely apologetic. "I didn't meant to. Let's just...go to sleep." Then he kissed my forehead, rolled over onto his back and encouraged me to rest my head on his chest.

I didn't know what to say. Didn't know what to think. With a sigh I dutifully rested my head on Lir's chest, tracing small circles on his stomach whilst he did the same thing on my back, until it became clear that both of our rapid heart rates weren't going to slow down any time soon.

It was a long time before either of us came even close to unconsciousness.

Chapter Eighteen

When Lir asked me the next day if I wanted to meet up with Max for lunch I was more than a little surprised, though I happily agreed to it.

"I didn't think you actually socialised with anyone from your course outside of classes," I admitted. It was reasonable to believe this, after all: Lir hadn't spent a single evening with anyone other than me ever since we got together nearly six weeks ago. That was half of the entire semester. Aside from his weekends spent outside of Glasgow, and the occasional late night he spent in the library instead of at mine, I could see no possible time during which he hung out with other people.

He chuckled good-naturedly. "I don't often. Whenever I have free time I usually spend it swimming, to be honest. But it's not as if I don't *like* socialising...sometimes. And I've seen Max a few times for a pint or two over lunch to break from studying."

Oh, yeah. Day time. It was stupid of me to have believed Lir spent *all* his time in the library or his flat, alone, before he came to mine. But that made me think about the night before, when he had very obviously not even been in Glasgow before getting to my flat when he said he'd been studying and training all day.

I shook the disconcerting memory of wind and seawater from my head. I didn't want to dwell on it, nor on the way Lir had overreacted to my stupid joke. I wanted things to be good between us. I wanted us to exist together in easy harmony, like we did ninety percent of the time.

I wanted Lir to not have sharpened teeth.

Max had picked a small bar in town which I actually liked and used to frequent with Louisa and Josh. They served two-for-one pizza and, because they actually had a wood-fired oven, said pizza was very good. Lir, of course, was no doubt going to order the fish, but I was long past caring about his dietary quirks by now.

Something told me Max was the type to be late to literally any plans he made, and I wasn't disappointed. We'd been sat at the table for twenty minutes, having almost finished our first round of drinks and about to order our second, when he finally showed up.

With a girl I didn't know.

I stared at Lir in horror, running my hands over my hair as if that would somehow make it less flyaway. "You didn't tell me this was a double date!"

He shrugged. "Does it matter?"

"I...guess not." It did matter, of course, but not in a way I imagined Lir thought was significant. But I'd have put more time and effort into my outfit. I'd have painted my nails, and curled my hair, and applied eyeliner instead of only mascara.

I sighed when I realised how stupid that was. Lir was right; it didn't matter. I'd spent so much of my life putting on an unnecessary front for other people, and now I had to unlearn that behaviour. It was for my own good that Lir hadn't told me this was a double date.

"Well aren't the two of you a sight for sore eyes!" Max said when he reached the table, posture so relaxed that for some reason I wondered if *we'd* been early rather than Max being late. *Nope, he was definitely late,* I thought, sparing a moment to double-check the time on my phone.

Max indicated towards the girl he'd brought with him. She was very pretty, with long, golden-blonde hair, perfectly manicured nails and the most immaculate red lipstick I'd ever seen. "This is Ruby," Max told us. "Ruby, this is Dylan and Grace. Dylan's on the same course as me and Grace was one of our teachers in a couple labs, if you can imagine that."

As we exchanged greetings it occurred to me how weird it was to hear Lir being referred to by another name after weeks with no mention of 'Dylan'. At first I'd been pleased that he shared with me, and only me, his real name. It felt like a secret. Now I wondered why nobody else was close enough to Lir to know that he preferred his middle name.

But I supposed that was a bit like the pot calling the kettle black. It wasn't as if I had loads of friends. Still, I had Louisa – even if I was currently avoiding her – and I had Josh – even if he'd been a dick to me in the past – and I had David – even if he still wasn't really talking to me properly and I hadn't seen him since Millport.

Okay, yeah. Pot, kettle, black.

"I didn't have you pegged as a gentleman, Max," I joked when he pulled out Ruby's chair for her before sitting down himself.

He gave me the finger. "Even sheep shaggers have manners, you know. But what's this about you finishing your thesis? Congrats! You Dr Ferguson now?"

A pleasant wave of embarrassment and delight washed over me at the compliment, especially because it meant Lir had been talking to Max about my accomplishments. It was the kind of comment I'd been longing for – something that confirmed that what I had achieved was significant. That I should be proud of it.

"I won't be a doctor until I pass my *viva*," I explained to Max, "and I'm bloody dreading that. But I appreciate the sentiment."

"The *viva* won't be a problem for you," Lir said. "When you talk in front of people you always impress them. Like in the lab."

It was a compliment and a very, very nice one at that. But I saw the second meaning of Lir's words clear as day: that it wasn't me who impressed people but, instead, the role I hid behind to avoid being myself. The person I was in front of everyone else was false, and he knew it. We both knew it. But I didn't want to always live my life that way. I wanted at least part of the fake me to be real...some day.

138

I wondered if Lir wanted that for me, too, or instead wanted things to remain exactly the way they were. As it was now, only I knew his core and only he knew mine. It was romantic and addictive.

But was it limiting, like my friendship with Louisa had been? Or was it freeing, because Lir simply wanted me to be myself without any of the fronts I put up?

I honestly didn't know.

Max very quickly took over the conversation after we'd ordered our food, regaling us with his big sister's recent break-up from her boyfriend. She was desolate, he said, and furious that the guy left her because he'd always had feelings for someone else.

I couldn't imagine being in a relationship when I liked someone else.

"What's even worse for Lauren," Max continued, after we had all finished our food and he was on his third pint of cider, "is that she works in the same place as this arsehole."

"Do they work in an office or something?" I enquired politely. I was eyeing up the dessert menu, which I didn't normally do when out for a meal with people. But I was enjoying myself; Max and Ruby made for easy company.

"Doctors," he replied, taking a napkin from Ruby when he spilled some cider on the table. "Children's ward, of all places. She wouldn't stop going on and on about how kind this guy was, how she thought they might get married eventually. And here's the kicker: the guy's fucking ginger. *Ginger!*"

Ruby giggled. "You'd think your sister would have better taste."

"What, like me?" Max replied, winking at his date. But then he caught my ashen expression out of the corner of his eye and frowned. "What's wrong, not-quite-a-Doctor Ferguson?"

I was aware that I had everyone's undivided attention, especially Lir's. I didn't have to look at him to know he was intently trying to work out what was wrong with me. "Um," I began, tapping my fingers on the table even though I hated displaying my nervousness in such an obvious fashion, "this arsehole ginger doctor wouldn't happen to be called Josh MacDonald, would he?"

"Holy fuck, yeah he is," Max said, disbelief plain as day on his face. "You know him, Grace? Sorry if I was hating on your friend."

"Nah, he deserves it." Because he did, even though we were on sort-of good terms again. "He's my best friend's older brother. I'm sorry he put your sister through all that."

Max immediately pulled out his phone without explaining what he was doing. Wordlessly he scrolled through his screen, eyes widening as he apparently read something of interest. "Fuck again," he said, laughing softly. "You're the lass he left her for, right?"

Oh, wonderful.

Lir narrowed his eyes at his friend, evidently suspicious. "What do you mean?"

"Lauren told me this Josh guy left her for his sister's friend," Max explained, holding up his phone to show Lir a message from his sister. "Who is clearly Grace, going by her face right now. Small world, huh?"

From the way Lir's hands curled into fists beneath the table I imagined he didn't like the small world notion one bit. I'd never seen him react like this before. Then again, he'd never found out until now that a man had left his girlfriend for me.

"C-can I just clarify that Josh didn't leave your sister *for* me," I stuttered, desperate to clear my name. "I didn't even know he was going to break up with her until after it happened."

Max laughed easily, which under normal circumstances would have put me more at ease. But Lir was clearly furious about the entire situation, though it was hardly one I could control. Perhaps he was angry that I never mentioned anything about Josh's feelings for me after the two of them met in my flat.

"It's obvious you're head over heels for this weirdo," Max said, pointing towards Lir in complete obliviousness of his friend's stark change in mood. "But, weirdness aside, Dylan is clearly a far superior choice to that ginger doctor, so well done avoiding that train wreck."

I appreciated Max's comments, though I'd have appreciated them more if they'd relaxed Lir out of his tense, sharp state. I risked brushing my hand across his, out of sight of Max and Ruby, hoping he wouldn't move away from my touch. Instead Lir did the opposite: he grabbed my hand so tightly I almost winced.

I would happily take that over being ignored any day.

Our double date finished a short while after, Ruby citing that she had to study for her politics exam whilst Max begrudgingly commented that he should study, too. He and Lir had their final exam on the twenty-seventh – just two days from now – so even Max could admit that it was worth putting in the effort for the final hurdle.

Lir and I walked back to mine along the riverfront because the weather was once more glorious and sunny. I couldn't remember an April as good as this one in years, which only solidified my desire to get the hell out of Glasgow.

"Where were you planning to go this weekend?" I asked, keen to strike up a conversation. Lir had barely spoken a word since we'd said goodbye to Max and Ruby.

"Loch Lomond," he replied, stiff as the breeze currently blowing through his hair. Lir didn't even look at me as he spoke, choosing instead to keep his eyes on the other side of the river.

If I never ask him the answer will be no, I thought, considering how to voice my next question. I'd avoided asking Lir if I could join him on his weekend trips before, but this one was straight after exams and would be a good opportunity to celebrate. Besides, Loch Lomond during springtime was beautiful.

"Oh, that sounds amazing," I said, keeping my voice bright and airy and not at all anxious in the slightest. "The forecast is so good for the weekend. Do you mind if I come along?"

"Yes."

His reply was so immediate that I stopped walking. "...why

can't I come?" I asked, when Lir was several feet in front of me.

He paused when he realised I'd stopped walking and turned around to face me. "I'm training," he said, tone cold and final. "The last competition of the year is on Wednesday. I can't afford to get distracted." Then Lir closed his eyes and drooped his head, splaying his fingers across his forehead as he did so. "You know what? I'll just stay at mine tonight. I need to study, anyway. I'll see you when I get back on Sunday night."

What?

"Wait – Lir!" I exclaimed, too slow to catch his arm before he crossed the road without even looking for oncoming traffic. "Is this about Josh?!"

But Lir didn't reply. He simply walked away.

Chapter Nineteen

I was watching the news. It was just about all I ever did in my spare time these days. I couldn't stop; it was like watching a train wreck in progress. Only this time, the oncoming train was in my neck of the woods instead of somewhere far off and unimportant to me. I was beginning to see a worrying pattern to where the attacks were occurring across the west coast of Scotland.

There was a new attack near Loch Lomond.

I could no longer ignore the fact that, wherever Lir went, something seemed to happen close by. When a man in his twenties had been murdered on Islay I'd been so worried that Lir was the victim. But what if...

I shook my head. I couldn't bear the thought. Lir couldn't be the attacker...could he?

I knew the coincidences were stacking up. The Volvo was missing, and the only person other than me who had access to it - especially considering the alarm never went off - was Lir. The first reported attacks were in Millport and then Largs, after which there was also Islay, Glasgow and now Loch Lomond. But the other attacks didn't line up with every place that he said he was going to for the weekend, so it was entirely possible that everything was a coincidence.

"But what if he's lying about where he's going?"

I didn't want to think about it even as I spoke my fears aloud. For how could Lir - gentle, soft-spoken, sensitive Lir - be capable of something so monstrous as what had been happening all across Scotland? His behaviour right before he left for the weekend notwithstanding, he really was the calmest person I knew. And that behaviour I could chalk up to him being jealous rather than having a temper. I mean, after finding out about Josh leaving his girlfriend for me he was *allowed* to be pissed...right?

But something was turning my stomach nonetheless. There was something I needed to know – something I'd wanted to know for a while now – that I could no longer ignore.

I phoned Josh.

The call rang several times with no answer, and I was hit with the stupidity of my fear. Lir hadn't stolen the damn Volvo. I was looking too much into this. People went travelling to seaside towns to surf and swim all the time, especially when the weather was as nice as it had largely been the past month. The perpetrator of the attack could be any one of thousands of people. *I should just hang up and –*

"Grace?"

My heart thumped painfully. "Um, hi Josh," I said, dithering about what to say next. "How are you?"

"Dead on my feet at the hospital," he sighed, "but when is that anything new?"

"Working a double?"

"The back end of one, yeah." He coughed to clear his throat. "I don't mean to sound rude but is there a particular reason you called? It's just that I have the get back to –"

"The attacks," I blurted out before I could stop myself. "Were any of the victims children?"

A pause. And then: "Grace, what are you talking about?"

"I just wanted to know if any of the attacks that have happened lately were on children. Glasgow has the closest large hospital to most of the places where the attacks have occurred; I figured everyone would eventually be flown over to get treated if their wounds were bad enough. And since you work in the children's ward..."

144

"Grace," Josh said, slowly and carefully, "why do you want to know this?"

I tried to work out how to voice my concerns without obviously sounding like I was hiding something. That I was lying. "It's just – the news hasn't said who any of the victims are, apart from the man who was murdered on Islay. I guess it's just, um, morbid curiosity."

There was another pause. I bit at my nails, realising that all of this was a foolish mistake. I was drawing suspicion to myself; suspicion I didn't need. That Lir didn't need.

Another pause. "No," Josh said eventually. "No, none of the attacks were on children. Grace, this is a really disturbing thing to be interested about. Tell me honestly: why do you want to know?"

"I... I don't have an answer for you, Josh," I said, because I most certainly didn't have one I wanted to willingly give. "I guess I'm just worried about it. After Terry and all."

Josh sighed heavily. Even over the phone I could tell how exhausted he was. "Yeah, I guess that's a pretty valid reason to worry about it. You *are* being careful when you go out, aren't you?"

"When I go out, yeah. What with my thesis and studying for my *viva* and all I'm not exactly leaving my flat that much right now, anyway."

"Good," Josh said, obviously relieved. "Yeah, that's good. And...look, Grace, I don't want to act like a middleman, but you must be aware of how upset Louisa is that you're ignoring her, right? Can you please call her and make up or whatever? What even happened between you two?"

I was taken aback by the sudden change of subject, though of course Louisa had complained to her brother. I really had been ignoring her calls – deliberately this time. I didn't want to have to listen to her insist that I spend less time with Lir and more time with the friends she'd made for me before she left for Australia. I didn't want any criticisms from her.

So why did I still feel guilty?

"I promise I will," I told Josh. I exhaled deeply, inclined to fall into bed and sleep even though it was barely three in the afternoon. "Look, I better go. Thanks for answering my questions. I hope the rest of your shift isn't –"

"Grace. Please tell me what's worrying you – for real. No lying this time."

"Bye, Josh," I cut in, then hung up.

No children were being attacked. That was something at least. But then I bit my lip to keep in a wave of tears, heading through to my bedroom to fulfil my urge to nap (or fretfully worry over everything with my eyes closed). For what did it matter that this person going about violently attacking and murdering people hadn't attacked a child? This person was reprehensible. This person was a monster.

But if it was Lir...

I couldn't believe I was considering it. Worse, I couldn't believe I was finding myself trying to lessen the severity of his crimes if it *was* him.

Don't let it be him, don't let it be him, don't let it be him.

For if it was, I would either lose Lir forever or lose myself by protecting him.

Chapter Twenty

After spending much of my time lately wishing I could get out of Glasgow I decided it was time to do something about it. My lease was up in June so I chose not to renew it. Louisa wasn't happy when I emailed her to let her know but ultimately understood why I had to do it; she knew we'd never be able to afford a rent increase *and* council tax when she came back, anyway.

I resolved to finally ask my parents to let me stay with them until I could get back on my feet. A month or two, tops. This gave me enough money to simply live a little for the rest of May.

Which meant I could finally leave the city for longer than an afternoon.

I had a car, after all, and if the only things I had to pay for were petrol and lodgings in cheap hotels or B&B's then I wouldn't run out of money for a while. It was the first of May now; if I spent a few days planning out the route I wanted to take and booked my accommodation in advance I could realistically spend three weeks travelling.

My heart soared at the thought of it, though my mood quickly plummeted when my attention invariably returned to Lir. Or, rather, the lack of him. He hadn't called or messaged once since our fight that wasn't really a fight, and after hearing of the attack in Loch Lomond there was a part of me that was scared to see him. I'd wanted him to come on this trip with me, since I knew his birthday was soon and his exams were over. I'd wanted it to be an extended celebration before I had to sit my *viva*. I'd wanted...

I'd wanted us to escape our lives, together.

My feet were dragging as I returned from the supermarket. It was ungodly hot and I had definitely not dressed for the weather before heading out. Sweat was running down my back between my shoulder blades, making my skin tingle and crawl unpleasantly. I knew the moment I got in I'd throw myself in the shower and blast myself with cold water.

I walked back to my flat via the riverfront to catch any kind of non-existent breeze I possibly could to cool me down, which meant I passed my terrace on the way to enter the building instead of coming round the back. It was in this way that I found Lir sitting on one of my deck chairs, waiting for me.

His eyes followed my every move as my footsteps slowed to a stop in front of him.

I pulled up my sunglasses, wiping my forehead in the process. "...what are you doing here?" I asked, entirely unsure about how to feel.

Lir immediately stood up and leaned over the railing, holding out a hand for my shopping. I didn't give it to him. "I want to apologise," he said, a very sorry expression colouring his face. "Of course I want to apologise. I've been awful lately."

And, just like that, I exhaled all the stress and negative energy that had been bundled up inside me. Lir wasn't a bad person. He wasn't unreasonably jealous or violent or a murderer or anything. He was just an ordinary guy, even though he was anything *but* ordinary to me.

I handed over my shopping bags. Lir's fingertips brushed mine as he took them from me, a gentle, deliberate motion that set my cheeks blazing. "I'm sorry," he said again, eyes wide and lovely and genuinely apologetic. "I really am."

"I believe you," I replied, barely able to keep hold of his gaze without crying. God, I was so stupid. I'd been overreacting all on my own, working myself up until I could barely function any more. "You can make it up to me by throwing together some mojitos. There's ice in the freezer. I'm going to wash off in

148

the shower first."

Lir beamed at me. His smile was so infectious I had my own enormous one plastered to my face as I clambered over the railing in lieu of using the front door, Lir laughing heartily at my ungainly landing on the other side.

"Mojitos, then," he said when I was safely back on my feet. "Want me to put the shopping away?"

"Obviously. I'll just be ten minutes."

By the time I'd washed, braided back my hair, slathered on sun tan lotion and frantically searched for my favourite blue bikini, Lir was back lounging topless on the terrace with a mojito in hand. He'd brought out my wireless speaker, too, which filled the air with Latin American pop from the late nineties.

I raised an eyebrow at Lir, though he couldn't see it through my sunglasses. "Did you search through my iTunes again to see what I've been listening to?"

He gave me a sly smile. "Maybe. To be honest I could have put any kind of nineties crap on and you'd have liked it."

"That's so insulting," I said, fake affronted. "I'll have you know I have *impeccable* taste in music."

"Sure thing. Now sit down and drink your damn mojito before all the ice melts."

It was an order I was only too happy to follow.

For a while all we did was listen to music and talk about nothing in particular and drink, Lir getting up to fill our glasses every time we finished our cocktails. We basked in the sun, and for a moment I wondered if I was mad for not renewing the lease. But I was no longer a student; my landlord was going to increase the rent and there was no way I could afford paying council tax, anyway. And if I was going to say goodbye to the place...

It may as well have been like this.

"How was your final exam?" I asked Lir an hour later, sucking on a piece of ice as I turned onto my front and unlaced my bikini top so my back wouldn't get tan lines. He lifted his own sunglasses and sat up, an incredulous look on his face.

"You really going to ask me a question like that when you're undressing in front of me?"

"Yes," I replied, grinning at his comment. "And you're going to answer."

"It was good. The end. Do you think people walking along the riverfront would see us if we –"

"*Lir we are not having sex on the terrace.*"

"It would make for a pretty interesting show for anyone who saw us," he chuckled, sauntering over to my sun lounger and pushing me to move a couple of inches so he could sit by my side. Because I was lying on my front I found it next to impossible to crane my neck around to look at him.

"I'm not turning back over just to look at you," I insisted, resolutely keeping my gaze in front of me. "You just want me to – *ah!*"

Lir rolled me onto my side so that he could lie beside me, pressing his body against mine so neither of us fell off the sun lounger. A foolish, playful grin danced on his lips as he slid his hand between us to grab my bikini top and remove it entirely, tossing it onto the floor with no regard for how I was supposed to get it back whilst retaining any dignity.

I clucked my tongue. "This is very inappropriate behaviour, Mister Murphy."

"Oh, use your teacher voice on me again, Doctor Ferguson. Tell me off."

I kissed him instead, giggling until his tongue found its way into my mouth and we grew too distracted to speak. Every inch of us was hot and slippery from the heat of the sun and the lotion rubbed into our skin, and when we finally pulled away just enough to catch our breath Lir had what must have been the most insistent hard-on in the world pressed against my thigh.

"Can't we...?" he whispered, all puppy-dog eyes and innocent eagerness.

At this point I was very, very close to giving in. But there were still some questions I wanted to ask. I kissed him softly, then said, "How did your training go in Loch Lomond?"

"Do we really need to talk about that right now?" Lir replied, making a face. "Because it went horribly, and my dick's shrinking merely *thinking* about –"

"Okay, okay, I get the picture," I cut in, forcing down a laugh at his humorous reply. "Will you be okay for the competition?"

"You and I both know I'm better than anyone on the team." There wasn't an ounce of arrogance in Lir's answer; it was simply the truth. "Why are you asking me that?"

"Just, because..." I filtered through my rum-fuzzed brain for the right words. "Well, I decided not to renew my lease."

A raised eyebrow. "Where are you going to live instead?"

"I was...going to travel, for a few weeks at least. And then work it out. Talk about procrastinating, but –"

"Travel where?" An immediate glint of interest lit up Lir's eyes, and I knew then and there what his answer would be.

"Around the west coast and the Highlands," I replied. "A road trip. I know Scotland hasn't exactly been the safest place these days but Glasgow is absolutely killing me. I need out. And I wanted to ask you to come with me – a celebration for me finishing my thesis and your exams ending. And presumably smashing this competition." I smiled softly, tracing a finger down Lir's arm to his hand. "And for your birthday. I mean, I know you like to keep your weekends to yourself but I thought that, maybe, you'd want to –"

"Grace." My name hung between us, full of meaning. Lir's hand wrapped around mine. "I'd love to. That sounds bloody great. You know I've been a bit of a mess lately. The city's suffocating me as much as it is you...you're just better at hiding it, clearly."

Lir really was looking more feral than normal. Hungry. Sleep-deprived. There were dark shadows beneath his eyes that hadn't been there when we met. "I'm better at hiding a lot of things," I said, which was a sad truth I was determined to change.

151

I wanted to be as honest as Lir was being right now, always.

"I'm sorry I didn't want you to come to Loch Lomond. I *was* jealous of Josh," he admitted a few moments later. "It was stupid. I know you don't have any feelings for him. And if I'd known my training wasn't going to go well, anyway, then I'd definitely have –"

My lips on his once more cut off Lir's apology. I didn't need to hear it. "It's okay. You don't have to explain yourself. Just win this competition and we can run off for the rest of May."

"Or forever."

It was then I realised I truly didn't care about his odd behaviour over the past few days – the lack of sleep, the sharpened teeth, the mad bout of jealousy – nor the coincidences surrounding the attacks. That's all they were, after all: coincidences.

If Lir wanted to run off for forever I'd gladly follow him.

But we could start with three weeks on the road.

Chapter Twenty-One

The last time I'd been in Glasgow University Union I was stalking Lir. This time I was in the union because he'd invited me.

How times had changed.

I put some effort into my appearance, curling my hair and putting on pretty, delicate make-up to complement the white sundress I was wearing – it had been a very hot day so far and the dress was the airiest piece of clothing I owned. Even now that the sun was setting the heat didn't seem to be dissipating all that much.

Several of the guys sitting in the beer garden openly stared at me as I walked past them; one of them even wolf-whistled. Normally such behaviour made me wildly uncomfortable. Because I was meeting Lir I didn't care.

A barrage of shouting, laughter and general revelry met my ears when I opened the door to the bar, and I wasn't surprised to recognise many of the louder students in the bar as members of the swim team. Glasgow had, of course, beaten their opponents (I couldn't remember which university they were from), with Lir in particular winning all of his races by a considerable margin. It filled me with pride to be the girlfriend of the team's most talented member, and that he wanted me to celebrate with him.

Then we'd be on the road in a few days, and it would be just the two of us with zero responsibilities for weeks. No worries, no weekends apart, no days where Lir had to lie about where he'd been or get jealous over Josh.

Just the two of us, together.

As I wandered through the crowded bar I struggled to locate Lir. He'd messaged me to say he was sitting near the back but I could hardly see through the throng of people, but then I noticed someone else sitting in a booth who I was decidedly happy to see.

David.

I beamed at him when he, in turn, noticed me, and when David waved me over I eagerly complied. "Hey, stranger," I said, noting that I didn't recognise any of the people David was sitting with. Friends from outside of his degree, clearly.

"It's been a while, Grace," David replied, a small but genuine smile on his face. "How are you? Are you...still seeing Dylan?"

"I'm great now that my thesis is done. And...yeah, I am," I added on, feeling a little guilty even though I had nothing to be guilty about. "Things are going well. And how about you? Do you have any injuries left from the attack?"

David looked good. His hair had been cut, and he was wearing his contacts, and all in all he absolutely did not look like he'd spent two weeks in hospital. But a shadow crossed over his face at the question nonetheless, and I immediately regretted asking it.

"One of my ribs is still healing," he said gloomily, "and there's something up with my left knee that feels kind of permanent." A pause. David turned his head around the room as if looking for someone. "Is Dylan here?" he asked. "Or are you meeting someone else?"

"Um, L-Dylan. The swim team won all their races today so they're celebrating."

David's face darkened even more. *Does he still like me the way he did before?* I wondered, unsettled by his expression. *Or does he not like Lir? But Lir said they got on well enough...*

"Actually, I was hoping to talk to you about that night in Millport, Grace," David said, motioning for his friend to get up so he could slide out of the booth. "Is it okay if we –"

154

But someone bashed into me before David finished his sentence, pushing me against the table so heavily all the air was knocked out of my lungs.

"Oh, excuse me, love!" a male, Irish-accented voice said, a pair of hands helping me back to me feet and turning me around in the process. The student in question was tall and well-built, with closely cropped, dark hair and ruddy cheeks. He raised his eyebrows when he took me in, gaze not-so-subtly lingering on the neckline of my dress before creeping back to my face. He grinned. "Let me buy you a drink as an apology."

"No, it's okay," I mumbled, glancing at David who had stood up to help me, an outraged expression on his face. "I'm with my friend, so –"

"Don't be ridiculous!" the stranger cut in, throwing an arm around my shoulders and steering me towards the bar before I could say a word in my defence. "I'm Cian, by the way. And you are...?"

"My girlfriend."

"Lir!" I cried, delighted and beyond relieved to see him, though his expression was mutinous. He grabbed my hand and pulled me away from Cian. "I've been looking everywhere for you."

"Sorry," he said, kissing me softly. "I was in the bathroom. You look gorgeous."

I flushed at the compliment. "Thank you. And congrats on today! What are you drinking? I'll –"

"I already got you a drink," Lir said, smile not quite covering his obvious anger. "It's back at the table."

"Does your girlfriend have a name, Lir?" Cian asked, interrupting our conversation. He was still eyeing me with an interest that I didn't like at all. But then I realised something.

He called Lir by his name.

"Grace," I said, answering Cian's question. I glanced at Lir. "Do the two of you know each other?"

"We go way back!" the Irish man exclaimed, thumping Lir's

shoulder as he spoke. It was clear from Lir's face that he didn't appreciate this at all. "We were next door neighbours before he moved away from Bundoran."

Oh.

"Come on, Grace," Lir said, a gentle hand on my back directing me towards the table a couple of his teammates were sitting at. "I don't want someone else taking our seats."

But Cian did not get the message that he was unwelcome. He followed us to the table, squeezing himself in beside us with an oblivious grin on his face. "Still can't believe I met you today after all these years," he said. "And to think we're both swimmers! He absolutely thrashed as, Grace. Man's a monster."

I flinched at the word.

"He really is something," one of Lir's teammates said, before turning to his friend and asking if he wanted a smoke. When the two of them left Cian spread himself out in the space they left.

"Ah, that's better. Hey, John, grab me a cider, will you?" he called out to a red-haired man who was queueing at the bar. He gave Cian a thumbs up in acknowledgement.

"I was kind of hoping to spend some time alone with Grace," Lir told his friend. He was making no effort to hide his displeasure at Cian's presence, though now I knew they were childhood friends I desperately wanted him to stay.

"It's fine," I smiled, squeezing Lir's hand. "It's hardly like we were gonna be left alone in here, were we? Your whole team is here. Let's just have some drinks together for a while."

Cian slapped his hands together. "A girl after my own heart! So how have you been, Lir? You're like a ghost on social media..."

After a few minutes of general conversation Lir finally seemed to relax. He began to smile and, when Cian cracked a joke, he even laughed. It was nice to see him talking to someone that wasn't me. Other than Max and the occasional person on his degree course I'd never seen him talk to anyone. It was reassuring to know that Lir actually existed outside of the bubble we put around ourselves, though it reminded me that I was just as bad, lately, at talking to other people.

I'd been avoiding Louisa's calls and messages for weeks now.

"God, this piss-poor excuse for whisky is flowing straight through me," Lir said half an hour later, stretching his arms above his head before standing up. "I won't be long. Don't go talking about me while I'm gone."

He smiled when he said this, though there was a warning in his eyes that I found alarming. But it wasn't directed at me; it was aimed at Cian.

His friend sipped his drink without a care in the world. When Lir was well and truly out of sight he sidled up beside me until his arm grazed mine. "*So,*" he drawled, a smirk on his face that disgusted me. "How long have you been going out with Lir, then? The guy was so fucking weird as a kid I thought for sure he'd be in a psych ward by now, especially after everything that happened to him."

"What happened to him?" I asked immediately, forgetting my dislike of the man in my haste to learn more about Lir. Though I'd decided I could wait until he told me about his childhood himself, being handed an opportunity like this to find out about him from someone who actually knew him wasn't something I was about to pass up.

Cian stared at me in disbelief. "You mean you don't know?"

"I...know what?"

"Well, it's only right that you know what you've let yourself in for," he said, far too happy about this prospect than seemed appropriate. His arm crawled over my shoulders to pull me closer, squeezing me against his chest. My heart hurt, and when I breathed in it seemed as if no air filled my lungs, and all I wanted to do was push Cian away.

But I wanted to know. I needed to know.

"What do you mean, then?" I asked, keeping my face politely curious. "What happened to Lir as a child?"

Cian bend his head until his lips were right by my ear. "His parents offed themselves when he was, like, four," he murmured. "Filled their pockets with rocks and walked straight into the sea."

Oh my god.

"Lir was left alone on the beach watching them do it with no clue what was going on," Cian continued, in a tone of voice that suggested he was reciting the latest plot of a television show he liked rather than someone's real life. "It was all anyone talked about for years in Bundoran – the poor, sick Murphys and the son they left behind. It was when his aunt took him in that I became his neighbour. Could tell he wasn't right from the moment I met him."

I couldn't speak. Couldn't get my brain to process what I'd just heard. Even when Cian's hand squeezed my shoulder I didn't have the wits to claw my way out of his grasp.

But Cian kept talking, completely oblivious to my shock. "Total nut jobs, clearly. I was too young to understand what happened back then, though, so I just thought Lir was odd for no reason. And then his aunt –"

"Cian." Lir's voice was friendly when he interrupted his friend, but there was an unmistakable bite to it that warned him not to continue. I hadn't even noticed him getting back from the bathroom. "Next round was on you, if I remember correctly."

To Cian's credit he looked wildly uncomfortable at being caught out both telling me about Lir's parents and having his arm around me once more. He pulled away, head bowed slightly, and left the table to buy the promised round.

Lir slid in beside me without saying a word. He looked at me through locks of messy, overgrown hair yet remained silent as if waiting for me to talk first. But I didn't know what to say, so all I did was stare right back at him.

It was like I was looking at Lir in a new light. Suddenly the innocence in his grey eyes – so at odds with the sharp planes of his face and his punishingly fit body – made perfect sense. He was a child who had lost his parents too young. A child who had witnessed something nobody should have ever had to witness. And that child was still there, hiding beneath the façade of an adult.

Searching for something. Longing for something.

As he reached out his hand for mine I realised he was shaking.

"I don't need to know," I said in an undertone. "You don't need to talk about it."

He squeezed my hand too tight. "Thank you."

As I rested my head against his shoulder I couldn't help but wonder: was *I* that something? Could I ever fill the hole Lir's parents left him with, which I had always noticed but never fully comprehended until now?

I wanted to. I sincerely, desperately wanted to, now more than ever before.

After another hour in the union I let out a yawn, and Lir laughed softly when he ruined it by sticking a finger in my mouth. "Why don't you head back home?" he suggested.

"What about you?"

Lir indicated towards Cian, who was too busy talking to his friend John to notice Lir pointing at him. "I want to have some words with him, then say goodbye to the team properly. I won't see them again until after summer."

I nodded in understanding. I was glad that Lir was going to talk to his former friend. I hoped that he called him out on being inappropriate as well as a complete and utter arsehole.

"I'll see you back at mine soon, then?" I asked, leaning forwards to kiss Lir on the cheek. He turned his face so the kiss landed on his lips, instead, and we both giggled.

"Of course," he said. "Hopefully I won't be long. Get home safe."

"You, too."

As I left the union I struggled to comprehend what I had learned from Cian. Lir's parents had committed suicide *in front of him*. It was sick. It was cruel. They really must have been mentally unwell to do something like that. Either that or they didn't care for their son, though I dismissed the notion immediately.

Lir had been loved, that much was obvious. But that love had been taken from him by the sea.

The sea.

Was that where his obsession with it all began?

Lir, Age Twenty-Three

After Grace left the bar Lir was quick to buy another drink for his childhood friend. Cian was only too happy to accept the offer of free alcohol. He was a student, after all. His stipend only went so far. He did not notice that for every vodka or pint or shot he did, Lir drank only water.

It was in this way that, by the time the bar closed, Cian Byrne was so drunk that he blearily agreed to Lir's suggestion of breaking into the university gym to use the swimming pool.

"It's not really breaking in," Lir assured him as they reached the side door into the building. "I have all the passwords for the doors, alarms and cameras."

"H-how?" Cian hiccoughed.

Lir flashed him a grin. "I have my ways."

When they reached the swimming pool the cavernous hall that accommodated it was lit only by the orange glow of the street lamps filtering through the narrow windows high up on the walls. Lir was quick to strip down to his underwear so Cian followed suit.

"What we gonna do? Race? We both – *hic* – know I can't beat you," Cian said, knowing his own limitations against his childhood friend even in his wasted state of drunken overconfidence.

But Lir laughed easily. "You give me too much credit. I'm drunk, too. You could win."

"Bull shit. You should be on the Olympic team, you son of

a bitch. Why are you wasting your time here?"

"I like being at university," Lir replied simply. He rolled both of his shoulders back until his spine popped in an entirely satisfying kind of way. "And I never wanted to swim competitively. I only joined the team here to make my folks happy."

Cian frowned. "Your mum and dad?"

"My aunt and uncle in Campbeltown," Lir corrected.

"Ah, so they're the ones who took you in after –"

"Do you wanna swim or not?"

Even drunk, Cian could see he'd crossed a line. He ran a hand through his close-cropped hair, walked over to the edge of the pool and prepared to dive in. When Lir did the same thing he turned his head to stare bleary-eyed at him. "Hey, I didn't mean anything by telling your girlfriend about your parents, Lir. I thought she knew."

"It's fine."

It wasn't.

"And..." Cian laughed awkwardly. "I'm sorry for hitting on her. She's hot and I was wasted. *Still* wasted. No harm no foul, right?"

Lir gave him a practised smile. "Of course. It's all good."

It really wasn't.

A dozen blue tetras, Lir thought as he poised himself above the water, muscles tense and ready to dive right in. When the second hand on the clock looming over the pool hit twelve the two swimmers crashed into the water and began their race.

Ten threadfin rainbow fish.

Lir cut through the water well ahead of Cian until he reached the deepest part of the pool. Then he paused, taking a deep breath as he watched Cian reach him.

Eight blood orange mollies.

Lir launched himself at his former friend, locking his arm around Cian's neck before he had a chance to work out what

162

was happening.

Cian's bloodshot eyes widened. "What the fuck are you doing?!" he spluttered, scrabbling at Lir's arm with alcohol-slow fingers.

Four red swordtails, who tried to jump out of the tank whenever the lid was removed.

Lir said nothing, using all his energy and focus to tighten his grip on Cian's neck when he tried to kick him beneath the water.

"This isn't – let me go, *let me go!*"

Three stripy loaches, who rooted around the plants and gravel like dogs picking up a scent.

Cian's movements were slowing and losing their strength. Lir knew he had to hold on just a little longer, so he swallowed back the bile that rose in his throat as he watched Cian's eyes grow ever more scarlet from broken blood vessels.

Two dwarf gouramis, that were inseparable from one another.

Lir pushed Cian's head beneath the surface of the pool so the water could finish him off. It seemed only fitting. When his childhood friend stopped twitching and grew still Lir let out a slow, staggered breath. Tears stung his eyes: the product of rage, disgust and relief instead of sorrow.

A mad grin spread across his face as Cian bobbed, lifeless, across the surface of the water.

"That was for the fish."

PART THREE

Lir, Age Six

Though Lir was supposed to start primary school the summer after he turned five, Orla grew increasingly concerned that he was not yet mentally ready for it. Lir was sensitive, imaginative and quiet, and she loved him fiercely, but onlookers knew there was something not quite right with the boy.

Orla did not want to admit that she agreed with them. But, to be sure, she decided to keep him back from school for a year. She reasoned that a few extra months to help Lir develop before throwing him into such a loud, demanding environment would do him good.

This led to the third and final moment that defined Lir's childhood – his sixth birthday.

Lir had become embroiled in fairy tales and folklore surrounding the sea, which Orla knew she had a heavy hand in enabling. She was the one who told him the stories, and bought him the books, and found all the television shows airing about Greek and Celtic and Norse mythology for him to watch. So when she asked Lir what he wanted to do for his birthday Orla was not surprised when he responded that he wanted to go to the beach.

"Which beach should we go to?" she asked him. "There's –"

"I want to go to the one mum and dad took me to."

Orla did not like the sound of that at all. But Lir was looking at her with big, hopeful eyes, and she knew that as he got older he'd have to process the death of his parents for what it was. Perhaps visiting the place where they'd left him would give Orla an opportunity to broach the subject in a more direct manner with Lir.

She couldn't let him believe they 'went home' forever.

So, after eating cake for breakfast and packing up towels, buckets and a huge lunch, Orla took Lir to the beach. The weather wasn't as glorious as it had been on his fourth birthday – dark, ugly clouds intermittently covered the sun, and the wind promised rain in a few hours – but Lir didn't care.

He was on a journey. A mission. A quest.

The weather didn't matter.

"Do you think selkies come to this beach?" he asked his aunt as they built a sandcastle. He carved an octopus into the moat with a skill that belied his young age.

"Maybe," she said, smiling when Lir pretended to strike the castle with lightning, obliterating it. She hadn't seen him so content and genuinely happy in months; the excitement in his eyes was infectious. "What do you think?"

"I think they do. All kinds of magical creatures live along the shore here."

"Is that so?"

Lir nodded seriously. "Someone in town could be a selkie."

"Like Miss Campbell in the post office?"

"No."

"Why not?"

"Because she's boring and ugly."

"*Lir!*" Orla chastised, though she couldn't help but laugh. "That's not a very nice thing to say."

"It's true, though," he muttered, staring at his hands. Then he jumped to his feet and tried to pull his aunt up, too. "Let's go swimming."

When Orla scanned the sky she didn't like the look of the clouds looming overhead; they had the beach largely to themselves because of them. The waves that crashed into the shore were anything but gentle. "I don't know, Lir..."

"*Please?*" Lir begged, hopeful and desperate as only a child could be. "Please, please, please, please?"

With a sigh his aunt relented. "Only for a little while, okay? And we're not going in far. Do you understand?"

But Lir was already gleefully running towards the sea.

"Slow down, Lir!" Orla called out as she splashed through the waves after him. "I said not so deep!"

But Lir didn't stop. His tiny frame travelled out further and further, Orla beginning to panic even as she marvelled at how quick the boy was. He'd been able to swim even before she took him into her home, so she had signed him up for swim club at the local pool in the hope he would make some new friends. He never made any friends, but clearly he'd gotten even better at swimming.

"Come on, Aunt Orla!" Lir shouted over the noise of the wind and the waves. "Mum and dad are waiting for us."

Orla's blood froze in her veins. "They're...what? Lir, come back, stop swimming so far out!"

When she finally reached him they were far from the shore, and Orla could no longer feel the seabed beneath her feet. She grabbed Lir's arm, pulling him back with all the strength she could muster. But Orla was frail. She always had been. Though Lir was only six he had a boundless amount of energy and a drive in his eyes to reach something Orla knew did not exist.

"We have to get home," Lir insisted, spitting out a mouthful of water when a wave tumbled over his head. "Which way is it, Aunt Orla?"

"We're going back to the beach," she scolded, trying to sound firm even though her voice was shaking. "Lir, come on – *Lir!*"

Lir slid out of her grasp and dived down, down, down into the water, and Orla screamed. Taking a deep breath she plunged beneath the surface after him, salt stinging her eyes as she searched for her nephew.

When she finally spotted him he had a large rock in his hands. Orla tried to take it from him and failed, twisting around to try and catch Lir when he swam around her. But she needed air, so she swam back up to gulp some down, instead. And then –

A dull thump to her head. Then another, and another.

"We have to go home," Lir said again, though his voice was hazy and faraway. "Don't be scared. Mum and dad will get us soon."

When Orla sank beneath the waves she did not get back up.

"Aunt Orla?" Lir wondered aloud, diving after her only to see the current pulling her away faster than he could swim. But he swam after her, anyway, excited that the sea was now helping them on their journey. Soon they would be reunited with his parents. Soon they'd all be together again.

But no matter how fast or how far Lir swam, home never came. His limbs grew tired, and he lost sight of Orla's body being carried by the current. So he treaded water as he tried to remember everything his swimming teacher had taught him. Deep breaths. Don't panic. Lie on your back until your strength returns.

Lir closed his eyes as he floated along on the sea.

When he opened them he was in hospital, and his aunt was dead.

Chapter Twenty-Two

I woke up on a beach I didn't recognise, though part of me was aware I was dreaming and not, in fact, awake at all. Perhaps it was more accurate to say I was having a nightmare.

However, after I woke up I wasn't sure if 'nightmare' was an accurate description of the dream after all. Maybe 'omen' was a better term, though I'd never been one to believe in anything superstitious before.

So maybe it *was* just a nightmare and not a harbinger of doom. A series of chemical impulses gone awry in my brain.

That was most likely it. Probably.

The sand between my toes was dense and damp, littered with stones and small twigs that pricked the soles of my feet. I was wearing one of those floaty, almost translucent white night dresses that the heroines from Louisa's Gothic and historical romance novels often adorned. The material whipped around my ankles as a surge of wind pulled me forwards. I fought against it.

Everything was dark – the moon and stars were covered by thick, ominous clouds – so I had to rely on my other senses to navigate my environment. In front of me was the sound of waves cresting and breaking on the shore, not very far away from me at all. Behind me I could hear...nothing at all.

I turned around, peering through the blackness. Was there really *nothing* there? Had my dream constructed itself only to exist in front of me and never behind? It was a disconcerting thought. My subconscious wanted me to move forwards, into the sea.

"I will not do it," I said, so quietly that the words were lost to the howling wind. So I screamed it, instead. "*I will not do it!*"

Silence followed my proclamation. The wind died in an instant, my dress no longer flapping and twisting around me but instead obediently lying flat against my skin. I couldn't even hear the waves.

Above me the clouds began to clear and the moon and stars were finally revealed. With them came an almost dazzling quantity of light, silvering the edges of the waves and making the sand glitter like a hundred thousand diamonds. My vision was swimming simply trying to take in all the new visual stimuli, and it hurt my head, so I closed my eyes for a moment to ground myself.

That was when I heard the voice. A familiar voice. A voice aching with longing and sorrow.

Lir's voice.

"Lir!" I called, opening my eyes and darting around the beach in bursts of frantic energy, desperate to find him. But he wasn't anywhere to be seen on the sprawling, lonely beach.

And his voice was coming from the sea.

Without another thought I closed the gap between myself and the water, the bite of it not bothering me in the slightest as I stumbled into the waves lapping at the shore. Lir's voice urged me deeper and then deeper still, until the sea was up to my thighs and the wind sprayed me with froth and salt.

"*Lir!*" I cried again, trying my best to focus on the exact direction his voice had come from. But the breeze grew stronger once more, carrying it around me until all I could hear were echoes and memories of his call built on top of each other in an endless loop.

He wanted me. He *needed* me. Though I could make out none of the words Lir was saying I was sure with every fibre of my being that it was imperative I reached him. It occurred to me, then, that although Lir always called me *his* siren, in my dream our roles had been reversed. But no part of me could stop moving through the water in search of him even as I acknowledged what sirens were supposed to do.

Lir would never kill me. He was not luring me to his side to die. He needed my help. He needed *me*.

A gust of wind blew through my hair, causing my scalp to tingle. I was up to my neck in the water and yet that gust was somehow all I felt. The smell of the sea followed the wind, all dark, pungent, salty waves, strong enough to throw me to my doom. It was overpowering. Even as I struggled to reach Lir's haunting, keening call, that smell and the wind on my scalp was all that consumed me.

A wave crashed over my head, filling my mouth and throat and lungs with stinging, freezing water. But when I tried to cough it up I simply ingested more water, and the current carried me further and further from Lir. No matter what I did I was never going to reach him. The sea was going to drown me first, dragging me down to its dark and unknowable depths.

I woke up.

My eyes flashed open and I sucked in a breath to make sure I was still alive. Cold, feverish sweat coated my skin; I was too afraid to wipe it away. The salty air from my dream refused to dissipate. It was stuck in my nose, stabbing at my eyes and pulling me back down under. *Go away,* I begged, turning on my side to huddle into a ball and try to fall into a decidedly dreamless sleep. But I rolled right into another person.

Lir, finally home from the union. I hadn't even heard him come in and yet here he was, barely-there breathing telling me he was dead to the world. I didn't have to look at my phone to know it was very, very late.

The smell of the sea wouldn't disappear.

With extreme hesitation I grazed my fingertips across Lir's arm. He was freezing to the touch – too cold to have been the result of walking back from the union on a warm May night. He had been somewhere else before coming back to mine. Somewhere far away.

171

When I nuzzled my face between his shoulder blades I came to the stark but somehow not surprising conclusion that Lir was the source of the salt air that had woven into my dream and woken me up. The memories of his siren call, luring me to his side as the waves crashed over me, kept me clinging to him even though I so badly wanted to recoil.

"Where have you been?" I mouthed against his skin, sliding my arms around Lir's chest to try and heat up his body with mine. "What did you *do*?"

But Lir did not respond. He was lost to sleep – far heavier than my own had been. *No person could sleep so soundly after doing something heinous...right?* I thought. It had to be true. Lir had simply gone on a miles-long walkabout. He'd been drinking, and it was so late. If he'd been wandering about for hours with no jacket or jumper rather than coming straight home then that would explain his cold skin. And the salt...well, sometimes the wind along the river blew from the west, from the coast. I knew this perfectly well.

I could account for Lir's current appearance as easily as that. There was nothing to be worried about. Of course there wasn't.

Inhaling deeply, I closed my eyes and forced my heart to slow down. It was in my best interests to go back to sleep. If I was asleep then I couldn't worry that my explanations for Lir showing up late, freezing cold and smelling of the sea, were anything but the truth.

Come morning everything would be okay.

Chapter Twenty-Three

My eyes flashed open after a long, restless night – the only proof I had that I'd fallen asleep at all. Lir was lying face down on his pillow, still dead to the world. I didn't want to wake him.

I didn't know what I'd say.

I slipped out of bed on whisper-quiet feet and padded to the bathroom, taking a deep breath when I got there. I needed to do something normal to take my mind off things, so I smoothed back my hair into a ponytail, washed my face and brushed my teeth. My usual routine. But something felt wrong nonetheless. Something had changed.

When I reached for my contact lens case a blurry, indistinct movement flashed across the mirror, and I froze.

"Morning," an out-of-focus Lir yawned, stretching his arms above his head until his spine popped. "Why didn't you wake me?"

"You...were so peaceful," I mumbled, struggling with the top of my contact lens case as I tried to stop my hands from shaking. Wordlessly Lir took it from me, opened it, then handed it back. "Thank you," I said. And then: "You got in really late last night."

"I didn't know you were up when I got in," he said. If Lir had physically reacted to my comment I couldn't see it without my contacts.

"I wasn't. I woke up after you fell asleep. You were so cold."

When Lir came up behind me and wrapped his arms

around my waist I prepared to flinch. But his skin was no longer freezing. It was warm, and comforting, and easily moulded to my body.

"I was drunk," Lir chuckled against my ear. His breath smelled faintly of whisky. "So drunk, in fact, that when Pete and the other guys on the swim team suggested a walk I thought it was a great idea. It was only after we'd walked to the other side of the city that I sobered up enough to realise where I was. Then I walked back along the river to yours. I'm an idiot. I know I said I wouldn't be long last night. I'm sorry."

I let out a breath, relief washing over me at his explanation. Lir had gone on a stupid, drunk walk, just as I'd suspected. That was it. There was nothing more to be worried about.

"It's okay," I said, meaning it. I turned my head slightly to brush a kiss past his lips: they were chapped and flaking. "Are you hungover?"

"Oh yes," he admitted, grimacing in a performative manner. "I'll be better after some water and breakfast."

"I'd kill for a McDonald's right about now."

"How's their fish?" Lir asked, kissing the back of my head before letting me go, freeing my arms up to put my contacts in.

I glanced at him in the mirror. "I don't know. I'm all about the Big Macs and chicken nuggets."

A pause. "I guess it doesn't hurt to try new things sometimes."

"I can't believe you've *never* had a McDonald's at almost twenty-four years of age, Lir Murphy."

"We don't have one in Campbeltown!" he countered, fake-affronted.

I couldn't help but laugh. "You've lived in Glasgow for almost three years, though."

"You've lived here for eight but still haven't set foot in about ninety-five percent of the restaurants in the West End alone."

It was hard to converse with Lir *and* put my contacts in, so I ignored his last comment in favour of giving myself the gift of

174

sight. The left lens went in easily; the right, however, was being a pain. I poked my eye and blinked out the lens twice before it, finally, sat in place. My eye was stinging and slightly red by the time I was finished.

Lir was wincing at my reflection. "I don't understand how you can touch your eyes every day. It's disgusting."

"I didn't have you pegged as a squeamish person," I said, genuinely surprised.

He shrugged. "I can't stand the sight of blood. The idea of touching eyes and bones and stuff creeps me out. Why did you think I wasn't squeamish?"

I didn't have an answer for him. At least, not one that *didn't* make me sound like an overly-suspicious, paranoid woman.

I left the bathroom, then, to give Lir an opportunity to use the toilet and brush his teeth, and wasted time picking out my underwear. But by the time I put some on and reached for a dress from my wardrobe Lir reappeared and grabbed me, pulling me down onto the bed to plant kisses all over my face.

"Lir!" I giggled. "What about food?"

"It's still the breakfast menu right now," he said, pausing from his entirely welcome assault to glance at the clock. "I thought you wanted chicken nuggets?"

"How do you know when the breakfast menu is on when you've never set foot inside a McDonald's before?"

"You spend bloody ages staring longingly at the damn place whenever we walk past it," he explained. "It's like you're addicted. How often did you eat from there before we started going out?"

"Um...too often, I suppose." I nuzzled into Lir's neck and thought about it. Louisa and I used to have a McDonald's every week. It was our thing. After she left I still went fairly frequently and then video called her so she could keep me company whilst I ate.

As if she knew I was thinking about her my phone began to vibrate on my bedside table, and when I reached over Lir to grab it I saw I had an incoming call from my best friend. I was divided on whether I should answer; I'd ignored so many of her calls lately. Me ignoring her wasn't *entirely* warranted, but she didn't make things easy when all she did was criticise me for spending time with Lir.

But if all I do is ignore her then she'll never, ever like him.

I gave Lir an apologetic smile. "I should get this."

When he pouted it was somehow both ridiculous and beautiful. "I'll make some tea, then. Lemon?"

"Just regular for me," I said, before rolling onto my front to accept Louisa's video call. A flash of genuine surprise crossed her face when she realised she'd actually gotten through to me. I waved sheepishly at her pixelated appearance. "Hey, Lou," I said. "How are you?"

Her surprise was quickly replaced with annoyance. "So you've finally dignified me with some kind of response?" Louisa huffed. "It's not like I haven't called a dozen times, left you loads of messages and tagged you in a tonne of photos on Instagram, you know."

I didn't have a good excuse, but an excuse I gave anyway. "I've been busy."

"Yeah, busy with your *boyfriend*," she said, as if the word disgusted her. Her response left me immediately on edge, reminding me why I'd been avoiding her in the first place.

"What's wrong with me wanting to spend time with him? He's my boyfriend, as you so kindly pointed out. What else am I supposed to do *but* spend time with him?"

"Oh, I don't know," Louisa said, rolling her eyes as she pretended to consider my question. "Maybe call your best friend? Let me know what's going on in your life?"

"I don't want to talk to you when all you do is judge me."

Louisa stared at me like I'd shot her. "Gracie, I'm worried about you, that's all! You've never been like this before."

"What, not dependent on you?"

"That's not what I –"

"You say you want to know what's going on in my life but you disapprove of what I'm doing. What you *really* want is for me to live the life you've decided I should have."

Even over the terrible video quality I could see that Louisa's eyes had grown too bright. She shook her beautiful mane of auburn hair. "You're putting words in my mouth. Look, I know things haven't been easy with me out here. But that doesn't mean things have to change so much between us."

"But they *do*," I insisted. "I'm tired of spending every day missing you, wishing you would come back but then hating myself for thinking that when you're just living your life. And I'm happy for you. Of course I am. But what you want for me and what I want for me are different things. *We're* different, Louisa. And if you can't accept that then – then –"

I hung up.

"That didn't sound too good," Lir said, lingering by the doorway with a cup of tea in each hand. He frowned at me in concern. "Everything okay?"

"Absolutely peachy," I said, clearly lying. God, I needed a Big Mac. "She's just so full of herself, you know? She decided she doesn't like you, which means I'm not allowed to spend any time with you. I think Louisa would only be happy if we broke up."

Lir sat down beside me on the bed, encouraging me to sit up, too, so he could hand me my tea. I held it between my hands, savouring the warmth it sent through me.

"That might be true," he said softly, "or it might not. Either way, the best thing for you to do is cool off and think about this later. Friends grow apart from each other all the time. How long have you known Louisa? Like, eight years?"

I nodded.

"So you're both completely different people than who you were when you first met, Grace. All friendships are subject to change and, well..." Lir picked up my hand and kissed my knuckles, grey eyes never leaving mine. "Louisa's on the other side of the world. She isn't in Glasgow. If you don't want to be

177

bothered by her all you have to do is stop picking up her calls and answering her messages. It's that simple."

He had a point. But even through my anger I knew I was sad, too. I didn't really want to stop being friends with Louisa. We'd never spent so much time apart; of course things were different between us. The dynamic of our relationship just needed to change a little for the better. That was all.

I sighed heavily into my tea. I needed to calm down. "I'm glad we're leaving in a few days," I told Lir. "God knows I need the break."

"Um, speaking about that..."

I froze immediately, staring at Lir in horror. "Oh, please, don't tell me you're not –"

"No, no, no!" he laughed, rubbing my shoulder reassuringly. "Of course I'm going. It's just, I couldn't wait for the trip so I... may have booked a hotel in Dunoon. For the next two nights."

"You what now?"

"I booked a hotel," Lir repeated, voice endlessly patient like I was a child he was explaining a difficult concept to. "Seems kind of arbitrary for us to leave in a few days. Why not now?"

"And you booked this when you were drunk?"

He shrugged. "Just did it on my phone on the walk back along the riverfront. I can cancel it if you want. Won't get my deposit back, though. Would you really rob a poor student of his money?"

I could only laugh. Lir didn't care about the money at all. If I said I didn't want to leave today then he'd accept that as my decision. But he was right. Why wait a few days? Getting away now was exactly what I needed.

I stood up, grinning at Lir. He responded eagerly in kind. "Let's pack, then. McDonald's on the road?"

"Of course."

All good road trips started with one.

Chapter Twenty-Four

The last time I visited Dunoon my parents had wanted to spend the day walking through Benmore Botanic Garden and then Glen Massan, but I was only seven and couldn't possibly manage such a long walk. We'd gone to Morag's Fairy Glen, instead, which was a much easier, shorter hike, and the entrance to it was conveniently right beside a play park. I spent almost an hour on the swings and slides, content to let my parents sit on a bench and watch me play. Since I had no siblings they took it in turns on the seesaw, though I liked it best when my dad was on it with me. He'd press down so hard on his seat that I'd go flying into the air, and my mum would scream in concern as I collapsed into a fit of laughter.

But I wasn't seven now, and I figured my parents' original plan for Dunoon was a good enough plan for Lir and I to follow.

The air was muggy and uncomfortable when we got out of my car and paid for our entrance to the Botanics, soaking our skin and clothes in sweat within minutes. "I hope the sun comes out," I told Lir, buying two bottles of ice-cold water from the café for good measure before leaving the wood-panelled building for the gardens proper. "It might help the air feel less...thick."

Lir nodded in thanks when I handed him one of the bottles, quickly unscrewing the lid and pouring the liquid into his mouth like he'd just walked through a desert for days on end with no water. I watched him swallow it all, admiring the curve of his throat with every gulp he took. How was it fair that Lir was in such fantastic shape? Okay, he spent half his time training so it wasn't as if he just naturally looked this way, but still. The fact he

179

had a perfect damn *throat* felt wildly unfair.

"At least we're outside rather than stuck indoors," Lir said, wiping his mouth as he recapped the bottle. Then he eyed me carefully, suspicious of the way I was staring at him. "Why are looking at me like that?"

"Like what?"

"Like you're...objectifying me."

I choked out a laugh. "Am I not allowed to objectify my boyfriend?"

"Only with his permission," he joked. He glanced up at the sky. "It might clear up, though. The weather. The sun is just behind the clouds."

"I bloody hope so. I might die in such oppressive conditions."

Then Lir pushed me into the gardens, hands lingering on the small of my back a second too long to be innocent. "A bit of heat never hurt anyone. Let's just enjoy ourselves."

"And if the heat gets too much?"

He gave me a look so filthy I could do nothing but gape at him in response. He smirked. "Then we find somewhere to rid ourselves of our clothes."

"We can't really – oh. *Oh.* Lir, look!"

For the scenery around us immediately threw my urge to flirt into the non-existent wind: after walking but a minute or two from the entrance we found ourselves in an outdoor corridor made for creatures much larger than mere humans. Giants, even. On either side of the grassy causeway was a line of redwood trees which dwarfed every other tree within my line of sight. Their trunks were as wide across as a horse, with exposed roots large enough to comfortably sit upon. It felt as if the rust-coloured length of them never stopped, simply continuing on forever into the sky. I had to tilt my head up and up and up to spot the tops of their leafy, crowning branches.

Lir let out a low whistle, hand over his eyes as he peered at the treetops. "Wow. Those are some big trees."

"Big is an understatement," I said, lowering my voice as we began walking between the redwoods. It felt disrespectful to be loud and brash and inappropriate in front of them. Like they were judging us. Like they were lords or kings or gods.

Clearly Lir felt the same way for he, too, grew quiet as we padded along the grass, eyes always on the monolithic trees. Even the air itself seemed silent; only after we passed through the walkway could we hear the birds sing to each other once more.

I exhaled deeply when the redwood trees were well and truly behind us. "That was kind of - kind of -"

"Scary," Lir finished for me, a look of awe on his face. "In an amazing way."

I nodded. There was surely a more eloquent way to put it but Lir's description worked well enough. Scary in an amazing way.

I wondered what the rest of the garden had in store for us.

But there were no more godlike trees or hushed, imposing silences for us to experience. The rest of the Botanics were beautiful - heavenly so, almost - but it was simply a garden. A very, very large garden, which fed into the forest, but a garden by any other name nonetheless.

There was a large, sweeping pond, with several willows hanging overhead. Their trailing leaves broke the surface of the water, sending ripples out in concentric circles until they disappeared as if they had never existed at all. Sometimes a bubble or two broke the surface, too, and when I looked closely I saw that they were the result of tiny fish coming up to eat flies and other insects that skated across the pond.

"I bet this place looks amazing in autumn," I thought aloud, pointing to the willow trees. "When everything's gone red and orange and gold. Don't you think, Lir?"

"The reflection in the pond would be beautiful," he agreed, kneeling down to slide his hand through the water. He disturbed a shoal of very tiny fish, and he chuckled.

I frowned. "What's so funny?"

"I'm just imagining what the fish think when they see my

hand. Am I a giant? An alien? Do they even have a concept of what I am at all, outside of me being a new obstacle for them to get around?"

"I've never really thought about things that way," I mused, pulling Lir back up to continue our winding path through the garden, "though it's probably the latter."

Lir pondered this for several long moments of silence. When we reached a huge but simplistic maze built of perfectly maintained hedgerows and rose bushes he took a seat on one of the few empty benches situated within it. Most of them were occupied by elderly couples, which I thought was adorable, but Lir took no notice of anyone else.

He slashed his hand through the air just as he had done in the pond. "Do you think we'd know what a god looked like, if it interfered with us the way I did those fish?"

"I...what?"

"Like how people insist terrible tragedies and apparent miracles are an *act of God,*" he continued, gently taking hold of my hand and pulling it through the air with his own, "do you think we even have the capacity to know what a god or a titan or any other *supernatural* force is? Or do we just see their acts as obstacles and interference?"

I tried to consider Lir's question, though in all honesty I didn't know what to say. He'd always been obsessed with mythology and tales of gods and monsters but I hadn't realised he thought about their existence to such a deep extent. Well, insomuch as it never occurred to me that he believed the tales he adored so much were anything more than fiction.

"Magic is simply science we do not understand," I eventually said. I couldn't remember where I'd heard that before, but it seemed fitting.

When Lir beamed at me I knew I'd said the right thing. "Exactly!" he replied, very enthusiastically. "We don't understand anything until we actively try to. But once we work things out - *bam*! It seems so obvious. Which means the gods could be playing with us at all times and we simply lack the knowledge to understand what they're doing."

"For now," I added on, going along with his train of thought, which made his smile even larger. I loved when Lir was excited about something and wanted to share it with me, even if it was a hypothetical discussion about how humans would react to gods. It made me feel like I was the only one who understood him – the only one who was important enough for him to share his secrets with.

After a few minutes of rest we continued through the Botanics, admiring the explosions of colour the late-spring flowers afforded the place, and ventured into the forest. It was marginally cooler beneath the trees, something both Lir and I appreciated. I watched him wipe away a drop of sweat before it could roll down his forehead, all the while thinking about his previous comment about removing our clothes.

"Can we get to Glen Massan from here, Grace?" he asked me when we reached a small clearing at the top of an incline in the trees. The view was amazing, all greens and yellows and bursts of pinks and reds and purples everywhere I looked. I could see the willow-framed pond, which was just a sparkle of sunlight on water from where I stood.

"The sun!" I cried, ignoring Lir's question as I closed my eyes to the heavenly rays that hit us a moment later. It broke through the mugginess like a sword, clearing the air even though it made the day even hotter. "Ugh, it feels so good."

"Glen Massan?"

"What now?" I asked Lir, staring at him in confusion. I genuinely could not wrap my head around the words he'd been saying, so absorbed in the joys of being anywhere but the city as I was. But Lir wasn't annoyed at me; rather, he grabbed my waist and pulled me in for a kiss, though the two of us were too warm and slick with sweat for it to be entirely pleasant.

He bopped his forehead against mine. "The glen," he repeated, smiling against my lips, "can we reach it from here or do we have to walk back to the car park and head from there? I'm dying for a swim."

God, he was right. A swim sounded amazing right now. I was so glad I'd put on a bikini instead of underwear before heading out today. "We have to go back to the car," I said, breaking away from Lir to begin heading down through the forest: I'd Google Mapped the journey that morning. "Unless you want a three-mile hike to reach the glen?"

"Another day, maybe," he laughed, eagerly following me along the path with renewed vigour.

Because we didn't stop to appreciate the scenery we made it back to the car in good time and, after a short drive, arrived in the dirt-and-gravel car park by Glen Massan. The clouds had cleared in their entirety by the time we began walking, the sun punishingly hot as it beat down on the backs of our necks.

"We're gonna have sun stroke for sure in an hour or so," I said, though I didn't care. It was evident Lir didn't care, either.

As we traversed the path through the glen the sound of water grew stronger and stronger until it was all we could hear. The ground beneath our feet changed from dirt and moss and ferns to stone, and then, after an abrupt turn, we were faced with the most beautiful series of pools I'd ever seen in my life.

"Okay, this might convert me to fresh water over the sea forever," Lir said, a gleam in his eyes that told me he couldn't wait to jump in. The water crashed beneath bridges of grey and bone-white stone, formed through years and years of erosion until they looked so deliberate it was difficult to imagine they had formed naturally at all. Other structures of rock looked positively alien, pock-marked with holes and recesses that could have hidden a small child from sight.

In the distance I could hear laughter, which meant further along the glen we'd meet other people. "Let's just swim here," I said, though the current in the water was clearly strong. From the looks of things it crashed into a much larger, shallower pool in the direction of the voices, which would have made for an easier swim, but I wanted to remain alone with Lir.

He didn't need to be told twice. In fact, Lir had already removed most of his clothes before I finished my sentence. "Be careful in there," he told me, before diving off one of the stone bridges with infuriatingly elegant efficiency.

"You could at least – wait, Lir!" I called out, hurrying to

remove my dress and trainers before leaping into the water after him. I immediately regretted it; the water was as bitingly cold as the sun was hot. When I resurfaced I couldn't breathe. The water was made of a thousand knives all stabbing at my lungs, and if I inhaled they'd go all the way through. But then I grabbed at a rock for support, closed my eyes for a moment, and risked a breath.

It wasn't made of knives, merely air.

"I told you to be careful!" Lir laughed when he caught sight of me. He swam backstroke against the current so well I was almost convinced I could do the same. He made it look so easy. But I knew better: Lir was a pro, and I was not.

"I n-never thought it would be so *cold*," I spluttered. "It's s-sore!"

Lir splashed me almost lazily. "You'll get used to it. Come on, let go of the rock. Let's swim through the tunnels!"

It took me a few minutes to get used to it but, true to Lir's word, after treading water my body finally adjusted to the temperature. It was almost pleasant, especially with the sun beating down on my head. When I swam over to where Lir was waiting for me I looked around, confused.

"Where are these tunnels, then?"

"Underwater, obviously."

"But the current, Lir!" I protested. "It's going against us. I don't think I'm strong enough –"

"Of course you are," Lir cut in. He reached over and squeezed my hand. "Come on, just follow my lead, okay?" And then he was gone, diving beneath the water before I had a chance to take a breath. I followed after him in a flurry of panicked bubbles, feeling blindly around me for the hole in the stone I was supposed to go though.

Once I found it and began swimming I realised that it was, in fact, pretty easy to go against the current, so long as I kept my wits about me and never stopped pushing forward. But when I reached the end of the tunnel and resurfaced for air Lir scared the life out of me by swimming between my legs and placing me on his shoulders. I clung to his head, screaming in fear and delight as he slowly made his way to the shore with me on top of him. He tossed me onto the moss and dirt, collapsing beside me with a voice full of laughter.

Then we passed a few minutes in contented silence with the sun on our faces, happy to simply exist in this moment, together.

"This place is unreal," Lir finally murmured. "I can't believe how beautiful it is."

I turned my head to face him, reaching out my hand for his to interlace our fingers. "We got so lucky with the weather, you know. If it had been raining –"

"Trust me, I'd have still gone swimming even if it was a bloody downpour," he laughed, squeezing my hand. "I feel like I can just be – me – when I'm in a place like this."

"You know I feel the same way."

"I know. That's why I love you."

For a fraction of a second I stilled, then my body relaxed as if it had never known how to do it before. "I love you, too," I said, shuffling closer to Lir to nestle in the crook of his arm. He stroked my hair the way I always did to him, and we closed our eyes, and allowed our confession to simply hang in the air between us for a while.

It was weird; neither of us had ever said we loved each other out loud before. But I was certain we'd felt this way since...well, since Lir spent the night with me in Largs. Louisa might have believed I was rushing into things but it simply wasn't like that.

Lir and I were meant to be together. That was all there was to it.

We spent another two hours in the glen, swimming and then sunbathing and then swimming again until the two of us had to admit that we were starving and tired. So we walked back to the car and drove to Dunoon, picking up some pizzas from an American-style diner on the way back to our hotel. Lir didn't even order fish.

After we ate we tumbled into bed together, too exhausted to even shower before doing so. It struck me that Lir and I could not have planned our day better if we'd tried. Everything had been so easy and carefree and unbridled from the troubles of our lives back in Glasgow. It truly was a perfect day in every possible respect, from the moment we woke up to the moment we closed our eyes to sleep.

I did not know, at the time, that it would be our last.

Chapter Twenty-Five

When we left the hotel it was raining, which was long overdue. We parked my car outside a little place called The Rock Café to eat chips and drink milkshakes, which even Lir, surprisingly, consumed. The next ferry was due in twenty minutes and then we'd continue on our journey around the west coast. Though first, I realised, we had to work out *where* our next destination was; going by my original schedule we weren't due to arrive in Campbeltown for another couple of days.

"I actually meant to bring that up last night," Lir said between one mouthful of chips and the next. "It's my aunt and uncle's thirtieth anniversary today. They're having a party tonight. If it isn't too awkward for you I thought we could maybe...go?"

I knew I was staring instead of answering. But this was Lir, the boy who never talked about his life before university. Lir, who didn't want his only friend from childhood telling me about his past. Lir, whose parents committed suicide in front of him, leaving him alone in the world.

But of course he had other family. He didn't reach his twenties raising himself, after all. And Cian had mentioned an aunt before Lir cut him off in the union.

"Grace?" Lir worried aloud. "We don't have to go if you don't –"

"I'd love to!" I cut in, far too enthusiastic for my own good. "Of course I do! So did they raise you, then? Your aunt and uncle?"

He nodded. "Tommy is my dad's brother and Róisín's his wife. They took me in when I was six."

"So is that when – when –"

"When my parents went away?"

The way Lir just went out and said it took my thoroughly aback. But there was no pain in his eyes. No sadness. The fact they 'went away' seemed like just another fact to him. I suppose I couldn't dictate how he processed his grief. It was *his* grief, and his alone.

"Yeah," I said, regretting asking the question in the first place. But to my surprise Lir shook his head.

"My mum's sister looked after me for a couple years first."

So that was the aunt Cian mentioned. Well, she did *live in Bundoran instead of Campbeltown so I guess that makes sense.*

"Why didn't you stay with her, then?" I ventured. "Did you not get on well?"

This was the question that caused Lir's calm veneer to crack. His hand tightened into a fist on the table until his knuckles were bone white, and his lower lip wobbled for just a fraction of a second. Lir closed his eyes and took a deep, shuddering breath.

"She died," he said, and that was that.

By the time we were on the road to Campbeltown all such tragic conversation was long since over, and Lir returned to being happy and excited. It was clear he was pleased to be introducing me to his family. I was too, of course, though as we covered another mile on the road, then ten, then twenty, I grew nervous. When I got nervous I got fidgety. I didn't want Lir to *know* I was nervous, so I turned the radio on and searched for a Glasgow-based music station and took my phone out of my bag simply to occupy my hands.

I had no messages from Louisa, which didn't surprise me at all given how I left things with her last time, but I did have a few messages from my dad (wishing me a good trip) and from Josh and David. As the woman on the radio told us to expect the rain across the west coast to dissipate by evening I filtered through the messages, a frown forming on my face as I did so.

Josh's messages all largely contained the same topic of conversation: *Please call Louisa and patch things up. She's so upset, Grace. I'm not just saying this as her brother. You're not acting like yourself, and something's been bothering you for weeks. Please tell me what's wrong. Has your boyfriend done something to you? You know I'm always here to help. Just say the word.*

I told him I was fine, and that I'd make up with Louisa when I cooled off. Both statements were basically true, after all. Yeah, I *had* been worried for weeks but it had all been in my head. Well, aside from Terry's stabbing and David's attack and my cat going missing and the Volvo being stolen.

Fuck. So much had happened since March. Had I gone numb to the real things that had occurred in my life during the process of worrying that Lir was somehow responsible for all the horrible attacks in Scotland? When I got back from our trip I'd have to sit down and have a long, hard think about my mental state.

I turned my attention back to my phone. David's message read: *Really wanted to speak to you the other night. Can we meet up for coffee and talk? It's important.*

I replied saying I was on a road trip and wouldn't be back for a few weeks. Though David said it was important it could probably wait until I got back. Besides, it wasn't as if I was going to travel back to Glasgow just for one conversation. If it was truly important then David would call me, instead – though I shuddered at how awkward such a conversation might end up being.

Lir glanced at me in concern before returning his eyes to the road. He was driving, since he knew the route to Campbeltown far better than I did. "You cold?" he asked, reaching a hand out to turn the heating on.

I reached out my own hand to stop him, squeezing his fingers before he returned his hand to the steering wheel. "No," I smiled, "I'm fine. It was just a shudder."

"Something about the weather report creep you out?" Lir

190

joked. "Or did someone send you something weird?"

When he tried to spy a look at my phone I turned it away from him. "Just messages from some people. Nothing serious."

"From Josh?"

I stuck out my tongue. "So what if he did message me?"

"Just because I overreacted last time doesn't mean I'm not allowed to be wary of the guy," Lir said. "I mean, he literally left his girlfriend for you. That's not something you do for just anyone."

"Well if he liked me so much he wouldn't have run off after sleeping with me," I muttered, then immediately regretted it.

Lir's hands tensed on the steering wheel. "He what?"

"Nothing."

"Did you just say you slept together?"

"It was practically a year ago," I explained, not wanting this to become more of an issue than it had to be. "Louisa had just left for Australia. We were drunk and I was sad and when Josh told me he'd always liked me I was exactly the right amount of weak to fall for it. But then he went back to his girlfriend, anyway, so to be honest I wouldn't be surprised if he just used his *feelings* for me to get out of a relationship he no longer wanted to be in."

"That's...what a fucking arsehole."

I could only laugh. "You've got that right."

"Then why on earth are you still friends with him?" Lir asked, seemingly no longer angry but simply curious. He shook his head. "I don't get it. I couldn't be friends with someone who did that. He and his sister seem as bad as each other for wanting to control your life."

"It's not -" I began, but then I corrected myself. "Okay, I suppose it kind of *is* like that, but things are complicated. Josh and Louisa are like family to me. You don't just throw away family."

A raised eyebrow. "You don't fuck them, either."

"*Lir!*"

"I'm just telling it like it is!" he protested, taking his hands off the wheel for a second in a gesture of surrender. But he was smiling, so I knew he couldn't be *that* pissed off.

"...found dead in the supply room by the pool," a reporter on the radio said, immediately cutting through the easy atmosphere of the car like a hot knife through butter. Both Lir and I stilled. I turned up the volume so we didn't miss a single word of the news.

"Coroner's report determined that the man, identified today as Trinity College student Cian Byrne, was drowned, though there were marks on his neck that suggest strangulation was also involved. Byrne, age twenty-three, was staying in Glasgow for a swimming competition held at the University of Glasgow. Police are treating the case as a murder and are encouraging any witnesses who may have seen him in the hours before his death to come forward."

Even after the news turned to more banal topics like sports and the music charts neither Lir nor I spoke a word. Silence stretched between us for what felt like hours.

Eventually I said, "Lir, I'm so sorry. To lose your friend like that...I can't imagine it."

But Lir did not seem in the least bit upset, nor was his face blank like it had been as he talked of his parents' deaths. No, he seemed – I wasn't sure what he seemed – but if I was going to pick a word for it I'd have said he seemed *vindicated.*

Lir unclenched the steering wheel and all the tension left his body. He turned his head, cocked it to the side and beamed, the epitome of an angel fallen down upon the mortal earth.

"He was never my friend."

Chapter Twenty-Six

By the time we reached Campbeltown I'd forced thoughts of Lir's reaction to Cian's grisly death out of my head. It hadn't been how I'd expected him to react, sure, but who was I to understand the full extent of their childhood 'friendship'? For all I knew Cian had done something horrific to him when they were kids. That I couldn't imagine what kind of horrors a child might inflict upon another didn't mean those horrible things never happened.

So I pushed Lir's eerily angelic smile into a dark corner of my mind.

Despite the fact we would be spending most of our time in his adoptive family home Lir had booked us a lovely waterfront cottage (complete with a refurbished bathroom containing a shower big enough for two) for the duration of our stay in Campbeltown. I appreciated the gesture: though I looked forward to meeting the people who had raised him for most of his life I was so nervous I was sure I'd vomit if I so much as opened my mouth.

"No need to be nervous, silly," Lir reassured me as I fidgeted with my hair, my ear, my sleeve. I'd agonised over what to wear to his aunt and uncle's anniversary, rueing the fact I hadn't packed anything appropriate for a semi-formal event. I'd settled on the one long-sleeved dress I'd packed, which was floral and floaty but entirely backless. I'd meant to wear it to dinner somewhere nice with Lir, just the two of us.

Now that we were outside the door of his family's house I

sincerely wished I'd worn something else.

Lir laughed when he caught my eyes scanning over my outfit. I hated how effortlessly good he looked in a pale blue shirt – two buttons undone at the collar and the sleeves rolled up to his elbows – paired with grey linen trousers cuffed at the ankles and smart, straight-out-of-the-box white trainers.

"You look amazing, Grace," he said, lacing his fingers with mine as he opened the door. "My folks are gonna love you. Just try not to be sick the moment you have to say hello."

"Why would you say that to me *right now*?!" I cried, though my complaint was entirely lost in the cacophony of voices that met our ears as we stepped foot into the hallway. For a moment my new surroundings overwhelmed me as I took them in, from the vaulted ceiling overhead to the white-painted walls adorned with tasteful artwork to the sheer size of the house's interior.

Lir's aunt and uncle were very evidently well off, which for some reason surprised me. Lir himself had always come across as someone who came from very little and thus was happy with very little. He wasn't materialistic in the slightest, and most of his favourite sports and hobbies required next to no money to pursue them.

But, then again, he also spent over two hundred pounds on a single book and could afford not to have a part-time job whilst he studied at university. Both were signs of a financially-secure individual.

At least two dozen strangers filled the gargantuan open plan living room and dining kitchen, almost all of whom stared at us as we made our entrance. My grip on Lir's hand grew so tight I saw his brow twitch a little in response but I didn't dare loosen my hold. I was so nervous. This was a terrible mistake. I'd never had a long-term boyfriend – much less met their parents – and somehow I'd thought I'd be able to manage an entire party full of extended family and friends?

I must have gone mad.

A woman with artfully greying hair secured in an elegant knot at the base of her neck rushed over to us immediately, a wide smile on her face as she slung her arms around Lir's neck.

194

Her embrace forced him to let go of my hand; I clasped my hands together, behind my back, to stop myself from fidgeting.

"Dylan!" the woman cried, delighted. "You never told me you were going to make it. Oh, Tommy, look who's here!"

A middle-aged man quickly appeared by her side. His tawny hair and grey eyes were so startlingly like Lir's that I literally took a step back when I saw him. The man – Tommy – gave me a warm smile before clapping his nephew on the shoulder when the woman who was presumably Róisín finally let him go.

"Leave it to you to surprise us like this, Dylan," he said. "But the last thing I expected was for you to bring a lassie with you. So who might you be, young lady?"

"This is Grace," Lir said, speaking for me on the off-chance I really *was* going to throw up. "She's my girlfriend. I'm really excited for you to finally meet her."

I jutted my hand out towards Lir's uncle, who shook it confidently and easily. I realised that I quite liked him based on first impressions alone. "I – um – it's really nice to meet you," I stammered, then took a second to collect myself. All I had to do was breathe and talk and listen. It was just a party. My teaching persona could help me out a lot here. I relaxed my posture and said, brightly, "Happy anniversary! My parents celebrated their thirtieth last year but they spent it in the South of France for a month without me."

At this Lir's aunt burst out laughing. "We were almost tempted to do the same thing! My mum insisted we had to celebrate properly, though. Of course, she fell asleep drunk in the corner about an hour ago, so maybe I shouldn't have listened to her. It's lovely to meet you, Grace. Would you like a drink?"

"We'll get them," Lir said, taking my hand once more and guiding me through the small crowd of people towards the fridge. He was greeted by many of them as he poured a glass of wine for me and, after searching through the cupboards, a measure of whisky for himself.

"Why do they all call you Dylan?" I asked him in an undertone, deeply curious. "I thought your family would surely call you Lir. I mean, Cian did, didn't he?"

"Ah, that's my fault," Tommy said, surprising the both of us. He took the whisky out of Lir's hand and poured himself a glass, winking at his nephew as he did so. "Thought you could pull out the good stuff without telling me, huh?"

Lir shrugged, a small smile on his face I'd never seen before. It was...relaxed. Effortless. He and his uncle clearly had a strong, comfortable relationship, just like the one I had with *my* dad. "I know you have another bottle of it in the study," Lir said. "You'd never miss this one if I drank it all."

"Precocious little brat, isn't he?" Tommy said, directing the jibe at me. "When we took him in Dylan insisted on using his middle name. It's the one my brother, Sally, and her sister all used, so he wanted to stick to it. I told him the kids in school would tease him to no end for having a strange name. You know what they're like."

I did, and for the first time it occurred to me that I'd never asked Lir if he'd been bullied before. But he seemed too - I wasn't sure how to put it - *aloof* to be bullied.

"My uncle was right, of course," Lir easily admitted, pouring me another glass of wine in the process. I hadn't even realised I'd finished the first one. "I was torn to shreds by them. I hated it. I didn't want everyone's attention on me. So I used my first name and the other kids finally started ignoring me." He chimed his glass against Tommy's, and they both drank heavily before doing the same with a second round.

"I didn't want him to be *ignored*," his uncle clarified after a moment or two. He sighed in satisfaction when he took another swallow of whisky. "But I suppose with all the swimming and studying he didn't really have time for lots of friends, anyway. And for what - a marine biology degree at Glasgow! I'll tell you again, Dylan: it's a waste of your talent and you know it."

Lir narrowed his eyes at his uncle. I could tell this was a conversation they'd had many times before: a point of contention between two otherwise very close individuals. "Grace just handed in her thesis at Glasgow," Lir told him. "She'll be a doctor soon. Is *that* a waste?"

Tommy turned to me in interest. "What's your doctorate in?"

"The use of recombinant proteins in targeted gene therapy," I immediately replied, so used to giving my rote answer to students that I forgot to use my 'simple' answer. I gave Tommy an apologetic smile at the blank expression on his face. "Molecular biology."

"Aha!" Lir's uncle exclaimed, triumphant. "See, Dylan? That's a *useful* subject. You should have let that scout sign you for competitive swimming back when you had the –"

"Thomas Murphy, will you leave your poor nephew alone?" Róisín cut in, appearing from behind her husband with a knowing look on her face. "You're going to scare off his lovely girlfriend."

"Oh, I'm enjoying this," I chuckled. "He never talks about his life before university. I'll take any and all information I can get."

"*Don't*," Lir warned his uncle, when Tommy slapped his hands together and poured another whisky, a mischievous gleam in his eye.

"If she wants to know she wants to know! I think it's little Gracie's right, don't you think? Is Gracie okay? Or is it just Grace?"

I smiled softly, a glow filling up my chest at the familial nickname. "Gracie is fine. I like it."

"Well then, Gracie, let me tell you about the time..."

For the next hour or so his uncle – and, sometimes, his aunt, when she stopped by to check on us and top up her wine – regaled me with all manner of stories from Lir's youth, Lir all the while sighing and tutting and throwing in protests when a story was 'untrue', 'exaggerated' or 'just plain embarrassing'. It was a whole new side to Lir that I had never seen, and by the time I reached the end of a bottle of wine I was more in love with him than I had been before the party, somehow.

Eventually I needed to pee so badly I began squirming on the spot.

"The bathroom's down the corridor," Lir said, noticing my discomfort immediately. "Second door on the left. Want me to show you?"

"I can manage it myself, I'm sure," I said, not wanting to interrupt his time with a now very drunk Tommy.

Feeling warm and tipsy from both the wine and the pleasant trip down memory lane with Lir's aunt and uncle, it occurred to me as I locked the bathroom door behind me that I was actually having a good time. Not only that: after my initial nerves had passed I'd felt like *myself* around Lir's family, rather than having to put up a front. I realised that could only mean good things for us as a couple.

I wondered if I should add a visit to Largs into our trip so Lir could meet my parents.

After fussing with my hair for far too long in front of the mirror and reapplying my lipstick, I left the bathroom and began making my way back to the living room. But then I heard a snippet of conversation between an ageing couple that gave me pause.

"...still don't understand why they took him in after what happened. The boy wasn't right in the head."

"Oh come now, Mary. Dylan seems fine now, doesn't he? After what happened to his parents I'm not surprised he was a bit of a broken child."

I hid behind a tall fern in a humongous, elaborately tiled pot, heart hammering painfully in my chest. Of course I was madly curious. Just what on earth had Lir done?

The woman called Mary tutted at her companion's remark. "Dragging your aunt to her death hardly counts as being *a bit of a broken child,* Harold. It's the mark of a sociopath. And all to get 'home', he told his uncle! Home? Ha! What on earth was that supposed to mean?"

"I'd rather you didn't talk about such things in front of my girlfriend, Mary," Lir said, surprising myself, Mary and Harold all at the same time. The couple stared at him, wide-eyed, then spied me hiding behind the fern.

Mary had the sense to look ashamed. "You know what I'm like when I'm drinking, Dylan dear," she said, though her flushed cheeks had nothing to do with the brandy in her hand. "What happened was a tragic accident. But one can't help but gossip about such things!"

Lir didn't move, standing perfectly still as he gave Mary perhaps the most chilling smile I'd ever seen. It was all gleaming white teeth, pulled-back lips and emptiness. It was a threat if ever I'd seen one. "If *one* gossips about a six-year-old deliberately murdering their aunt then perhaps *one* should entertain the notion that they themselves are mentally disturbed," he said, each word intonated in an identical, almost poetic fashion. And then, in a completely different voice: "Grace?"

He indicated towards the stairs with his head, breaking from his eerily calm composure in the space of a second. Numbly I followed him, stumbling up the stairs without looking at anyone – especially Mary, who was now complaining to Harold about the manners of 'kids these days'. I didn't know how to process what I'd just heard. For how could I?

Lir hadn't *really* killed his aunt, had he?

When we reached our destination I realised Lir must have taken us to his bedroom. The place was impeccably tidy, though the walls were adorned with multiple shelves bursting at the seams with books as well as drawers and carved wooden boxes filled with even more books. The curtains were a tasteful, seafoam green; they matched the duvet on the double bed. Going by the colour I knew Lir himself must have chosen both of them.

He sat on the pale green bed now, patting the space beside him until I, too, sat down. Neither of us spoke for several minutes; below us the noise of the party carried through the carpet, muffled and unrelenting. I wished we had silence.

After a while I realised my hands were shaking so I stuck them between my knees to try and make it stop. A lock of hair came loose from behind my ear. I didn't move it back, but Lir did.

"Grace," he said, very softly and with none of the venom

with which he had spoken to Mary lingering in his voice. His fingers moved from my hair to trail down my jawline. "Grace, ask me to tell you what happened to my Aunt Orla."

I didn't dare look at Lir, though I knew he desperately wanted me to. "Y-you didn't, did you?" I stuttered, keeping my gaze firmly on my hands. They began to make the entire length of my legs shake. "You didn't murder her, did you?"

Lir placed a hand on my right knee. He squeezed it so hard my chin jutted up in response, and he turned my face to look at him with a gentle finger on my cheek. His grey eyes were too bright, like he was on the verge of crying.

"I didn't murder her," he said. "But I *did* kill her."

A sound came out of my throat that was somewhere between a sob and a choke. "W-what does that mean?"

"It means I'm the reason she died. I made her take me to the beach where my parents...where they walked into the sea." There *were* tears in his eyes now, which Lir made no attempt to brush away. He squeezed my knee again, and the next words tumbled out of his mouth so fast I didn't think Lir could have stopped them even if he'd wanted to.

"I made my aunt come into the waves with me," he said, "to follow the path they took back home. I knew we could reach them. I just *knew* it. But Aunt Orla...she didn't believe me, even though she was the one who told me where they went in the first place!" I wanted him to stop talking – so desperately wanted to cover my ears with my hands and block out his recount of what happened – but Lir just kept on going.

"And she panicked, and I tried to calm her down but she just wouldn't. I didn't mean to hit her with the rock – I didn't know that would make her fall unconscious or that the current would carry her away from me. I thought we'd go home, together. But I lost my strength and when I woke up in the hospital...well, she was gone. She was gone and it was my fault."

Lir wasn't the only one crying now, and I wasn't the only one trembling. Hot, ugly tears were running down my face, dripping off my chin and landing on my chest. This was all too much. Lir's *childhood* was too much.

"I'm so sorry," was all I could croak out. "Lir, I'm so, so sorry. At least...well, at least she's with your parents now. She isn't alone." Not that I'd ever believed in an afterlife, but who was I to deny comfort to a grieving boy?

The blank stare Lir gave me was as unsettling as the smile he'd given Mary mere minutes ago. "No she isn't."

Something told me I didn't need a clarification over what he meant. Or, rather, didn't want to hear it. I asked anyway. "I... what do you mean, Lir? They're all –"

"My parents aren't dead," he insisted, standing up so abruptly I flinched in surprise. He began riffling through a bookcase, tossing a leather-bound tome on the bed, then another and another. "They went home. They're where they're meant to be. I'll reach them if I can make things right." He carefully extricated a roll of parchment scrolled all over in blue ink from a box, then moved over to a second bookcase for...whatever it was he was looking for.

Through my tear-blurred vision I began reading the titles of the books he was pulling out and working out their subject matter. Greek legends. Celtic folklore of the sea. Welsh river gods. The dark elves of Norse mythology. Japanese spirits and demons. Jinns and other beings from Arabian stories. And that was just the books Lir was immediately placing before me.

As I wordlessly surveyed the hoard of books, notes and drawings Lir continued to remove from his drawers, his boxes, his shelves, his wardrobe, a sick feeling began to ball in my stomach. Something wasn't right here. This was too much...stuff. And he wasn't even finished pulling it all out. It was a never-ending sea of manic interest.

When finally Lir stopped bringing out all of his things I gulped down the rising bile in my throat. I knew I was looking at something gravely wrong. I just didn't know *what.* So I asked the only question I could think of.

"What the hell is all this?"

Chapter Twenty-Seven

"What the hell is all this, Lir?" I repeated, when Lir did not reply immediately.

"It's research," he said, as if it was obvious.

I stared down at the mess of paper covering his bed and floor. Between the books, scrolls and leaflets were drawings in a similar style to the one Lir had been working on in the library back when we first spoke. Some were drawn in pen, some in watercolour paint, others in graphite pencil; all of them contained the same manic, frightful energy of a sea crashing into the shore, even when the subject matter was a lone shark or the regal yet twisted figure of a person I could only assume was some tragic character from one of the plethora of mythologies Lir adored so much.

"This is...this isn't a hobby, is it?" I murmured, slowly standing up from the bed as if I meant to back away to the door. But I stopped by Lir's side, staring at him until he gave me his undivided attention. "This is a full-on fucking obsession. But *why?* Why are you...what's the point of it all?"

He blinked. "To get home, like I already said. To reach my parents."

To reach his parents.

I spoke my unfiltered thoughts out loud, too shocked as I was to do anything else. "They're *dead,* Lir!" I exclaimed. "You must know this. It's important to me that you know this."

When Lir laughed and shook his head it was with the

amusement of a person discovering their friend believed the earth was flat. "That's what everyone wants me to think. Of course that's what you would believe, too. You've never known any better. But Aunt Orla knew – that's why she told me what really happened. That's why she started teaching me about myths and legends from across the globe. But they're not just *stories,* Grace. They're all bound in a truth nobody wishes to remember."

I could only gape at him. He couldn't be serious. He *couldn't.* But the way Lir's eyes lit up as he ran his hand across a well-worn volume of Norse mythology suggested otherwise.

In a fit of panic I grabbed a book at random from his bed and riffled through it, landing on a section about offerings to the gods in Ancient Greece. "So you're tell me all of this is *true?*" I said, knowing I was beginning to sound hysterical. God, I regretted drinking an entire bottle of wine within an hour. It had all gone to my head, making it difficult for me to think clearly. "Sacrificing alcohol and fruit and – and *goats* to appease the gods?"

"People have been sacrificing things to the deities of their cultures and religions for about as long as society has existed," Lir replied, calm and solid where I was twitchy and upset. He took the book out of my hands and turned a few pages over until he reached a section which was scrawled over in notes of his own handwriting. "It's a common practice, Grace."

"But it doesn't *work!*"

"How do you know?"

It was my turn to blink at Lir in confused disbelief. "How do I – how do I *know?* C'mon, Lir, you're a bloody scientist. How could you possibly –"

"There's no empirical evidence that sacrifices do not work," he said. "Why shouldn't I keep an open mind about them?"

"You could say that about anything! Fire-breathing turtles, vampires and unicorns, God –"

"Exactly."

"*Lir!*"

"What?!" he fired back, calm exterior shattered in a moment as he rose to his own defence. He loomed over me, making me feel as if he was four feet taller than me rather than four inches. "Why am I not allowed to believe this, Grace? Why am I not allowed to do my own research – it's clear I've done a lot of it – and come to my own conclusions about my beliefs? My parents aren't dead. They went back to where they came from. A plane of existence or a realm or a world that humans cannot venture into. They were special, Grace. They were different. *I'm* different. So I'm going to find my way to the place I belong."

I forced myself not to immediately retort the way I had done so far. I bit my lip, forcing tears from falling as I absorbed what Lir was saying. "...why haven't you reached your parents yet, then?" I asked, which was a fairly rational question. There was no way Lir could wave it off.

When his anger broke and I saw a hint of sadness creep back through, however, I knew it was the wrong question to ask. Without speaking a word he put down the book about offerings and sacrifices and searched through the mess on the floor until he found a small tome entitled *Prometheus.*

I didn't like where this was going.

Lir returned to my side and gently pushed me back onto the bed with him to listen, then he cleared his throat as if preparing a speech.

"Prometheus stole fire from the gods to gift it to the humans he loved so much," he began. "I mean, he shaped them from clay, didn't he? Of course he loved them. Of course he wanted them to evolve – to build a civilisation. But for that, Zeus punished him. Prometheus was bound to a rock in the sea and doomed to have his liver pecked out by an eagle. Come nightfall it grew back, and the process would start all over again for eternity. He angered the gods by going behind their back and doing something they didn't want, and wasn't saved from his tragic fate until Heracles came to his aid. I've angered the gods, too, and now I can't go back home where I belong. I should have followed my parents into the waves. I shouldn't have sat on the beach, watching them and wondering what was going on. I was being tested and I failed."

Going by Lir's clean and practised words it was evident that he well and truly believed this, and had thought it over hundreds – perhaps thousands – of times.

He continued, more manic and undone with every word that left his lips. "Aunt Orla died because she didn't believe. I was wrong to take her with me at the time. She died because of me: I know that. I accept that. If I'd only gone by myself then... then..." Lir pressed the heel of his hand against his right eye and wiped away a tear. He let out a long, shuddering breath. "But it doesn't matter now. I tried to go back alone so many times when I finished high school and it never, ever worked. So I went searching for answers, and it became clear I had to give something up to the gods so they would help me. But nothing's worked so far! No matter what I do I *can't do it.* And I –"

"Wait."

For a few seconds I didn't elaborate on the reason for my interruption. My brain was playing catch-up with all of the information that had been offloaded on me in such a short space of time.

Animal sacrifices to Greek gods.

"You killed my cat," I whispered, certain. "You killed Tom. You sacrificed him to your – your gods."

A pause. And then: "He wouldn't keep quiet!" Lir said, so easily admitting to the murder of my pet that I recoiled from him, intending to back away once more to the door. But Lir grabbed my wrist to stop me from leaving and fell from the bed to kneel in front of me. He turned his face up to me, eyes pleading and desperate. "I didn't mean to kill him. I really didn't. I wasn't going to sacrifice him. But he *wouldn't keep quiet.* You'd have known I was outside your house for days before I finally had the guts to knock on your door."

"*You killed my cat!*" I screamed at him, once more trying to break away from his grasp. Yet his grip was strong as steel, and when I tried to stand up Lir pulled me to the floor, instead. I couldn't stop crying. "You killed my cat. You killed my –"

"Because I love you!" he keened, stroking my hair with his free hand even as I sobbed and sobbed. "I loved you long before the first night we slept together. I just wanted to be close to you. But the cat wouldn't be quiet."

I could hardly breathe. "W-why didn't you just *talk to me,* then?"

"Why didn't *you?*"

"I never went about killing your pets, Lir!"

"I'm sorry," he said, kissing my forehead and my cheeks and my lips because I no longer had the strength to fight him. "I'm sorry. I know that doesn't make up for what I did. Killing your cat was wrong; I knew it in my heart as soon as I did it. I should have told you what I'd done at the time but I was so afraid you wouldn't want anything to do with me. And I...Grace, I need you. I love you. Please don't leave me. Please, please..."

It was Lir who was crying worse than me now, head bowed against my chest as he clutched at my arms to stay upright. "I want to go home, Grace. I want it so bad. I want to see them. My parents. I want you to meet them. My dad would adore you, Grace; he loves boats just like you and *your* dad. If I can go home then we can finally be happy. Everything will be right. Everything will be complete. Will you help me? Please, Grace. Help me. *Help me.*"

Lir was trembling. I was trembling. I was furious and upset and so deeply disturbed by what I'd learned.

I knew it wasn't just my cat he'd killed in his quest to return home.

But I loved him. I couldn't turn that feeling off even now, faced with what Lir really was.

I didn't know what else to say but, "Yes."

Chapter Twenty-Eight

To say I had not slept all night was an understatement. I spent my time watching Lir, instead, who in contrast to me slept more soundly than I'd seen him do in weeks. Everything we had discussed in his bedroom, if it could have been considered a discussion at all, had clearly been weighing heavily on his mind. Now that he'd told me what was going on – what he wanted, what he *needed* – it was as if he could finally exhale and relax.

I doubted I'd ever be able to feel that way again for the rest of my life.

Lir was sick, of that much I was certain. He needed help. And I gladly wanted to give him that help before his behaviour deteriorated any further. The only problem was that I didn't know *how* to help him.

"You're very fidgety today," Lir said from his position on the couch, flitting through a magazine on fishing that had been left on the coffee table for us by the owner of the cottage. He watched as I paced into the kitchen and threw open the fridge only to immediately close it once more, returning to the living room to stare out of the sizeable bay window that took up much of the sea-facing wall. "Are you okay?"

"I'm...not really," I admitted, not looking at him. "Last night was a lot." *Understatement.* "I just need some time to adjust." *Another understatement.*

I heard Lir sigh from behind me. We'd spent the entire day like this: me pacing and him sighing. "I guess I should have expected that. I should have told you about everything sooner."

I wondered how I would have felt if Lir told me about his parents when we first got together. His aunt. His reasons for obsessing over the sea. His complete and utter psychotic break that he evidently wasn't aware of whatsoever.

"Come sit with me, Grace," Lir said when I didn't respond to his last comment. It felt as if I was going through the motions of walking over to sit down beside him rather than actively choosing to do so, but it got me to where he wanted me to be nonetheless. Lir put down the magazine he was reading and took my hands in his, a genuinely excited smile on his face. "Everything will change when I get home. I'll see my parents again and they'll see how worthy I am to be part of their world as well as this one. And -"

"Lir -"

"And then they can come back here to meet you!" he continued, too overwhelmingly eager with his own delusion to take note of the unsure expression on my face and the rigidity in my hands. He leaned towards me so close that his breath, warm and tasting of lemon, fanned across my lips. "Or I could bring you to meet *them*. They must have been so tired of the human world to leave it when they did." Lir nodded, firm in his decision. "Yeah, I should bring you to them. That makes so much more sense."

I got up abruptly.

"I need some air," I said. "You're right. I'm restless. I need to get rid of all this excess energy."

"Why don't we go for a jog?" Lir suggested, making to get up from the couch. "We don't have anything for dinner. We could go to the shops and -"

"I'll go by myself," I said, too quickly. I grimaced at the hurt expression on Lir's face. "Sorry. I just..."

He sighed again, drooping his head in understanding. "Need some time. Okay. I get it."

Now I felt terrible. I forced a smile on my face. "I'll pick up some wine or something. I probably just need to relax for the evening and then I'll be fine. Have you seen my phone?"

"Your phone?"

"Yeah. I haven't been able to find it all day."

Lir frowned. "Go get changed and I'll look for it in here."

I dutifully moved through to the bedroom and changed into my jogging gear, twisting my hair up into a bun and furrowing my brows at my pale face in the mirror. I'd thought I'd been developing a tan thanks to all the lovely spring weather we'd been having but I looked stark and sick.

If I was going to help Lir I had to buck the fuck up and sort out my head.

When I passed through the living room again Lir chucked my phone at me, which I only just caught with clumsy hands. "It was down the back of the couch," he said. "Could you get some painkillers at the shops? I think I'm getting a headache."

"Of course," I replied, forcing myself to bend down and kiss his forehead before grabbing a bottle of water from the fridge and a couple of bags for the shops. "I won't be long. Love you."

Lir beamed at the words. "I love you, too."

For a while I genuinely did exactly what Lir suggested I do: I ran. The three and a half months of solid exercising I'd completed this year meant that I actually *could* run now, rather than struggling to breathe after barely five minutes of jogging. I relished the sea breeze blasting my face as I traversed the waterfront and the pounding of the tarmac beneath my trainers, making absolutely sure to keep my mind as blank and steady as possible. So long as I focused on putting one foot in front of the other over and over and over again I could drill any and all thoughts from my brain.

I was empty. I was still. I was nothing.

Twenty minutes later I reached Campbeltown Harbour. The jetties were fairly devoid of people given that the weather today hadn't been that great, but now that the sun had finally come out to drench the early evening in warmth a couple of children came to sit by a yacht tied to the pier, legs swinging as they devoured rapidly-melting ice cream cones. Their chins were sticky with the stuff, and when a man appeared from the yacht to warn them to keep clean - lest their mother find out he ruined their appetites before dinner - I couldn't help but laugh.

Eventually I came across a bench and sat down, breathing heavily and wiping my brow of sweat. I guzzled down most of the contents of my bottled water. Then I stared at the horizon as the sun bled ever closer towards it until spots of darkness clouded my eyes and I had to blink a dozen times to remove them. Dread and peace fought within me, one second turning my stomach to lead only to leave it dizzyingly empty the next. Something about this particular moment felt like the calm before a horrible, inevitable storm.

I pulled out my phone to call Josh.

I had a missed call from him dated at four o'clock this afternoon in my call log. *Strange,* I thought. *There wasn't a notification to say I had a missed call.* I checked to see if he'd left a voicemail before calling him back, and though I had no new messages I had a saved one, when that morning I'd had none.

I didn't like this at all.

My hand was shaking as I played the voicemail and lifted my phone to my ear. The call was abuzz with noise, like wind whooshing past the receiver and the roar of an engine. "Grace," Josh's voice said, in a panic that set my teeth on edge and trailed ice down my spine. I straightened on the bench, keeping my eyes on the sun even when it began to blind me once more. I didn't want to keep listening to the voicemail simply from the way Josh said my name.

I had to.

"Please pick up the phone as soon as you can. The police are looking for your boyfriend in relation to that student who was killed on campus," he said, and I choked. "They want - Grace, they think he did it. I believe them. Ever since you asked me about the attacks I knew you had some suspicions about them. It's because you thought Lir might be responsible, right? God, please pick up the phone. I'm heading to Campbeltown now: your parents gave me the address of where you're staying." A pause. A sigh. "Please, please get away from him, Grace. You aren't safe with him around. I'll get there around six to pick you

210

up, okay? Just...don't do anything stupid until I get there. I love you. If you want to shout at me for saying that out loud then stay safe until I can take you away from him. I love you."

When the message ended I kept my phone held to my ear, listening to the automated voice on the other end asking if I wished to play the message again or delete it. I couldn't process what I'd just heard, but part of me...

Part of me had expected it, too.

Finally, with what felt like enormous effort, I wrenched my phone from my ear to check the time on the screen. It was quarter past six. My phone clattered to the ground, an ugly crack spreading across the glass the second it hit the tarmac. I barely had the wits to pick it back up and shove it in my bag before I bolted away from the harbour.

I needed to get back before Josh arrived. I *had* to. I couldn't fathom what would happen to him if he got there and I was missing.

Please be safe, I thought. *Be safe. Be safe. Be safe.*

Even though I was running faster than I'd ever done before, with more efficiency and intent than I was likely to feel again in my life, I already knew it was too late by the time I approached the cottage ten minutes later. Josh's car was in the driveway, and all the curtains were closed despite the fact the sun was slanting through the windows.

I heaved the moment I stopped moving, hands on my knees as my lungs cried out for air and my calves twisted in the throes of painful cramps from running so quickly. But I pushed through it all and reached out a shaking hand to open the door. It was locked. I listened carefully for shouting. Fighting. Anything. But there was nothing; only silence.

Just run, I thought, blind with fear. *Run away and you can pretend you don't know anything.*

But I couldn't do that. On the other side of this door was a scene – whatever that scene might be – that I had to face up to. In reality it was one I had long since believed would happen, down in the darkest recesses of my mind. Only so many coincidences could stack up before they became correlation, after all, and I was a scientist. Looking for correlations was my literal job.

I pulled out my key and shoved it into the lock before I gave myself enough time to over-think the decision. The click as it unlocked seemed far too loud to be real, and raised all the hairs on my arms and spine until I shivered. With hands so tired of shaking they had eventually come full-circle to be steady with dead calm, I pushed open the door.

My immediate reaction was to take a step back and wrinkle my nose in disgust. The stench that filled my nostrils was overpowering. A smell so primal, metallic and innate that, though I had limited experiences with the scent in the past, I knew at once what it was.

Blood.

"L-Lir?" I called out, wavering and insubstantial. I stumbled down the hallway towards the tiny living room where he'd been lounging when I'd left for my jog. My vision was hazy at the edges, like when you play a video game and you reach dangerously low health. Given the situation I was in the comparison seemed more than appropriate.

Lir didn't answer my call, though I heard a shifting of limbs through the open door frame before I reached it that told me he'd heard me. My stomach lurched; the smell of blood grew ever more sickening as the distance between me and the living room decreased with every step I took.

Don't go in. Just run. Run, run, run away.

But Josh was in there. I could feel it in my very core. I couldn't run away and leave him alone with...whatever Lir was.

I took a deep, shuddering breath and turned into the living room.

Lir was kneeling over a horribly familiar body cut wide open from neck to navel, every inch of his skin slick with dark, crimson blood. In his hands was a heart. To my eyes it looked like it was still beating.

Josh's eyes stared at the doorway, dull and lifeless and so at

212

odds with the panicked expression on his face that I could do nothing but return his stare. I wanted him to wake up. To be *able* to wake up. *He isn't dead,* I thought, even as I looked at the gaping hole where his heart used to be. I fought back the urge to vomit. To cry. To scream.

To run.

Lir dropped Josh's heart back into his chest. "Grace," he said.

I backed away towards the front door.

Chapter Twenty-Nine

"Grace, don't go!" Lir cried out after me. I took a slow step back into the hallway, then another, then another, all the while never taking my eyes off Lir as he staggered upright and came after me. His bare feet trailed blood through the living room carpet like some kind of horrific ghost story come to life.

"Don't!" I cried, holding a hand out in front of me when Lir reached the doorway for all the good it would do. "Don't come over here. Don't – don't – just let me leave."

He didn't reach out to grab me. He didn't demand I follow him back through to the living room and face Josh's mangled corpse, either. What Lir *did* do was smile at me through a face spattered in blood and gore.

"I had to do this," he said, as if that explained everything and made it okay. "He was my rival. I had to sacrifice him for me – for *us*. The gods like those kinds of tributes much better. The ones that personally affect us. Don't you see, Grace?" Lir let out a laugh, as if he couldn't believe how blind he'd been up to now. He pointed back through the doorway towards the massacre he was responsible for. "I should have thought of this so much sooner. Thanks to this the gods will forgive me and I can *go home.*"

I lost my capacity to speak about anything other than the facts that lay in front of me. "You *killed* him."

"And? I had to."

"*No you didn't.*"

214

"Animals aren't enough, Grace," Lir argued, eager for me to understand. "I worked that out a while ago. But strangers...they don't seem to work, either. I could have saved so much trouble had I just gone for someone who directly affected my life from the beginning."

All I could do was stare at him. I couldn't believe the words that were coming out of Lir's mouth. They didn't belong – didn't sound *right* – in his lovely, lilting voice.

"What else have you done?" I asked, so quietly even I barely heard the question. So I cleared my throat and asked it again. "Who else have you *sacrificed* to your gods?"

"I think you know. I think you've known for longer than you care to admit." The smile slipped from Lir's face, leaving only an impassive expression that dared me to contradict him. But I couldn't: he was right.

I knew exactly who he'd hurt.

"You attacked David," I said, very slowly. "You even told me you were the last one to see him that night."

"Yes," was all Lir said in response. "And?"

"And...Terry. Oh my – oh my god," I uttered, as the memories I'd repressed up to this point hit me like a brick violently smashed into my face. "He told me someone was watching my parents' house. I could barely understand him. But he was warning me about *you.*"

He nodded. A drop of Josh's blood fell from his chin and down onto the carpet. I watched the grey fibres soak it up instead of having to look at Lir's face. "He didn't believe me when I said I knew you," he said. "Even when I tried to reach your door to tell you I was there, he pulled out his phone to call the police. So I tried to silence him and things went too far. Somewhere along the line I figured he'd make a good sacrifice. He obviously cared about you – wanted to protect you. But then you showed up and I had to stop!"

"Oh, so it's my fault I prevented you from murdering someone?!" I cried. Part of me knew I shouldn't upset Lir. He was unhinged. A literal murderer. I should have felt unsafe but, for some reason, I knew he wouldn't hurt me. Not physically, anyway. So I continued being brutally honest: "When you were late coming back from Islay do you know how afraid I was that the man who'd been killed was *you*, Lir? But you murdered him, didn't you? And you murdered Cian! Every attack the news has been following – doubtless so many more they don't know about – it was all you, wasn't it?"

"Well, yes, but –"

"There's no *but*, Lir! How in the world do you justify all of – all of this?"

I moved through to the living room despite my better judgement, forcing myself to face up to the disembowelled body of Josh MacDonald. Age thirty. A paediatrician. Older brother to Louisa MacDonald, age twenty-five, who was my best friend. He'd always wanted to be a doctor, even when he was little. Children and elderly folk alike adored him. Josh knew this made him more attractive to women and so utilised it to his advantage, but that didn't mean he didn't love his work or genuinely care for his patients. He was a flawed human being with a frustrating sense of entitlement but was, nonetheless, a good man.

He didn't deserve to die.

He never deserved to die.

Lir had killed him. And for what?

"Why..." I began, pointing at Josh with a finger that shook so much I looked like I was having a seizure. "You said – you said a personal connection. Why Josh? Why David? Why my *fucking neighbour?*"

"Your neighbour was in the way," Lir explained simply, though his veneer of calm seemed to be cracking as if my questions were making him address things he didn't want to talk about. "Like your cat. I didn't want to touch him. But since I had to...I was as well making the most of it."

God, I was going to be sick. Every word out of Lir's mouth pushed the bile further and further up my throat until every swallow was actively pushing it back down. Somehow, impossibly, it was looking at Josh – at his entrails pouring out of his stomach across the floor, at his hands now forever curled into fists to try and defend himself, at the resignation in his eyes as he realised he was going to die – that calmed the nausea.

I knelt down beside him, not caring about the blood that covered my skin in the process. It was cold. Disgustingly cold. But Josh deserved someone to be by his side so he wasn't alone with the monster who had killed him. I reached out a hand to close his eyes...and faltered. The logical part of my brain knew I shouldn't touch him. My DNA couldn't go anywhere near him, otherwise the police –

The police.

I forced my eyes from Josh to Lir, who was watching me with obvious upset on his face. Clearly he didn't like seeing me displaying even an ounce of sympathy for the man he'd killed. I hated seeing him jealous like that because a twisted part of me wanted to soothe him and tell him not to worry. The fact my love for Lir hadn't magically disappeared after witnessing what he'd done was the worst feeling in the world.

I knew I had to call the police. He needed to be locked up. Someone far more qualified than myself needed to help him through his psychosis.

So why couldn't I pull out my phone and call them?

"Did you go to Islay fully intending to kill someone?" I asked Lir, buying myself some time to fight with my conscience whilst getting answers to the questions I'd wanted to ask him for weeks now. Months. "All the attacks before that never ended in you taking a life."

Lir seemed relieved by the question which unsettled me to no end. "The man on Islay...that was an accident," he said, cocking his head to the side as he considered his answer. "Well – kind of," he corrected. "After your neighbour I thought I had it in me to sacrifice a human being but it turned out I was wrong. I was so sick that night, Grace. I couldn't stop throwing up. Thinking about the way his body bloated – the colour of his face, the way his whole body went rigid like it was made of wood – I couldn't take it. There was no way I could have come back to Glasgow that night and pretended everything was okay. So I

217

waited until the next day to return."

"I thought *you* were the victim," I whispered. "I thought you'd been taken from me forever."

At this Lir came bounding over and knelt beside me, taking my hands in his and holding them to his chest. I was too scared to pull away even though his grey eyes shone with a fevered madness I couldn't possibly understand.

"Well I was, in a way," he said. "The victim, I mean. I'm not doing this because I'm evil, Grace. You must know that, right? I'm doing this because the gods wish it to be so. I just need to find the right sacrifice."

"And how do you know that to be true?"

"They'd have let me go home if I'd done it right, wouldn't they?"

"If the sacrifice is supposed to be a personal one then why didn't m-murdering Cian work?" I stuttered, forcing myself – as I had done the night before – to make Lir face up to rational questions and answer them properly.

A flash of disgust crossed his face at the mention of his childhood friend. "He killed my fish. Then he kept hitting on you even when I was *right there*. I thought my hatred for him would be enough but clearly it wasn't. Maybe it's because he wasn't a good person, so the gods didn't want him. Maybe if I'd been able to follow through on killing David –"

"You planned to *kill David*?!" I cried, wrenching my hands from Lir's grip. "He did nothing to you! He –"

"He liked you too much. Of course he had to go."

"Lir," I mouthed, my throat closing over so much that I could hardly make a sound. "I was going to turn him down. He'd never have pursued me after that. He's a good –"

"You're *my* siren, Grace," Lir cut in, sliding closer to me across the bloody carpet until his knee was locked firmly between mine. He pushed errant strands of hair from my face, smearing sticky wetness across my skin as he did so. "My siren, not theirs. They didn't deserve you. Couldn't have you. Not Cian or David and especially not *him*." He pointed towards Josh without looking at him.

For a moment neither of us spoke, our eyes on each other speaking volumes in place of our voices. I could tell Lir was trying to work out what I planned to do next. I wondered, if I decided to call the police, if he would do anything to stop me - to save his own skin.

"I would never hurt you," Lir said, as if reading my mind. "Not even if you...but please. Don't leave me. Don't let them put me in a box I'll never get out of. I just want to go home. I just want - out. I love you, Grace. I love you more than anyone or anything else on this earth."

And I could see he believed it was true. It was in his eyes and the way his entire being softened as he stroked my cheek.

That just made things worse.

Lir was a monster. A twisted, childlike, tragic monster, but a monster nonetheless. I had to leave him. I had to turn him in. I had to avenge Josh and David. Cian. My neighbour. That nameless man on Islay. My cat. Every soul Lir had ever hurt.

I *had* to.

"I won't leave you," I said, reaching a hand out to cup Lir's face, bringing his lips to mine for perhaps the most fragile kiss I'd ever experienced. But within moments it turned desperate, hard and sharp, Lir's predatory canines piercing my tongue until all I could taste was blood. I didn't pull away even though the taste made me want to vomit. "I won't," I repeated between stolen breaths. "I won't. I won't. I won-"

Lir broke the kiss to envelop me in a bone-breaking embrace, forehead resting on my shoulder as he leaned all his weight against me. "I knew you wouldn't," he whispered. "I always knew you'd stay. We're meant to be."

Until two days ago I'd eagerly believed that to be true. But if it still *was* true despite everything, and Lir was a monster...

What did that make me?

Chapter Thirty

When I walked to the bathroom I was too numb to notice where I was going. But clearly some part of my brain knew I needed to be clean. I was covered in blood – *Josh's blood* – and I needed it gone. Lir didn't even protest when I broke away from his arms without a word of explanation as to where I was going. Perhaps he understood my desire to be clean just as much as I did.

I could hardly bear to look at the shower as I turned it on and stripped off my clothes. I'd been so excited that it was big enough for two only yesterday, my head filled with lustful thoughts of me and Lir getting entirely lost in each other as steam and sweat became indistinguishable on our skin.

But all I had on my skin now was blood. When I caught my reflection in the mirror and saw the red streaks across my cheeks and forehead, stark and unsettling against my painfully pale complexion, I stifled a sob. It was on stumbling feet that I finally managed to slide open the glass door and step inside the promising, comforting heat the shower provided.

I hardly dared to exhale as the rush of scorching water poured over me, running down my face and chest and legs until I was soaked through. Crimson circled the drain for a while. Red, red, red. Then, slowly, pink, paler and paler with every swirl of water until eventually it was clear once more. But it wasn't enough. No matter how much I scrubbed and brushed and lathered myself I couldn't wash away the feeling that I'd never be clean again.

Lir had gotten under my skin. He'd fed me sweet nothings and promises of being soulmates, all the while ripping through my life until there was nothing left but the two of us. *What will he do to my parents?* I thought almost dully. I didn't think I had anything left inside me to react appropriately to the disturbing situation I was in. Lir clearly loved his aunt and uncle; perhaps family was off-limits. *But then what about Louisa?*

That was when I fell to my knees, hand to my mouth to mask the sobs wracking through me, agonising and bone-breaking. Evidently I wasn't as numb as I thought I was. I tried to imagine telling her about what happened to her brother all because of my boyfriend.

Because of *me.*

What was it that Louisa had seen in Lir to be so immediately suspicious of him? What had Josh? How had they worked out something was off about him before me?

At this I shook my head so vigorously I was in danger of hurting my neck. For they hadn't worked it out before me. I'd known right from the very beginning that there was something odd about Lir. Something different. Something...other. It's what had drawn me to him in the first place.

I kept scrubbing my skin, even when my arms grew irritable and red not from the heat of the water but from friction. All I'd wanted was someone on my level. Someone who understood me. Someone I could sit in a corner with and discuss the world outside, without having to put myself at the mercy of said world. Someone to hide beneath the covers with me on dark, windy days and not move for hours.

Someone to live my life with.

I guess that's ultimately exactly what I got.

When Lir came into the bathroom and stripped off his clothes I didn't immediately notice. It was only when he slid open the shower door, letting out my precious heat for a moment as he stepped inside and eased me back to my feet, that my brain finally acknowledged his presence.

He looked like he'd bathed in blood. His beautiful face was

covered in the stuff; it stuck thick and disgusting to the curls of his hair that swept across his eyes. Those eyes of his, that looked so innocent even as they hid the true extent of how wretched Lir had become.

"Grace," he murmured, so softly. When he pushed me against the tiled wall I didn't protest, even when his skin moulded to mine to smother it in blood once more. But it was his touches, his kisses, his proclamations of love that contaminated me, not what was left of Josh. Everything about him was poisoning me, seeping into the darkest, most distant corners of my very being until all I could think about was him.

I wrapped my arms around his neck, mouth hot and desperate on his as I begged Lir to get closer, closer, closer.

And so I got my fevered experience in the shower with Lir, after all. I just never imagined it would involve the blood of a man who loved me lying between us on our skin, and a fear of what would become of my soul hanging heavy in the air.

Later – much later – we finally emerged from the shower in a puff of steam and exhausted, shuddering breaths. No red remained on me or on Lir, not in his tawny hair or on his starved cheekbones or god-like body.

God-like.

How could it have only occurred to me now that every fibre of his being had aspired to belong in the tales he believed to be true? I'd been blind and stupid from the beginning.

As we crawled into bed and lay, silent, in the dark, my brain slowly came off its sick chemical high and crashed back down to earth. My eyes found the door. Though it was closed I knew exactly what was on the other side of it in the opposite room.

"What did you do with his heart?" I croaked out before I could stop myself. "Did you –"

"It's in the fridge. I –"

I ran to the bathroom and barely reached the toilet in time to throw up the contents of my empty stomach until I was gagging on nothing. *This is it,* I thought, when no air could reach my lungs. *This was how I die. Hyperventilating into a toilet and*

222

suffocating on bile.

My vision intermittently went white then black so I dug my fingernails into my thighs and forced myself to concentrate on my breathing. I just needed to make it to tomorrow. That was it. Come tomorrow I'd –

Well, I didn't know. But I had to do something. If I didn't have it in me to turn Lir into the police then I had to find some other way to stop him. For it was clear he wouldn't stop, otherwise. Gone unchecked he'd keep sacrificing people until he was caught in his own net and taken down for it. He'd be locked away from the sun and the rain and, most importantly, the sea. The light that burned so strongly within him – however perverse it had become – would be lost. Lir would become a shell of himself, and me with him.

There had to be another way.

When I returned to bed Lir pulled me into his arms, chin resting on top of my head as his long, nimble fingers trailed across my skin. It was supposed to be soothing: it felt like spiders were crawling across me.

"I have to keep it fresh for tomorrow," he murmured into my hair. "His heart, I mean. I probably should have done it tonight."

I really didn't want to ask. "Done what? Wasn't killing him enough?"

A small rustle as he shook his head. "I need to take it to the sea. Only through the waves can I return home. Why do you think I always went to the coast?"

"To swim and stuff," I said, because I had believed that. I tried to imagine Lir attacking a person one moment only to abandon them to go swimming. Actually, it was pretty easy to imagine. He was unhinged enough to do it.

He let out a soft laugh. "Well, I did do those things. I have to keep fit, after all. But it made a good cover story all the same. Nobody ever suspected what I was doing. Except you, but you never said a word."

And there it was. The truth handed to me from the

proverbial mouth of the devil. That Josh's death was my fault hurt all the worse for knowing I might have prevented it had I only had the courage to face up to the person I let crawl into bed with me every night.

"The Volvo," I whispered, because it was the only thing I hadn't asked Lir about at this point. "Did you steal it the night we slept together?"

Through the dark he nodded. "Public transport is terrible at getting to the really isolated parts of the coast. I needed a car and...it was there."

So simple. So emotionless. He never thought about how taking the car would impact me or my parents. The worry we felt. The impending trauma of knowing a creature like Lir was using it to scope out his victims.

"Don't think about things like that right now," Lir said, cuddling closer to me. "In the morning we'll go to Westport Beach and then...then you'll see, Grace. You'll see what I did this for."

"And what if it isn't enough?"

A pause. A shuffle in the dark, Lir turning me around to face him. "What do you mean?" he asked, voice slow and uncertain.

"I mean what if Josh's death isn't enough? Who's to say it will be? And if it isn't...what then? Will you kill your aunt? Your uncle? Me?"

Lir looked at me as if I'd personally shot him. "I would never sacrifice you. Or them. Grace, what will I do if it doesn't work? It *has* to. What else can I do, otherwise? Unless –"

Oh, no. I didn't like the new sheen in his eyes. Lir took my hands in his and squeezed them tightly. "What if you came with me, Grace?" he said, so fevered and excited I could do nothing but gawk at him. "I've never tried going through with someone who was willing before! Maybe my mum and dad could only go home because they were together. A couple. Soulmates. So will you, Grace? Will you come home with me tomorrow?"

The reality of his request was an incessant buzz in my brain,

224

indistinct and unreal. Lir meant for us to die whether he was aware of it or not. I knew that, deep down, he truly had no idea of what walking into the sea meant. His own reality had become too warped to see things clearly. And how could I blame him? After everything Lir had been through at such a young age it should have come to absolutely no surprise to me that his brain was fractured and wrong.

He needed help; he was beyond help.

If this was the only way I could save him...

"Yes," I said, turning so that Lir could not see the tears I spilled as I condemned myself to die.

This way I would never have to face up to everyone knowing what Lir had done. I would never have to leave him, and he would never hurt another living thing in his twisted attempt to return to a home that never existed.

Chapter Thirty-One

Lir drove us to Westport Beach just as the sun was beginning to rise...in my parents' Volvo. He'd been hiding it in a privately-rented garage fifteen minutes from his uncle's house whenever he wasn't using it.

Although he'd cleaned the upholstery the air within the vehicle still smelled of damp and dust and the vague, sweet smell of rot; as we drove through the dawn all I could picture were dead bodies hiding in the shadows of the back seat. It didn't matter that Lir assured me he never used the car to move them – he'd left the man on Islay where he killed him, on the beach, and he'd left Cian where he drowned him, in the pool, and what was left of Josh remained back in the cottage, where Lir slaughtered him – but none of that mattered to me.

Regardless of where I looked all I could see was red.

Lir was busy concentrating on the road. Though the sun was peeking up over the horizon the sky above us was grey and unsettled, and every so often a spatter of rain hit the windscreen and he had to put on the wipers and peer through the grey morning to see where he was going.

I used his temporary distraction to surreptitiously pull out my phone from my pocket. I hadn't touched it since I listened to Josh's voicemail. My one and only keepsake of his voice, forever telling me he was coming to get me. To save me.

My phone had very low battery which didn't surprise me in the slightest. What *did* surprise me were the number of missed calls, messages and voicemails I'd received. I'd never been so popular before.

All it took was finding myself a perfect, doting, criminally insane, serial killer boyfriend.

There were messages from Max and other students from the marine and freshwater biology lab, as well as my PhD supervisor and the head of Lir's degree group. They'd all evidently seen the news. David had called me, too, and left a dozen messages begging me to reply. Then there were the deluge of attempts from my parents to get in touch with me...and Louisa.

Louisa, Louisa, Louisa, over and over again.

Josh called me, she wrote in one of her messages. *He said he was going to get you, that Lir was...Gracie, he won't pick up the phone. What's going on? Please tell me he's safe. Please tell me you're safe. Oh my god, oh my god. Please pick up the phone.*

A knot formed in my throat, constricting my breathing as I forced back the tears my body wanted me to shed. I could see that my dad called the police barely ten minutes ago. They were probably on the way to the cottage right now, and when they found what Lir had left behind...

"I can't wait for you to meet my parents," Lir said, cutting through my invisible agony with his excitement. I put my phone back in my pocket just as he pointed through the windshield. "The beach is up here. Just think, Grace: in a few minutes everything will change for us. We'll both become part of a world that leaves this one completely in the dust. It's going to be...well, amazing doesn't seem quite right, does it?"

"Extraordinary," I suggested, surprised at how lovely my voice sounded. I knew I had a smile plastered to my face though I wasn't sure how I was managing to keep it there. "Breathtaking. Life-altering."

He slid a hand through mine and completed the drive one-handed. "You're so much better at describing things than I am. Maybe you're meant to be a poet instead of a scientist? You'll have all the time in the world to weave words once we start our new lives."

I didn't reply, merely squeezing Lir's hand before he pulled into the empty car park and slowed to a stop.

When we got out of the car I was immediately struck by a strong, sharp gust of wind full of salt and sand. I winced away from it, my back against the cool metal of the car, when Lir came in front of me to protect me from the worst of the blasts.

"I know you're scared," he said, reaching out for my hand to bring it to his lips. He kissed my knuckles ever so gently, his gaze never leaving mine. Everything about him was so soft. So affectionate. So tender.

It broke my heart.

"I love you," Lir said, and he pulled me along the beach.

For some reason I'd expected Westport Beach to be the one from my nightmare. It was stupid of me to believe that, of course: why would a real beach I'd never visited before be mimicked by my subconscious when I was asleep? Yet though the curve of the beautiful shore was different, and the shelves of rock jutting into the ferociously powerful waves hadn't been present in my dream, they seemed familiar.

And then I worked it out.

"Your drawing," I gasped, pointing at a part of the beach some ways off from us. "That's the bit from your drawing."

Lir beamed at me as he walked towards the shore, more insistent and impatient than ever. "I can't believe you noticed," he said. "It's the place where the water gets deepest quickest – where the current can help pull you out faster. Seems like the most efficient way to travel."

My stomach lurched. "I...guess so," I forced out, dread coiling inside me as we finally reached the waves. Lir let go of my hand to throw off his shoes, lightly jumping from foot to foot as if the adrenaline within him wouldn't let him stand still. He was literally shaking with excitement.

"This is going to work, Grace," he said after he'd pulled off his shoes, certain. "I can feel it in my bones." When he looked at me expectantly I realised I, too, was supposed to take off my shoes. I didn't want to. I really, truly didn't want to.

Under Lir's gaze I had no choice.

"My parents put rocks in their pockets and stuff when they went into the sea," he told me, taking my hand once more to walk along the shoreline in search of promising-looking stones. "Maybe if I'd done that when I first tried to reach them I'd have got there. Well...it doesn't matter any more. But we should replicate what they did as much as possible, right?"

I couldn't bring myself to pick up a rock when Lir found a pile of 'good' ones, so I let him fill my pockets for me. "...how old were they, Lir?" I asked, when both my pockets were full and heavy and Lir patted them down with a satisfied smile.

His eyes grew bright at the question once he worked out the answer, and he kissed me enthusiastically. "They were our age!" he gushed. "Twenty-four and twenty-five. Well, I'm twenty-five in two days, but I'm sure two days won't make a difference. Do you think age matters? I think it must. Why hadn't I seen that before? You're such a genius, Grace!"

"God, I really love you," I bit out, hating the words even more because they were true. Lir was just so...happy. I'd never seen him as content as this. He truly thought he was going home, and me with him. He thought we were going to have a glorious life together in the realm of gods and heroes, where his parents had been patiently waiting for him for twenty years.

He had done abhorrent, reprehensible things to get to where we were now, standing on a windy beach at dawn, about to die, and still I loved him.

I needed to end things.

When we set foot in the sea I shivered. The water was cold – bitingly so – but it didn't seem to affect Lir at all. He took the first step forward, and the second, and the third. It was only when I could barely reach out a hand to touch his back with my fingertips that I began to follow.

Every drag of my legs through the turbulent water was a challenge. My bones were steel; my muscles lead. The rocks in my pockets pushed the soles of my feet much farther into the sand that I had expected, and I held a hand to my mouth to keep in a scream.

Against the howl of the wind and the crash of the waves I doubted it would have been heard, anyway.

"Don't look back, Grace," Lir called out when we were up to our waists in water. It felt like in no time at all we'd be consumed entirely. I had minutes left to live. Seconds.

I concentrated on the curve of Lir's shoulder blades as he picked his way confidently through the sea. "What do you mean *don't look back*?" I shouted at him.

"Well," he began, pausing for a moment when a larger-than-average wave bowled right over our heads. I sucked in a lungful of air before it hit, expecting it to be my final breath as I staggered beneath the sheer force of the water, begging myself not to fall. But it wasn't my final breath; the wave abated and we were back to wading through the sea at waist-level after a few horrible, drawn-out moments.

"When Orpheus went down to the underworld to save Eurydice," Lir continued when he could speak once more, "he was ordered to never look back to see if she was following him out. If he did then she would be stuck in the underworld forever. But he doubted himself, and he looked back, and there was Eurydice following his every footstep. By looking back he condemned her forever. So I won't look back at you, and you don't look back at the shore. It's the only way we can both stay together, going forever forwards. We'll get there. We will."

All I wanted to do was look back.

By the time the water reached my neck I began trying to swim even though my body was dull and heavy and desperately wanted to sink. Since Lir was several inches taller than me he could still walk through the waves, and though he didn't look back he must have heard me struggling and worked out what I was doing.

"Don't fight it!" he shouted. I could hardly hear him even though he was barely a metre away. "Just a little further and we'll get there. Just a little more. You can do it, Grace."

When the water was too deep for even Lir to walk another wave buffeted us. This time it knocked me under the surface for a few seconds. I cried and screamed for all the good it would do, but all my mouth emitted were bubbles. No matter how I fought against the current I couldn't reach the air above my head. So I unzipped my jacket with clumsy, trembling fingers and wrenched it off me, feeling myself lighten immediately until I finally, finally broke through to the blessed, salty air above the waves.

"Stop fighting!" Lir yelled at me again, treading water as he resolutely did not look at me. So I launched myself at him, wrapping my legs around his waist for purchase as I tried to pull off his jacket. He struggled under my grip, much stronger than I was, but still I held on as I battled with his zipper.

"We – are – not – dying!" I gasped into his ear, pulling at his clothes and swatting off his hands whenever Lir tried to buck me off. "This is madness! We're going back!"

"We can't," Lir replied through gritted teeth. "This will work. You're just afraid."

His eyes were closed so he could avoid looking at me. I wondered if he knew he would see the truth in *my* eyes – immutable and completely at odds with his own beliefs – and was afraid.

Afraid to be wrong. Afraid for all his evils to have been for naught.

I fished through his pockets for a rock, and when my fist closed around one I tried to throw it away. Lir grabbed my wrist to stop me. "Of course I'm afraid," I got out, spitting salt water from my mouth all the while. It was so hard to stay afloat. "We're going to die, Lir. I don't want to die. I don't –"

"*Neither do I.*"

"Then don't do this!"

"We have to!"

With a tremendous amount of effort Lir wrenched me from him, turning with his eyes closed to try and push me beneath the water. I scratched at his arms the first time he ducked me down. I pushed at his chest and kicked his stomach the second time, swallowing mouthfuls of deadly, terrifying sea all the while. The salt stung my eyes but I didn't dare close them. If I did I was lost. If I stopped fighting I was lost.

The third time he forced me down I reached for Lir's pockets once more and finally found a rock.

"*You* might," I gasped, after I smashed the stone against Lir's head and used his stunned surprise to escape his grasp. My throat was agony as I heaved in a breath; oxygen had never felt so good. "You might," I repeated, hitting him again when he opened his eyes and tried to reach for me once more, "but I don't. I don't want this."

Blood began to trickle down Lir's temple. He didn't even seem to notice; all his attention was on me as his gaze grew hazy. "Don't you want me, Grace?" he begged, voice already so faraway. "We're meant to be. I love you. You love me. We're soul–"

I hit Lir again and his words were lost to the sea. I watched as his eyes fluttered closed and, between one stinging blink and the next, the current pulled his slack body away from me.

"I know," I told the waves, too weak and frightened and hysterical to move as his body was pulled beneath the surface and out of sight. "I'd rather not possess a soul than have one connected to you."

It took much too long to reach the shore – so long I thought I might end up losing all my strength and drift off after Lir despite fighting so hard to survive. At this point maybe that was for the best. But then, just as I considered closing my eyes for good, my feet touched sand and then my hands did, too, and I crawled and slid my way through the shallows until I was just barely far enough out of the sea that it couldn't sweep me back in.

When police sirens began to fill the air I could think of nothing but breathing and Lir. One breath, two breaths, three. I wondered how he felt the day he discovered his parents had left him forever. Four breaths, five. He'd been too small – too young – to be abandoned by the people who were supposed to have loved him more than anything.

Now I had done the same.

Six breaths.

When a faceless man approached me to take my pulse, wrap a blanket around my shoulders and ask me if I was okay I began to weep and weep and weep.

I didn't think I'd ever stop.

Chapter Thirty-Two

Louisa rushed over on the first flight back to Scotland after hearing the news of her brother's death...and what happened to me. She went home first, of course, and I was sent straight to Largs so my parents could look after me onces I was released from the hospital and the police station for questioning, so by the time I came face-to-face with my best friend almost two weeks had passed and it was the day of Josh's funeral.

I hadn't processed anything in those fourteen days. I was numb. It felt like part of me had died in the sea the moment I rejected Lir and left him to die, alone.

But now I was the one who was alone.

Neither of us said a word when we met outside the church, but we ran to close the distance between us and held on to each other so tightly I thought we might be drowning. I suppose we were. When her parents joined us to hug me just as tightly I couldn't stand it. The looks of pain and pity on their faces when their eyes caught mine...it threatened to break me.

I was a victim. I was supposed to be Lir's next victim. That was all they saw.

But that wasn't true. Not one bit.

At the end of the funeral, as I held Louisa's hand and walked with her between the pews, I noticed someone familiar standing awkwardly at the back of the church waiting for me. David. He smiled softly - so sadly - and with a squeeze of her hand I pulled away from Louisa to usher David outside to talk.

He shifted from one foot to the other as we stood in uncomfortable silence upon the gravelled driveway, by the church door, but quickly became surrounded by people giving their condolences to Louisa and her parents. 'Josh was such a wonderful son,' they said, and, 'A doctor – a kids' doctor! What a horrible loss,' and, to Louisa, 'What a saint he was, going to save your best friend. I heard he loved her. How tragic!'

Their words filled my head, spinning round and round until I was dizzy and sick. I couldn't breathe. My vision was going red and black and red again. Without a moment's hesitation David directed us away from the lot of them around the back of the church, until the two of us were hidden by perfectly maintained rose bushes and small trees.

"Th-thank you," I gasped, bent double with my hands on my knees until my vision returned. "I don't – I can't –"

"You don't need to say anything," David replied. "Hearing them say all that is bound to make you feel awful. It's okay to feel awful. You know that, right?"

I did, but what David had no idea about was the fact that I was mourning for Lir just as much as I was for Josh and his family. Possibly more so. That made me an awful *person.*

But I couldn't tell him that. I probably couldn't tell anyone that, ever. It was a secret I had to hold close to my broken heart until I died.

When it became clear I wasn't going to respond David coughed and ran a hand through his hair, unsure as the day he'd first asked me to lunch. "Anyway," he mumbled, "I just came along to support you. It can't be easy being with your friend's family after what happened."

"It's almost impossible," I found myself saying instead of lying. I held a hand over my mouth, shocked at my honesty and disgusted at how much of a coward I was. Josh's parents had lost their son. Louisa had lost her brother. And it was all because of me. Yet all I was thinking about was how difficult it was for me to be around them instead of the pain they themselves were going through.

When David reached a tentative hand to touch my shoulder

I let him, and when he wrapped his arms around me I let him do that, too. It was easier than looking at his face, especially when I began to sob.

"I'm s-sorry he attacked you," I cried into his chest, because I was. I was sorry about everything. "I'm sorry I didn't listen when you tried to tell me about him. I'm sorry he -"

"Shh, Grace, it isn't your fault. You didn't know. How could you have known?"

The signs had all been there. All I'd had to do was ask Lir to his face about what he'd been doing. If he was responsible for everything. He'd have told me, I was sure, if I'd properly confronted him about it. He hadn't believed he was doing anything wrong.

And so I cried and I cried and I cried about all the things I should have done but knew, in my heart, that I never *would* have done. For if I'd known what Lir was up to the very moment he started I wouldn't have handed him over to the police. I couldn't fathom doing that, even now. No, I'd have told him to run off with me - I'd convince him that he didn't need to go home, so he could stop with the sacrifices. He had me, and I had him.

We could create a *new* home.

I knew that would never have been enough for Lir.

That was how Louisa found me some time later, her face pale despite her tan and her cheeks streaked with tears and mascara. "I was wondering where you were, Gracie," she said, forcing a smile to her face when she caught David's eye. "I'm sorry, have we met?"

David shook his head as he gently extricated me from his arms. "David," he said. "Grace was one of the demonstrators in my labs. We got on well so we became friends outside of it." A pause. "I'm so sorry for your loss."

A practised look of - well, of nothing, really - was plastered to Louisa's face. She glanced at me. "So you *did* make friends when I was gone."

"One friend," I clarified, holding up a finger for emphasis. "One friend, who my boyfriend attacked and -"

"I don't think now's the time for that," David cut in quickly, noting the horror in Louisa's eyes. Another awkward pause and then: "I'll message you later, Grace, okay? And you have to answer because apparently I'm your second friend in the entire world."

I choked on a laugh that was more of a sob as he waved and left, leaving me alone with Louisa. For a couple of minutes neither of us said a word, and I wiped my tear-stained face until it was sort of dry again.

Then she reached for my hand. "Come on. The wake's in my dad's favourite pub. He and Josh used to go there for pints all the time even when Josh was only sixteen. I'd never have gotten away with it; I'm so short. But Josh was huge from, like, age twelve, so..."

I couldn't bear to listen to her talk about him even though I knew she was doing it as a coping mechanism. "Louisa, I can't go," I said over the top of her story, attempting to pull my hand away.

But Louisa held on fast. "No. I'm not leaving you alone. What the hell kind of friend would I be if I did? And what the hell kind of friend would *you* be if you made me go to the damn wake without you?"

She had a point and we both knew it. There was so much she didn't know, though. So much that would ruin our friendship forever. "Okay," I said. "Okay. I'll go."

The pub was exactly the kind of place I expected it to be, but that was a problem. It was so similar to the pub in Millport. The one where I thought my life had been transformed for the better only to discover, too late, that it had also been the beginning of so much blood spilled because of me.

Too much blood.

"You know, I'm glad my dad never took me here," Louisa said after we'd finished a bottle of prosecco whilst sitting at a sticky table hidden in the corner, out of sight. "It's just an old man pub, isn't it? Nothing special about it. Don't know why I was so jealous of Josh. It stinks of smoke. Is it the seats? It must be." She sniffed at the faded upholstery and winced. "Yeah, definitely the fabric. Ugh, I'll never get this out of my dress. Though I don't imagine I want to wear this again for the rest of my life."

She was rambling. Trying to make me feel better. I appreciated it more than she would ever know even as it sent daggers into my heart. Her brother was gone because of me. Not because he tried to save me from the villain of Scotland's west coast but because I was the one who put the target on his back that led to his doom in the first place.

I gulped down a sob.

Louisa, being Louisa, could tell what I was thinking. Well, at least part of it.

"This wasn't your fault," she soothed. "Everyone knows that, Grace. I'm just so glad you got away before – before...I don't know what I'd have done if he took you from me, too."

She couldn't even say Lir's name. I couldn't blame her.

When I downed my drink in lieu of responding Louisa gave me the smallest of smiles. She reached for my hand, though we'd spent so much time holding each others' hands that afternoon that I was surprised they weren't still desperately entwined.

"Come travelling with me," she said.

I stared at her. "Come...travelling?"

Louisa nodded her head in earnest. "Like hell are you staying here after everything that happened to you. Aren't you packing up the flat, anyway? Just throw everything out. Toss it all out and come with me to the other side of the world and let's just *live*. Mum thinks I'm running from my grief by going back to Australia, of course, but dad agrees with me that it's the right thing for me to do. And I think it's the right thing for *you*, Gracie."

I think she expected me to say no or that I'd need some convincing. "Okay," I said, instead, surprising both her and me. "Yeah, you're right. I can't stay here. I have nothing – no-one – keeping me here."

Because I condemned him to the sea.

238

The look of sheer delight on Louisa's face crushed me. As she began gushing about all the things she couldn't wait to show me - all the people she couldn't wait for me to meet - I found myself perfunctorily agreeing with her and forcing smiles to my face.

One day I would tell her. One day, when I could come to terms with the fact she'd never forgive me for it, I'd tell Louisa how I'd loved Lir to the very end despite all he'd done - that I'd been willing to die for him right up until the moment when I didn't. But I still needed her in my life. Without her I'd break down.

So, one day, I would tell her. But not today. Today I'd finish packing up the flat, and then I'd escape my fears and guilt and broken heart by living somewhere sunny and responsibility-free with the best friend I'd betrayed in the worst way possible.

After the wake it took lots of convincing for Louisa and her parents to allow me to go back to Glasgow on my own. In the end the promise that I'd video call Louisa whilst I finished packing everything up did the job, and I took an almost empty train back to the city.

When I returned to the flat I was greeted by a stack of flat-packed boxes that my dad had brought over the day before, knowing I had to have everything packed by tomorrow when I handed the keys to my landlord. I didn't have an ounce of willpower in me to even begin sorting through my stuff, but I knew if I didn't start now then I really would do what Louisa suggested and throw everything out.

When I walked into my bedroom to pack my clothes I knew immediately that something wasn't right. The sliding door to the back terrace was ever-so-slightly ajar, the translucent curtain hanging over it billowing softly in the breeze.

The air smelled of salt water.

I stood frozen to the spot, eyes darting around as if Lir was somehow hiding in some minuscule corner of my room. But he wasn't there. Of course he wasn't there. The surge of hope I'd felt the moment I'd smelled the sea crashed and burned around me, hearkening a fresh wave of tears. But then I noticed something fluttering on my pillow.

Slowly, very slowly, I approached my bed as if it might bite me. I perched on the edge of it, hands shaking as I picked up the lined piece of notebook paper that lay there. Its edges were mottled and soft as if it had been wet at one point, and deep creases running through the paper told me it had been folded into a pocket for a very long time. I knew what was going to be on the other side before I turned it over.

The sea, crashing upon the shore as a gull flew overhead. The picture Lir had drawn in the library, the evening we'd first spoken to one another. I could do nothing but stare at it, wiping the tears that spilled from my eyes before they could smear the precious blue ink upon the paper.

If Lir had truly returned home, I hoped the gods were pleased with him. I hoped that he was happy.

Excerpt from Invisible Monsters

What truly separates monsters from men?

Poppy King finds herself in trouble when she fails to book a two week retreat for her university sports club. Saved at the last minute when the handsome Dorian Kapros offers a massively discounted stay at his new facility, she happily accepts the too-good-to-be-true offer, enticed by the sound of Dorian's irresistible voice.

But when Poppy survives an accident that should have killed her, Dorian does not react at all the way she expected him to. For Dorian is not what he seems, and his shiny facility may just be a front for something far more sinister.

Read on for an excerpt from book one of H. L. Macfarlane's thrilling *Monsters* trilogy!

***

Dorian's safety talk was short and sweet. He went over how to use the equipment – all stuff that the group was familiar with – before Poppy promptly ignored it all and began nimbly climbing up the wall without any equipment whatsoever.

"King!" Fred exclaimed furiously. "What the hell are you doing?"

"Free-climbing," Poppy called back simply. "I won't go all the way to the top." She was lying, of course. Poppy loved free-climbing more than anything else in the world. She never, ever fell.

Except that, this time, she did.

Poppy King had almost made it to the top of the climbing wall, expertly navigating the hand and foot holds like it was second nature, because it was. But then she glanced at Dorian, curious to know if the handsome man with the beautiful voice was watching her.

He was.

Like a hawk analysing a rabbit two hundred feet away Dorian was watching her. Even from this high up she could see the blue of his irises peering, observing, calculating. They were too bright. They were a distraction Poppy had not prepared for.

And she fell.

A whoosh of air rushed past her ears before Poppy landed heavily on her right side, crushing her arm beneath her with a sickening crunch. For a few seconds she lost consciousness. For a few seconds nobody spoke. For a few seconds not a soul in the room seemed to breathe. A fall like that meant several broken bones at the very least, but the way Poppy had landed...

When she sat up, cringing in pain and barely able to see or hear or think, most everyone cried out in shock and relief.

"How the hell is she –"

"Oh my God I thought she was dead –"

"I've never seen Poppy fall!"

"Poppy, your arm..."

Poppy couldn't focus enough to look at her injury, though she didn't need the full function of her eyes to know that it was red and hot with blood. Before she had the chance to react, however, someone swept her into their arms and carried her away.

"I'll deal with this!" Dorian exclaimed as he clutched her to his chest, voice hazy and faraway in Poppy's ears even though she could hear his heart battering against his ribcage clear as day. "I'll call an ambulance if I have to. Fred, Andrew – can I leave it to the two of you to clean up here? There's some bleach in the kitchen!"

"What happened?" Poppy groaned in Dorian's arms as they left the cacophony of the central building behind them. Her eyes flickered beneath their lids until she forced them open. "I don't – I don't fall."

Dorian laughed humourlessly. "Seems like you do, Poppy King." He kicked open the door to the infirmary and placed Poppy on a bed before hurriedly grabbing everything he needed to clean and dress her arm.

There was so much blood. As her vision returned to her it was all she could see. Poppy had never considered herself queasy before but the sight of her *own* blood made her head spin painfully. And was that – bone?

Dorian made quick work of cleaning up the blood, brows knitted together in worry as he worked. Poppy could tell what he was thinking: if she'd bled this much then she must have hurt herself very, very badly.

But then Dorian's frown melted into confusion. "I don't understand."

Poppy risked looking down at her arm. Now that Dorian had cleaned up the worst of the mess she could see her arm was hardly even bleeding anymore. The exposed and broken bone Poppy had been so sure she'd seen had disappeared. Even as she stared the long slash that rent open her skin began to seal itself.

She didn't want to say anything. She didn't want *Dorian* to say anything.

Because Poppy knew this would happen.

There was a reason she never fell – that she climbed so recklessly. Because, as a child, when she *had* fallen, she'd never gotten hurt the way she should. When she realised that cuts and scrapes healed inordinately quickly Poppy learned to hide that she had ever been hurt at all in front of people. She knew it wasn't normal to heal this rapidly.

"You don't have any broken bones."

243

Not a question: a statement.

Poppy shook her head.

"Did you hurt yourself anywhere else?" Dorian asked. He began dressing and bandaging Poppy's arm, for all the good that it would do.

She shook her head again.

Dorian's frown returned, growing deeper and deeper as he continued working in silence. Poppy didn't dare say anything. She didn't know *what* to say, anyway. Then he rubbed a hand against his face, unwittingly smearing some of Poppy's blood across his mouth.

The man froze, a blank and unsettling expression plastered across his face as he stared at Poppy. She wanted to look away from his eyes; they pierced through her like knives. In that moment she knew that *he* knew something, somehow.

"Um, Dorian...?" Poppy asked uncertainly. Any normal person would have cleaned the blood from their face immediately. Dorian didn't. He continued staring at Poppy as if he couldn't believe what he was seeing. Considering how quickly she'd healed he probably couldn't.

Finally, after several interminably long seconds, Dorian averted his eyes and took a step back from her. "Go clean the rest of yourself up, Poppy," he murmured. "Maybe don't tell anyone about your...arm."

Poppy got up wordlessly – wobbling dangerously on her feet before regaining her balance – and when Dorian didn't say anything more she walked away. But when she reached the door to the central building, she paused.

What do *I say to everyone?* she worried. *Though only a handful of people actually saw the fall everyone will know about it by now. And I'm barely hurt.*

She glanced back at the door to the infirmary. She couldn't understand Dorian's reaction whatsoever. It wasn't how anyone normal would have responded to what he saw happen with his own eyes. Poppy was hopelessly, confusingly curious.

Looking upwards she saw that the ceiling tiles of the facility were akin to those found in offices and schools – the kind one could lift easily. Judging the height she'd need to get through the ceiling, Poppy kicked off the wall to gain enough momentum to grab one of the metal rails that supported the tiles. She swung in place for a few seconds then hauled herself up, head bumping the tile out of the way as she did so. Poppy winced at the pain in her arm when she put her weight on it.

With some effort she pulled the rest of her body through the ceiling before her arm finally gave way, taking a deep, shuddering breath after she put the tile back in place. "What the hell am I doing?" Poppy murmured, shaking as she crawled through the ceiling until she was certain she was just above Dorian in the infirmary. She just barely lifted the edge of a tile to confirm this: the man was pacing back and forth as he muttered to himself. Something about him seemed different.

Poppy wasn't sure what.

"...fucking blood. Immortal blood!" he hissed, running a hand through his hair with an anguished expression on his face. "I can't bid her off. God no. *I want her.* They can't know, otherwise –"

Dorian abruptly paused in his nonsensical rambling. With unnaturally keen eyes he located Poppy's position in the ceiling just as she replaced the tile. Her breathing came in loud, sharp, painful gasps that she could hardly control; everything about the situation she was in screamed *danger.*

Somehow finding the strength to turn around Poppy made to escape back the way she came. But then the tile behind her came crashing down and she felt an excruciatingly tight, cold grasp around her ankle.

With a scream Poppy was wrenched from the ceiling, landing heavily on the linoleum floor at Dorian's feet. She stared up at him in shock that quickly curdled into fear. Dorian didn't look like himself at all. He loomed over her, much taller than he'd been before. *Impossibly* tall.

The arm that hauled her from the ceiling ended with dark, gleaming, wickedly sharp claws. They were all she could focus on; one swipe of those claws across her throat and Poppy thought that even she might die before she could heal herself. Whereas before Poppy couldn't get air into her lungs fast enough, now she found she couldn't breathe at all.

Dorian's grin was feral as he continued to somehow change form in front of her very eyes.

"You really are too curious for your own good, Poppy King."

Acknowledgements

I came up with the idea for The Boy from the Sea after seeing The Lighthouse, which was one of the four films I managed to see in 2020 before lockdown began (the other three being The Invisible Man, The Hunt and, of course, Sonic the Hedgehog). I wanted to write a book steeped in mythology that wasn't strictly fantasy, and so it was that The Boy from the Sea was born.

I hope everyone enjoyed it. It took me months to work out exactly how I wanted the plot to go, and then it took me far longer than I thought it would to actually write the book. But I liked the end product so it's all good!

I'd like to thank Kirsty for not only editing The Boy from the Sea but also providing me with the absolute best comments, feedback and reactions as she read each section of the book for me. It provided me with more motivation to complete the book than I could possibly put into words.

This is the first book I've ever written that isn't part of a series or trilogy. Which is so bizarre! I want to write more standalones now. It's a completely different challenge to writing a story in multiple parts or having characters appear in other books to continue their story.

Thank you for reading The Boy from the Sea. I hope you look forward to more from me in the future.

All my love,

Hayley

About the Author

Hayley Louise Macfarlane hails from the very tiny hamlet of Balmaha on the shores of Loch Lomond in Scotland. Having spent eight years studying at the University of Glasgow and graduating with a BSc (hons) in Genetics and then a PhD in Synthetic Biology, Hayley quickly realised that her long-term passion for writing trumped her desire to work in a laboratory.

Now Hayley spends her time writing across a whole host of genres, particularly fairy tales and psychological horror. During 2019, Hayley set herself the ambitious goal of publishing one thing every month. Seven books, two novellas, two short stories and one box set later, she made it. She recommends that anyone who values their sanity and a sensible sleep cycle does not try this.

Printed in Great Britain
by Amazon

57133506R00149